HEART OF THE MACHINE

Tawnya Torres

ISBN-13: 978-1-958557-03-7

For Zac and Chance, the only people who know how I really feel about aliens.

CHAPTER ONE
EXSOMNIS

The equipment beeps and hums. It makes clicking noises. Rotating cylindrical pieces pump air into the artificial womb and filter it. The monitor has her vital signs up on the screen. Air bubbles escape the respirator and float to the surface of the tank. Bright white and blue lights glow from every direction. This specimen is important. She is humanity's savior.

My father started this company to propel humanity into the future. He revolutionized the modern world. Unfortunately, we were invaded before we could enjoy our technological advances. I was only twelve when it happened. The sky turned dark, and a song of trumpets broke the sound barrier. A maelstrom formed in the clouds that were black and slate. Everyone in the world looked up at the same time.

Creatures with wings and folded forearms flew from the whirlpool. No one knows their origin. They are from somewhere far away. Their heads are triangular and fitted with enlarged red eyes. Black bodies with thick exoskeletons were difficult for our armies to kill. Most of humanity has retreated underground. I am fortunate. My father built his lab within Mount Ontake. He always wanted to be secluded. His theory was that science needed privacy and to be protected.

This is the second attempt at making the perfect machine. My father, Adam Krim, started the Ex Machina Project over forty years ago. His approach differed from any other's. He took a human fetus and implemented it with the device. It looks like a metal flower on the side of her head. This enhances her intelligence. It gives her the mental speed and calculation of a supercomputer. The device augments what is already there.

Humans are smart, but the device is a welcomed advantage against the

Mantodea. That is what we named the creatures plaguing our planet. They look like a praying mantis but are as big as a luxury SUV. They screech and tear up the cities. The Mantodea hunt us down for entertainment and consumption. The female aliens are more brutal than the males. They aren't afraid to eat their own species or fight another female Mantodea. The males follow the females lead. They do what they're told.

This Ex Machina is special. My father became depressed when the first one didn't come to fruition. He didn't plan for her needs correctly. She is grown with a human fetus but is partially inorganic. Besides the device, there are a few more additions. Along her spine are three wires. They have metal jacks at the end of them. She moves them around in her sleep the way a cat would move its tail.

The first Ex Machina was named Nyx. She died within ten days of being born. My father didn't anticipate her need for complex emotional interaction and kept her isolated. His team of scientists found her dead. She committed suicide. The Ex Machina was safe from everything but herself. My father was distraught.

Nyx would have been fantastic because she had the intense need for human connection. This is what will persuade the Ex Machina to help us on their own accord. They have their own free will. My father had high hopes he could build a machine that was not only strong but also capable of love. Everyone in the scientific field called him crazy. Until now.

"She's ready," says my colleague Hotaka. His glasses have a glare on them from the bright lights.

"Let's do this then," I say and hit the button to drain the liquid. The Ex Machina ceases floating in the amniotic fluid and lays flat in the womb made of plastic and metal. Physically, she is twenty years old. Her hair is platinum blond and has grown to her thighs. She's never had a haircut. Her face is serene. I pull the respirator out of her mouth and she coughs. Her eyes are closed, but she reaches out and I take her hand. Gripping my palm, she opens her eyes. They are hazel but glow gold because of the device. "Welcome to the world," I say to her. She looks at me, then around the room and examines my team. They all wear white coats and anxious faces.

"Who am I?" she asks.

I help her sit up. The Ex Machina has a human body with robotic enhancements inserted during infancy to grow with her. On her shoulder blades are a set of metal plates extending out like small wings. They glow blue now that she's awake. These will allow her to fly through the sky or propel herself through water. The wires on her spine swish back and forth. With these she can sense something's presence and what it is from fifteen miles away.

"Your name is Gwen," I say.

To ease her, I smile, hoping it makes her trust me. She touches my face softly. It's gentle but electrifying.

"What's your name?" she asks.

"My name is Bellamy."

I put my hand over hers. She is real. I made her. It worked. I look over my shoulder and see my colleagues cover their mouths with shock.

"Where am I?" she asks.

I help her stand up out of the tank. She stands at 5'6" and weighs one-hundred and twenty pounds. Her hair is dripping wet, and she leaves a puddle on the sterile lab floor. She holds onto me and scans the room. The wires on her back move like snakes trying to take everything in.

"Mount Ontake. We are in Japan. This is my father's laboratory," I tell her.

The device on her head glows blue in the middle. Her eyes move over everyone's faces. They all stare at her in awe. Not only is she an amazing scientific achievement, but she is gorgeous. Her skin is fair but tough. The fluid she was grown in has given her a thin exoskeleton and fortified her bones. She is virtually indestructible. The Ex Machina is designed to withstand the pressure of the bottom of the sea and space. She can go anywhere.

"What am I doing here?" she asks. Her gold eyes look into mine and I see the clockwork pieces mesh together with her humanity.

"You're here to save the world," I say.

***

The day the Mantodea arrived, I was playing baseball. My team was losing, but I knew I could win the game for us. It was my favorite thing to do. I was just a kid, but I could hit that ball as far as any adult could. The sky was blue and bright. Not a cloud in sight. I was up to bat. The pitcher hated me. I knew he was going to throw me a curve ball, but I was ready for it.

I hit it with no problem. His face turned red and his eyebrows looked like they were going to touch each other. I laughed like a madman as I ran. My dad wasn't at the game because he was working, but my mom was there. She was always there. I saw her stand up and clap. She kept chanting my name. "Bellamy! Bellamy!"

As I slid into home, I cheered myself. I pumped my fist in the air with triumph. The dirt covered my face with glory. It wasn't until I opened my eyes I realized the sky had turned dark. Everyone was looking up, but I scanned the crowd. Their tense faces. Horrified expressions. Women covered their mouths and men took off their sunglasses.

My eyes turned to the dark clouds forming above. The maelstrom caused harsh winds and blew my baseball cap off my head. The kid next to me started crying. I was frozen, unable to comprehend what was happening. People looked to the sky, but I looked to them, searching for an answer.

The aliens were quiet at first. They didn't make a sound. Then there was the loudest song of trumpets I've ever heard. I had to cover my ears. All the other kids and I laid on the ground with our faces to the grass and our palms on our ears, attempting to drown out the sound. Many years later, it was described as God's Song.

Parents and siblings ran to each other. My mom picked me up off the ground, but my ears hurt. She didn't let me whine. We ran to the lab where my dad worked. His company was prepared with an emergency shelter in the basement. My father was called a lunatic, crazy, enigmatic. Now everyone feels guilty for shaming him. He was right about so many things.

He believed we would one day, not any day we would see he believed, be invaded. Not necessarily by extraterrestrial beings, but by other countries. The armies he predicted would still be human. His complex scientific advancements, strange personality, and odd behavior made him an outcast in the field. My father was a weird genius, but a genius nonetheless.

Nyx had already died at this point. My father was in his deep depression back then. We hid in the emergency shelter for six weeks before relocating to the lab in Mount Ontake, where I am now. After the initial invasion, the Mantodea spread out and weren't as clustered. My father's wealth allowed us militarized travel.

Two years later, Gwen was created. I was fourteen. My father was so excited to show her to me. She was small. Only twenty-four weeks old. This fetus was donated from Norway. Nyx was from China. My father was banned from certain countries for his practices. While the world used his creations offering them luxury, they scoffed at his personal integrity, and the integrity of anyone who would allow such a thing to happen to an innocent child.

It wasn't like that. I remember the way my dad touched the tank she was in. He loved her. Every day he read to her. He would play music for her. I often found him staring at her with his hand pressed up against the glass. My father might have been crazy, but Gwen wasn't just a project to him. He cared about her. Sometimes I think he cared more about her than me.

My father died three years ago. I'm sad he didn't get to see her birth. I know he would have been beyond himself. She is fantastic. In order to make her less daunting, we've fitted her with a strapless white dress. It hugs her waist and hits her knees. The metal plates sit above the back where the zipper is.

Gwen doesn't need shoes, but we gave her matching white flats. The fluorescent lights glare off her platinum blond hair. It's so pale it's almost white. Her skin is fair and has a slight sheen to it from the barely noticeable exoskeleton. The wires hang down her back and peek out from under her dress like a tail. She never stops swishing them about. The Ex Machina is always on alert. We are playing chess. She will beat me every time, but I want to offer her stimulation and company.

"How are you doing today, Gwen?" I ask.

"I'm okay," she says and moves her knight.

"Just okay?"

"Is that not an appropriate answer?" she asks as I move my bishop.

"No, it is." Gwen and I continue to play and she wins. I pick up the pieces and rearrange them back on the board. "Is there something you want?" I ask as we start the next game.

"Yes," she says.

Her tone is flat. Gwen's eyes flicker gold beneath the hazel. The device has grown with her all her life. It has connected the synapses in her brain with metallic thread. This gives her an intellectual advantage but dulls the emotional part of her brain. The thread has fused with her veins and lungs, enhancing their strength.

"Can you tell me?"

"I want to go outside," she says.

I sense she is bored.

"We can do that tomorrow if you'd like," I say and stand up. Sitting next to her, I admire my creation. Her face is youthful, but the eyes hold decades of information. The device appears as a decorative accessory. Gwen's hair is hanging off the chair and touching the ground. I pick it up. "Your hair is very long. I can have someone cut it for you," I say. Gwen snatches her hair out of my hands and holds it defensively.

"No," she says sternly. This makes me happy. I shouldn't, but I let out a small laugh. "Why are you laughing at me?" she asks.

"It's hard to explain. I'm not laughing at you. I'm just happy to see you feel so strongly about your hair."

Gwen's reaction shows me she is developing her own personality. Her own desires. My father made Gwen to defeat the Mantodea, but I still want her to be happy. She might be partially robotic, but underneath the exoskeleton and metallic threads she has a human heart.

"Do I have to cut it?" she asks in a sad voice.

Gwen is cradling her hair the way a child would hold a toy. I put my hand on hers.

"No, we don't have to do anything you don't want to. I like your hair. I thought maybe it was bothersome to you because it's so long."

"I want to keep it," she whispers.

"Can you tell me why?" I am interested to hear what Gwen has to say.

"Because it's mine."

CHAPTER TWO
DEITY

My name is Bellamy Krim. I'm thirty-four years old, but I look like I'm twenty-five. No one takes me seriously. I used to wear baseball tees and cuffed jeans. Now I wear a lab coat and slacks. I'm 6'0", one-hundred and seventy pounds. My hair is sandy brown like my mom's. I have misty gray eyes like my dad. All three of us have oval faces and chins that stick out. I don't have any siblings.

This may be the greatest year of my life. I was able to complete my father's dream. The Ex Machina continues to thrive. We let Gwen roam around the laboratory as she pleases. I don't wish to make the same mistake my father did.

The entire team is frightened of her. She has done nothing harmful or aggressive, but we all know her capabilities. She could fry us all. The metal jacks at the end of the wires in her back are not just sensors. She can draw power from the atmospheric electricity and use it as a weapon. If she chose to, she could plug into our system and turn us all to dust. I have faith she would never harbor such feelings towards me. Towards us.

Gwen looks like a little goddess as she wanders the halls. Her hair sways above the back of her knees. She appears completely human until she turns her head and the floral device is visible again. The wires peek out from her dress and hover above the ground. They rattle like snakes, waiting, anticipating.

I grew up playing baseball, but my dad wanted me to be a scientist. He let me be myself. I think he was quietly glad when the Mantodea came. It gave him a reason to work harder. To build it faster. Better. I spent all my free time with my dad and the baby Ex Machina. He showed me everything he knew. I'm glad he wasn't just a science nerd but also an excellent teacher. My mom read to me every morning and every night we would go over history and math. She died when I was nineteen. My father could take a human fetus and make a god, but there was no cure for the type of cancer she had.

My youth was an interesting time. I was a child when I first met Gwen, but in a way I feel fatherly towards her. The device took up a quarter of her head back then. She has grown into it. The metal plates in her back barely stuck out an inch. I watched her grow. We can do all sorts of things with science, but for this to work right, we had to let her mature naturally.

Twenty years I have waited to meet her. Her mind isn't fully developed, but my father's theory was to let her out before age twenty-five so additional synapses could grow in her brain outside the artificial womb. The new experiences from the outside world will greatly affect the way she reacts the day she comes face to face with a Mantodea.

Gwen's room was all white, but we let her pick out certain items to personalize it. She picked the grey blanket over the dark blue one. When we offered her an assortment of books, she chose a children's story. It's about a toy rabbit who wants to be real. This intrigued me. I wrote it down in my notes.

My colleague Hotaka gave her a sketchbook and pen. He asked if she would like to draw something. Gwen was able to draw a portrait of me with accuracy. Hotaka asked her why she drew me. She said I was the first person she ever saw, the first voice she heard. The hand she felt when she reached out was mine.

I am touched that Gwen is already showing an emotional connection. She hasn't smiled yet. I try to get her to, but she hasn't developed a sense of humor or she simply doesn't find me funny. Either way, it's great to know she thinks about me, not only analytically. The Ex Machina sees in ones and zeros, but also through the lens of an ordinary human. The heart may have metallic threads in it, but it's still a heart. We didn't alter that part of her.

"Are you ready, Gwen?" I ask. She stands beside me with a blank gaze.

"Yes," she says.

I open the steel door. We can't go out for long, but I want to make this special for her. She stands at the threshold, seeming unsure. I take her hand.

"It's okay."

We step out onto the grass. It squishes, soggy from the rain. It smells fresh and aquatic. The green and woody notes of the forest are refreshing. All I've been exposed to is metal, plastic, and cleaning products, making everything smell sterile. The cedars stand tall. There are daisies, dandelions, and ferns. A bird up in the elms calls to us. Gwen looks at it with curiosity.

The crater lake is navy blue with green around the edges. It's been a while since I stepped outside. It's shades of jade, cerulean, and gold. An agreeable change of pace from all the white and chrome I see. Gwen kneels down and cups her hands around something in one of the flowers. It's a ladybug. "What do you think?" I ask her.

Gwen holds the red and black bug with care. She scans the forest and looks back at her little friend. She turns to me.

"It's beautiful," she says.

***

When I was sixteen, I found out my mom was dying. She was sick all the time. The cancer had spread into every vital organ. There was no way to remove it without killing her. Even though my father was creating something to save humanity, he couldn't save his wife. It killed him.

I was depressed back then. A sad teenager with no siblings, no friends, only the people who worked for my dad and my dying mom. I've become friends with my colleagues, but I don't know if we would have been friends outside of the circumstances. Hotaka and I bond the most. He has short black hair and brown eyes hidden by the glare of his glasses. We talk about our favorite songs and the way music makes us feel.

My team is made up mostly of men, but there are two women. Yui is our youngest scientist at age twenty-four. She has a pixie cut and dark eyes like Hotaka. Although she is the baby of the family, she is the most serious. I don't think she has ever considered having fun. She is all about the discovery, the how, and the why.

Shira is the same age as me. Her demeanor is serious, but not as serious as Yui's. Everyone I work with is Japanese. My family is from Boston, where my dad's headquarters was. This laboratory here in the mountain was for "just in case." Good thing he planned for everything. The lab is spacious: 180,000 square feet. We have an indoor garden with limited crops. Most of our calories and vitamins are in powder form. It's nutritious but unsatisfying.

There is the room where Gwen was born and two other rooms holding artificial wombs made of plastic, chrome, and glass. In the future, we hope to be in the process of creating several Ex Machina at once. It has fluorescent lights on the ceilings and blank walls, but it's welcoming. Everyone is professional but casual. We've been in here so long it feels like home. Equipped with dozens of bedrooms with private bathrooms to accommodate our team. There are nine of us, including Gwen.

I'm watching the women have tea. Yui and Shira are making polite conversation with Gwen. She doesn't seem interested, though. I want her to smile. She hasn't yet. The ladybug interested her. A bird had her attention for a moment. Gwen seemed like she enjoyed her experience outside. She said it was beautiful. Yet she didn't smile.

Shira attempts to be sisterly and braids Gwen's hair. The Ex Machina accepts Shira touching it. She lets her play with her precious hair. This is a pleasant surprise. I thought Gwen would snatch it away from her the way she did to me. But she doesn't. She stares into her teacup and lets Shira braid her virgin hair. It's never been cut. Maybe this is why she is so attached to it. It's always been with her.

Yui says something that interests Gwen because she stops looking at her green tea with a thousand-yard stare. She stares intently at the young scientist. I wonder what she said to make Gwen look at her like this. I walk towards the women casually, but I'm nervous.

"Hello. How is everyone?" I ask and scan their faces.

Shira stops braiding Gwen's hair.

"Doing well. Thank you, Bellamy." says Shira.

"Good. I better get back to work, though," says Yui as she puts her teacup down. She stands up and hurries past me. Her lab coat is loose on her small frame. She wears high waisted skirts and silky blouses. A formal girl. I sit down and examine Shira's face. Then Gwen's. Shira looks embarrassed or like she wants to hide. Gwen's flat affect keeps me locked out.

"What were you talking about?" I ask and lean back.

"People, life, art..." Shira says each word with intention.

"Death," says Gwen. Shira sits up straight at the word. She pulls her lab coat tighter over her grey sweater dress like she is cold.

"What did Yui say about death?" I ask.

"That I most likely will never die," says Gwen.

Yui is correct. Gwen isn't immortal, but she is close. She won't die from the pressure of space or the sea. Penetrating her skin is nearly impossible. Her physical capabilities, such as high speed and immense strength, will keep her safe. So will the exoskeleton. The device will enhance her longevity. Her telomeres won't fray.

Killing Gwen would require a massive amount of electrical energy. Essentially, something would need to galvanize her. A source of catastrophic static to interrupt Gwen's core system. I can't think of anything on earth with that kind of power besides herself. In theory, Gwen could live forever.

If she does die, all her experiences will be uploaded onto the device. It will act as a black box. She is constantly recording and downloading information. I hope Gwen never dies, but if she does, she could continue to live on in another. Her body would be different, but Gwen could come back as an improved Ex Machina from her previous life.

"That's true. You're quite strong. You don't have to worry about dying," I assure her.

Gwen grips her teacup tighter.

"But what about you?" she asks. Shira puts her hands on Gwen's shoulders. Gwen doesn't respond, but I hope she feels cared about.

"I won't die for a long time," I say.

"But you will one day," says Gwen.

"Yes. That's true," I admit.

I lean forward and rest my elbows on my knees. Gwen won't look at me. I keep staring at her, hoping for her to reciprocate eye contact.

"I should help Yui," says Shira as she gets up to leave.

She is uncomfortable. I am, too. Gwen is intelligent beyond humanity's wildest dreams but has childlike emotions–they are difficult for her to comprehend. I sit next to Gwen. She might not want me to, but I do.

"Don't worry. We'll have lots of time together," I say. Gwen reaches for my arm. She squeezes, but not hard.

"No matter what, no matter who I love, I will always be alone. Everyone I know will die and I will remain alive. What is the point of having a heart if I am to feel things like this?" she asks.

The Ex Machina's eyes haven't left the amber water of her teacup. I run my hand through my disheveled hair and take a deep breath.

"The hurt that you feel teaches you things."

It's corny, but it's true.

"Pain is like a teacher. There is a lesson in the suffering. Is that what you are trying to tell me, Bellamy?" asks Gwen.

She looks at me with eyes flickering between hazel and luminescent gold.

"Yes. That's right, Gwen."

The Ex Machina lets me go and puts down her teacup. She gets up without saying goodbye and goes into her room. I think about keeping her company, but she closes the door and shuts me out.

CHAPTER THREE
COGNIZANT

After my mom died, my father worked tirelessly. He barely ate or slept. Me and a few of his colleagues had to convince him to take breaks. He said he couldn't stand leaving her alone. I made him rest and took over keeping Gwen company. She was physically age five, but her brain was showing rapid development. I could see it on the screen.

Her hair hung suspended in the blue liquid. It swirled around and reminded me of a tornado in a glass. The device was intermittently visible through the long locks of hair. Every so often, she would twitch or take a deeper or slower breath. She wasn't awake yet, but she was very much alive.

Gwen was my friend, my confidant, someone to be with. I found her enchanting. She was a child, but she would grow up to be the most magnificent being. The Ex Machina was a project, but I considered her part of our family. My dad did, too. I suspect he felt like she was his daughter.

He put in a tremendous amount of effort to make sure everything was perfect for her. At times, I was jealous, but I wanted Gwen to have everything. I had nightmares about her dying because she didn't have the proper care. Some nights, I sneaked out of bed and sat with her. The light blue glow of Gwen's tank soothed me and I fell asleep in the chair, leaning against the glass.

I was lonely. As the youngest person in the building, I had few people to connect with. Most of them were my dad's age. I hadn't learned to speak Japanese yet. That gave me something to do. I sat in my dad's chair next to Gwen's tank and read to her. Or I would play the alternative electronic music I like. I know my dad would disapprove, but this was my time with her.

My father and I had a strained relationship. Not that he was intentionally neglectful, he simply had other things on his mind. I would sit next to him and he explained the inner workings of his brain. A lot of it made little sense to me.

Now it does. I understand why my father was so obsessed with her. He really did love her. I know because I love her, too.

It was my twentieth birthday. I was listening to music through my earbuds and reading. That day, I sat next to Gwen with my hand to the glass. I wasn't really paying attention, but I felt a small vibration through the tank. Ripping out my earbuds with the other hand, I turned to see Gwen's hand was resting on the glass between us.

"I love you," I said it out loud.

She drifted after a moment. It could have been a coincidence, but I think she knew I was there. Her hair moved around her in thick ribbons. Since she was from Norway, I imagined her deep sea fishing and walking through snow in her dreams. I thought her eyes would be blue, but they turned out to be hazel. She is full of surprises.

It's time to feed Gwen and I should eat, too. Gwen can live on electricity or consume human food. I try to alternate between giving her strawberries and plugging her into the battery. Food is a human experience and I want her to retain her humanity as much as possible.

Sitting across from Gwen, I watch her bite into the apple I gave her with a steel jaw. She is polite, but something about her indestructible teeth and the ability to chew through ten feet of metal intimidates me. I know she's not doing anything wrong, so I look away. Gwen has been withdrawn from me. I think she is mad at me, but I don't know why.

I want Gwen and me to be close, but she is cold. This isn't her fault. I can't take it personally. She is meant to calculate the best way to defeat the Mantodea, not to entertain me. Still, I can't help but feel like I should do something to cheer her up. I look at Gwen's youthful face and wonder what she would have been like if she were an ordinary girl.

"Are you okay?" I ask.

Gwen rips another chunk of the fruit's flesh from the core with a precise razor bite.

"I'm fine," she answers.

I sense she knows how to lie.

"Do you want to play a game?"

"Not really," her voice is pretty, but her tone is flat.

The device glowing blue reminds me she isn't like the rest of us.

"What would make you happy, Gwen?" I ask.

She stares at the apple core. I see the wings glow behind her. They peek out from her small shoulders.

"I want to go outside again," she says.

"We can do that tomorrow if you'd like," I say.

"Bellamy, why do you care if I'm happy?" she asks.

Her eyes appear human, but light up with her racing thoughts.

"What do you mean?" I laugh.

This is good. Gwen is trying to understand her heart.

"You created me to save humanity. Why do you care if I'm happy? It doesn't make sense," she says.

"I want your help, but I also deeply care about you. I waited a long time to meet you," I smile at her. Maybe she will smile back this time.

"Really?" she seems surprised.

The Ex Machina doesn't smile but appears to be searching the vast library of her mind for an answer that is rational. She won't find one.

"Yes. I've been with you your whole life, but you hardly know me. It doesn't make sense...I missed you, but we didn't know each other yet."

"I heard you," she says as her glowing gold eyes bore into my gray ones.

"What?" I ask.

"The day you said it, I didn't know what it meant. But I remember three words. 'I love you.' Is that what you are talking about?"

My eyes are wide, and my heart is pounding. The Ex Machina has been aware of me for much longer than I thought.

***

My palms are sweaty. There are dark circles under my eyes. I haven't been sleeping well. In fact, I hardly sleep at all. This must be how my father felt. I've been so amped up on the adrenaline from Gwen being alive that I haven't been able to decompress. I feel great, but I look like shit. Splashing cold water on my face and running my fingers through my hair makes me feel human.

Gwen is sitting with Hotaka. He is showing her a song he likes. Gwen listens with enthusiasm. She is analyzing the alternative electronic pop song. There is no right or wrong answer. It is up to interpretation. I am excited to see her reaction. So far, there has been little that has touched her. The children's story and the ladybug stand out to me. I think these are clues into the heart of the machine.

"What do you think, Gwen?" asks Hotaka.

He is a year older than me. We like the same bands and have a similar sense of humor. I enjoy seeing him interact with Gwen. He speaks to her with gentleness. I think he cares about her, too.

"Why do you like this song?" she asks.

The Ex Machina stares at Hotaka. He is wary of the wires swishing around. I see him eye them. Gwen makes us all nervous. We don't want to admit it.

"I guess I like the feeling of it," he says.

There are beads of sweat forming at his temples, but he acts cool.

"Can I hear it again, please?" she asks.

Hotaka seems flattered. He plays it for her and she listens to it again, but with a new perspective. The song ends, and she is silent. Hotaka takes off his glasses and rubs his eyes.

"Do you like it? It's okay if you don't," he says.

Gwen considers what he is asking her. The eyes stop glowing and she looks completely human.

"Yes. I can't describe why though," she seems agitated.

Hotaka recoils slightly at her irritation. I walk up and act casual.

"Hey Hotaka. How are things with Gwen?" I ask.

He wipes the sweat from his hairline with his sleeve.

"Good. Gwen likes our music," he smiles, but I can tell he is anxious.

"You do?" I ask Gwen.

She has her fists on the table. I sit next to her, but she won't look at me.

"You like this song, too?" she asks.

Gwen relaxes her hands. She surprises me by reaching up and touching my face. Like the day I woke her up. I let her run her fingers over my cheekbone. My heart has stopped in my chest, but she isn't using electricity to shock me.

"I do. It's one of my favorites," I say.

Gwen puts her hand on my heart. Hotaka jumps in his seat. It startles him, but it startles me more. I try to stay still. Gwen's curiosity hasn't been dangerous—yet.

"Can we still go outside?" she asks.

Gwen changes the topic. I'll write it down later, but right now she wants to go out.

"Of course," I say and stand up.

"I'm going to check on the crops," says Hotaka.

He excuses himself. Gwen and I walk to the main door. I watch the wires peek out from her dress and survey her surroundings. Her hair sways from side to side. She walks with no bounce in her step. Once we're at the door, I turn to smile at her. She still hasn't smiled at me.

"Are you ready?" I ask.

Gwen nods her head. I push the button, and the door makes a mechanical noise as it opens. The sun is bright and warm on my face. I take in the earth tones. The green, blue, and gold. It's nice to be outside. Gwen picks a daisy and turns it over in her hand.

"Do you think it's pretty?"

"Yes," she says.

Her eyes are bright gold beneath the hazel. Her thoughts have to be going a million miles an hour. Suddenly, the wires on her back cease to move. She has locked onto something. We both turn and see a large elk. His gaze is on Gwen and hers is on him. I can't tell what she's thinking. The elk bounds off down the hill and Gwen takes off after it.

"Gwen!" I shout at her. She doesn't listen. The Ex Machina doesn't have to listen to me. She has autonomy. "Gwen! Wait!" I keep calling for her, but she runs out of my sight.

Does she want to hurt the elk? Or does she want to get a closer look? I don't know what she desires. The mountain is spectacular, but I can't enjoy its beauty knowing Gwen is gone. What if she doesn't come back? She touched my face so softly. I want to believe she cares about me enough not to run off.

"Gwen," I call her name and scare the birds out of the oaks and cedars.

The lab is further away now. I haven't gone this far. The lake is blue green in a gold bowl. Fluffy clouds pass by but don't cover the sun. I'm running and for some reason I think of playing baseball.

"Gwen, please come back!"

I'm distraught. I can't bear the thought of her not coming back. She isn't just a project. I care about her. Now I know how much I care. I'm willing to run into the dark woods for her.

"Gwen!"

My voice causes all the birds to flee from the pines. There are streams of light coming through the branches. Butterflies float in the air, suspended in time. I'm not watching where I'm going and step into a hole. It's not deep, but it trips me. My ankle gives out. Then it burns. My white lab coat is stained with dirt. I didn't break it, but I most likely sprained it. The sting is sharp and feels like it's on fire.

"Dammit," I growl to myself.

There is a grotesque clicking noise coming from beyond the foliage. I know this sound. It's a Mantodea. The creature appears to me. It stomps on the ferns as it nears. This one is a female. They are larger and obscenely vicious. She screeches at me. I try to stand up, but my ankle won't cooperate.

The female Mantodea's red eyes are soulless. Her folded arms have razor-like edges. The antennas quiver as she rears up and roars. I haven't seen one this close. They are uglier than I remember. The Mantodea appears to be praying, but she is readying herself to tear me apart. She lunges and I cover my face with my arms to block out the sight of her devouring me.

I think of blond hair and gold eyes, for it's the last thing I want to see before I die. The Mantodea never reaches me. I open my eyes to Gwen. She is standing over me in a protective position. The Mantodea is mere inches from slicing open my neck, but Gwen has inserted her wires into the beast's head and abdomen.

"Bellamy, get down and close your eyes."

The Ex Machina gives me orders and I do what she says. There is a bright light. It sounds like gravel in a blender. The noise gives me a stomach ache. A small screech is emitted from the dying Mantodea. I look up to see Gwen has fried the creature with electricity. It lays smoking with its exoskeleton in pieces around it. The naked Mantodea convulses, but Gwen reaches out with a wire and zaps it again.

She is holding my shoulders. I'm in a daze. The brilliance of the light and the horrendous sound stun me. She is studying my face. Gwen's mouth is moving, but I can't hear her. The cedars and elms move around us. The earth is spinning faster and faster. A shadow passes over us. Is it another Mantodea? Or is it a bird? Gwen is talking to me. I think she's saying my name, but I fade out.

CHAPTER FOUR
FASCINATION

I hear beeping. Machines are sighing. My head is throbbing. It's difficult but I try to open my eyes. The fluorescents are unbearable. I can't do it. The white light attempts to laser through my eyelids.

"Bellamy?" it's Gwen's voice.

She sounds sad. I feel her hands on mine. Now I have to open my eyes. My ankle is burning. It takes me a minute but I remember why. I've been out for hours. I'm so tired. Gwen wants me to wake up but I can't.

"Bellamy?" she calls for me again.

Her hand moves from my palm to my face. She seems interested in my hair because she takes it between her fingers. I haven't seen her express affection and wondered if perhaps those parts of her brain were inactive or numbed by all the synapses meant to increase her intelligence.

"Gwen," I whisper her name to let her know I'm awake.

I'm too tired to open my eyes, though. The lights are hostile. We are chest to chest. Her heart beats next to mine. She is part machine but also very much alive. The Ex Machina is embracing me. She is being sweet, but I have the disturbed thought she could crush me if she wanted to. Gwen's arms can bend steel. She could press molten rock into sapphires and diamonds. Gwen can rip through a military tank.

"I thought you were going to die," she says.

This time not as flat. She sounds genuinely upset. I don't want her to be sad, but I'm excited to see a wider range of emotion in her. If only I could open my eyes.

"You're okay."

It's Hotaka.

"Hotaka, can we dim the lights?"

He does as I ask and I'm able to open my eyes. Gwen looks at me with glowing gold orbs. Her coral lips are in a frown. The opposite of what I want, but her hand is on mine. She protected me. I'm glad she came back. I don't know what I'd do if she didn't.

"Where did you go?" I ask.

"I wanted to see where the elk went," she answers.

"Did it make you happy?"

"Yes."

"Can I get you anything, Bell?" asks Hotaka.

"Just some water, please. Thank you," I say.

Hotaka steps out of the room. I rest my head on the pillow and adjust myself to get comfortable. The consistent beeps and hums of the machines lull me into a relaxed state. Gwen chooses not to leave me. She is still holding my hand but is also touching my heart. The Ex Machina is trying to unravel mysteries I don't have the answers to. The heart is a strange and complicated thing.

"I'm sorry," she says.

"For what?" I ask with my eyes closed.

"For running off. If I stayed with you, this wouldn't have happened."

Gwen is showing she is not only worried, but remorseful. She is more empathic than I thought.

"You saved me from the Mantodea. I'm not mad. I understand you were curious about the elk."

Hotaka returns with my water.

"I'm glad you're okay," he says.

I sit up and take a sip.

"Thanks. Me too. I'm glad Gwen came back for me," I smile at her.

She is looking at her palm on my chest. The Ex Machina is focused on my heart. Hotaka and I glance at each other. I see him take out his notebook and write something down.

"I'm going to get ready for bed. Goodnight, Bellamy. Goodnight, Gwen," says Hotaka.

"Goodnight," I say as he walks out. My eyes are heavy. I close them and allow myself to drift in and out. My ankle keeps waking me up. First it throbs. Then it burns. I wake up to it stinging. The constant pain annoys me. I'm surprised to feel Gwen's hands on mine. She hasn't left my side. I turn to look at her. The Ex Machina doesn't need to sleep if she has sufficient energy levels. "I'm okay if you want to go to your room," I offer.

"I want to stay with you," she says.

"I'd like that." I rub the back of my head. It aches. I think Gwen's powerful electricity and blinding lights are amazing, but damn, they pack a punch.

"Why did you think I wouldn't come back?" she asks.

I massage my scalp, hoping to ease the tension.

"You have free will. I'm sure you have your own desires. If you did leave, I wouldn't hunt you down and make you come back or anything like that."

"Where would I go?"

"Wherever you want. You can go anywhere. To other countries. Deep space and the bottom of the sea. You're different from any being in this world," I say.

"I want to stay." This makes me laugh. She doesn't think it's funny.

"Good. I want you to stay."

I pull the blanket up to my shoulders. I'm about to close my eyes, but Gwen has more to say.

"Bellamy, can I ask you something?"

"Yes."

"What am I supposed to do to save humanity?"

"Well, today I saw how you fried that Mantodea. You're incredibly strong. The Mantodea have taken over our planet. They have decimated our armies and killed off seventy percent of the population. We need to find a way to destroy them without hurting anything else," I say.

I haven't told Gwen much about her purpose. I've been too busy trying to make her smile.

"If I get rid of the Mantodea, can we go outside all the time?" she asks in her childish way.

"Of course. We could go outside anytime we felt like it."

"Then I will do it."

"Really? You want to help me?" I ask.

"Yes," she says and her eyes stop glowing gold.

She looks like a normal girl with blue and chrome wings. Her blond eyelashes are noticeable without the mechanical lights.

***

When I was twenty-one, I met Sophia. She was eighteen. Her father came to work for my dad. I don't know if we actually liked each other, but we were the only people in the lab under forty, so we started dating. She had shoulder-length brown hair and blue eyes. I thought her laugh was adorable.

We dated for over a year. I lost my virginity to her. At the time, I was worried I'd be a virgin forever with the circumstances. Who would've thought aliens would be one of the many reasons I couldn't get a girlfriend? I liked Sophia, but I don't think I loved her. Her hair smelled like cinnamon. I think she used me the way I used her, but we were okay with what we had.

I remember getting out of bed to stare at the Ex Machina. Sophia's arm would be around me and I'd have to gently pull from her grasp. She wasn't a tall girl, but she had these long spindly arms. I would sneak out of my room and into the part of the lab holding Gwen. It seemed like she was waiting for me. My dad's chair is next to her tank. Her long hair swirling like a tornado in a glass.

Sophia and I said " I love you" all the time. We were young. It felt like love. I knew I meant it when I put my hand to Gwen's tank and said it. She hadn't touched the glass since. The respirator made wheezing noises. It unnerved me.

Slinking back into my room, I'd slip back into bed. Sophia never asked me where I went. She would put her arms around me and I'd fall asleep dreaming about blond hair and blue liquid. I was sad when Sophia and her father went back to the United States, but I was also happy that I could focus on Gwen. I had grown quite fond of her.

My ankle is in a brace. I have to use crutches. Gwen hasn't left my side. I think she is worried about me. We are playing chess again. She wins every time, but I don't mind. I enjoy being with her. She moves a pawn and so do I. We are examining each other. I sense Gwen looking at me differently. As more than an opponent or creator. I think Gwen is learning to love. Maybe I'm being too hopeful.

"How are you, Gwen?" I ask. She moves her rook.

"I'm fine. How are you?" she asks.

"I'm doing well. My ankle is almost done healing."

I move my knight, and she takes my bishop. Gwen is very good at strategy. I'm not only impressed, but I'm proud of her.

"Am I not allowed outside anymore?" she asks.

I stop playing to look at her. She seems cross with me. Her mood is usually mild, but she has instances of annoyance.

"We can go outside as soon as I'm all better."

I try to calm her down. The gold glow of her eyes seems increasingly sinister.

"Really?" She takes one of my pawns.

"Of course. I would never restrict your access to the outside. It's just that I want to be with you."

"If I were to walk out that door right now, would you try to stop me?"

She stares me down with a predatory glare. I've never been this frightened of Gwen, but her manners and line of questioning are making me suspicious. Perhaps the Ex Machina has motives of her own.

"I don't want to make you do anything you don't want to do. If you don't want to live here, I won't force you to. You're not my hostage," I say and take her rook.

"Why did you make me without any actual means of controlling me?"

Her awareness is astonishing, but I expected her to ask me this at some point.

"Because of my father's theory."

"What's that?"

"If you got to know us, you would help us willingly. Trying to create a machine, intending to manipulate it beyond its own autonomy, was never my father's style."

"I'm not a machine. I'm not fully human either. What am I?" she asks and takes my queen. I lose. She rearranges the pieces. Her wires swish around her, focusing, sensing.

"You're something completely different. An Ex Machina, if you will."

"I am to bring about resolution for humanity."

"That's correct." I start the game by moving a pawn. Gwen stares at the board and then at me. She takes a long time on this turn. "Are you okay?" I ask.

"What if I can't do it?"

"I trust you can." I smile at her, but she frowns at me.

"I want you to be able to go outside all the time," she says.

It's quite touching. She hasn't said anything this personal to me yet. I knew she cared about me when she saved me. She brought me back to the lab and waited for me to wake up. Gwen may have dulled emotions, but they are there.

"What would you want to do after you defeat the Mantodea?" I ask.

Gwen's wires dart in different directions, hypnotizing me. They make me nervous. The metal jacks can act as stingers.

"Stay with you," she says and takes one of my pawns.

"You don't have to."

"I want to."

"Really? Why?"

This interests me. Gwen is showing attachment. She embraced me. The Ex Machina held me the way a child holds a toy, but could crush me with minimal effort.

"I can't explain it," she says.

"I'm flattered you'd want to stay with me. I'm not that fun," I tease.

"I enjoy being with you."

"You do?" I ask.

Gwen has been curious about me. She shows me affection. I felt her touch my hair. She reaches for my face and heart if I am near.

"Yes."

She moves her bishop and swipes my knight.

"I'm glad."

"Is it okay if I stay with you?" she asks.

"Of course. You can stay with me as long as you like."

We continue to play. Gwen takes my queen. I lose again.

"Why do I want to stay with you?" she asks.

I rearrange the board, but Gwen doesn't want to play anymore. She gets up to sit next to me. Her hands are on my face. She is trying to read me.

"I'm not sure. You must like me," I joke.

This time the Ex Machina's face changes. She smiles.

"I do," she says.

***

Today we're observing Gwen's abilities. I'm working with Isamu, Katsuo, and Nori. They are all in their early forties. Isamu has round glasses and a square jaw. Katsuo has a youthful air about him but is ten years older than me. Nori is a quiet guy with straight black hair and bangs covering his eyes.

Katsuo has a son named Hikari. He is seven years old. They both have honey-colored eyes. Katsuo's wife was murdered by a Mantodea when Hikari was five. Although not the most ideal place for a child, the lab isn't the worst. I know because I grew up here. It's a sterile environment, but we try to make the most of it. We listen to electronic and rock music while we work. No one eats alone. We are a family of misfits.

Hotaka is my friend but I get along with everyone. Nori doesn't talk about much except work with me, but we like some of the same music and can bond over that. I think Nori is a soulful person but is too shy to express it. I can tell because he has deep eyes. Not everyone has deep eyes like Nori. When Gwen's eyes stop glowing gold, there is a mystery told in earth tones. Sophia had these strange blue eyes. They reminded me of delphiniums. They were a dark shade of cerulean but they weren't deep the way Gwen and Nori's are.

Isamu is a science nerd like me. He was always this way. I had to grow into it. We joke around about not actually being smart, only so curious it's foolish. He has shaggy hair like me and light brown eyes. His glasses give him an air of authority, but he is a laid back person. Isamu and I like the same comic books. We geek out about scientific theories, the human condition, and superheroes. It's ironic I grew up reading about heroes and then I made one.

The men and I wait patiently. Gwen is in the testing chamber. We have given her an assortment of tasks. She can extend the wires out thirty feet and grab, shred, or shock whatever her target is. Gwen hovers with ease, using her wings. The Ex Machina is graceful. She reminds me of a little goddess. Her skin is shiny under the fluorescent lights.

Gwen could have captured the hearts of many men if she were a normal girl in a normal world. I see her wearing a flower crown and a bunad. She could have been a Scandinavian princess in a festival. The sides of her head would be adorned with plaited blond braids. I wonder who Gwen would've been if she wasn't donated for my father's project.

Katsuo and Nori take lots of notes with vigor. Isamu can't look away from her. He is too enthralled. Me and him are the same. Gwen can solve complex puzzles in a matter of seconds. Her partially robotic mind allows her easy access to the secrets of problem solving. She picks up a metal bar and bends it without emotion. It creaks as she folds the steel.

There is a pile of sand. Gwen uses electricity from one of the wires on it. We put on sunglasses in order to watch her magnificence. She shocks the sand, and it cuts the power to the building for a second. We all go "whoa" at the same time. Gwen reaches into the sand and pulls out large pieces of glass that look decorative with floral elements. She holds up clear peonies and chrysanthemums.

The next test is underwater. There is a small reservoir in the mountain. We've equipped it with cameras so we can watch Gwen. The men seem shy when Gwen takes off her dress. Even though she is a machine, she is still a woman. The Ex Machina feels no embarrassment and dives in. Her wings propel her through the water. The aquamarine blue glow of the metal plates mixes with her white-blond hair creating the illusion of a mermaid. Gwen can go eleven minutes without breathing. Her lungs can store enough air for her to make brief trips to space and under the sea.

Gwen does something that has us all engrossed. She swims up to the camera. Her hair swirls around her, but her breasts are visible. I see Nori turn red and look at his notepad. She reaches for the screen and blows bubbles at it. Like she's blowing a kiss. She's gone in a flash and all I see is dark water.

My heart needs an electric shock because it has stopped. I'm not sure why, but I'm on edge. Gwen's attentiveness towards me and her strange behavior in front of the camera have me on high alert. What is going on with her? Perhaps she was curious. I'm not sure but I think the Ex Machina is aware of her sexual appeal and is flirting.

She darts back and forth. Then she stops in front of the camera. She pulls back and runs her hand down her flat stomach, almost salaciously. I'm not sure if it's on purpose or not. Gwen hovers in place and touches her collarbone. She disappears into the darkness but returns to blow bubble kisses. Maybe she is playing.

Gwen emerges from the water with soaking wet hair. It leaves large puddles around her feet. She doesn't put her dress back on. The men and I watch her approach the glass. The device on her head has tangled blond strands in it.

The Ex Machina has piercing eyes. I can see the hair on the back of the men's necks stand up as she steps closer. Gwen presses her small palm up to the glass. She's looking at me. The men notice this and begin writing it down in their notes. Gwen and I stare at each other, trying to understand, attempting to see inside the other.

CHAPTER FIVE
IMPRINTED

Things became more tense and unusual with my father after I turned twenty-three. I sensed he didn't trust me around Gwen. He would shoo me away from her. I would find him asleep in his chair with his head pressed up against the tank. I never did anything to warrant suspicion. My father's colleagues told me it was because he was losing his mind. They might have been right.

One day, when my father wasn't hovering around Gwen, I let myself admire her. The screens showed the device creating the additional synapses. Her brain activity was through the roof. The spiraling platinum blonde hair fascinated me. She was a tornado in a glass, getting stronger and stronger as the years went by. I anticipated meeting her just as much as my father did. My hand was on the glass and I heard my father say my name. "Bellamy?"

"Hey dad," I said.

He stepped next to me and studied my face before turning to Gwen.

"What are you doing?" he asked.

I could tell he was agitated by my presence. His work consumed him. He wanted Gwen all to himself, but I stole moments with her when I could.

"I just wanted to see her," I said and let my palm fall.

He didn't stop me as I exited the steel door. As long as he was in there, I couldn't see her. It drove me crazy. Now it would drive my father crazy to see how Gwen has grown. She's made such progress. Her strength is incredible, but it is her mind that is infallible. She can calculate and process faster than any computer. I'm intrigued by her choices.

When offered books, she chose another children's story. This one is about a little prince who travels through space and time to learn about the power of love. The other book she chose was a romance novel. Gwen can divide and conquer an army, but I believe she has a kind heart. The device has altered her brain, but the core of her humanity is relatively unchanged besides the metal wires protecting it.

Gwen has made efforts to be closer to Shira and Hotaka. She follows me everywhere, but she lights up for Hotaka if he asks to listen to a song with him. He reads poems, hymns from other countries, and haikus to her. Hotaka wants to introduce literature and music into her life. It's nice to see her build a friendship.

Shira is wary of Gwen, but they have a somewhat formal but sisterly connection. Gwen and her talk about paintings, landmarks, and girly things. Recently, Gwen allowed Shira to do her hair and makeup. I was astonished. Shira gave her traditional Scandinavian braids. It had to have taken hours. Gwen has so much hair, but Shira was patient and did something a female friend would do.

The Ex Machina goes back and forth between following me like a shadow and being distant. I can't tell if she retreats because I have upset her or because she wants to be alone. She's intimidating, but I don't mind her interest in me. I think she feels closer to me since rescuing me from the female Mantodea.

"Are you ready to go outside?" I ask her.

Gwen is happy my ankle is healed and excited to go out again. I hit the button for the heavy door and we step out into the bright day. The sun is the color of white wine. The wood and grassy fragrance are invigorating. I get sick of the scent of chemicals and metal.

Gwen's wires swish about. She is surveying the area. Her face is tense but relaxes. The Ex Machina senses nothing dangerous. At least not within fifteen miles. She is admiring the view. The sun is behind her. She is a little goddess. Her blue chrome wings glow and it adds to her magnificence.

"It's so beautiful," she says. I stand next to her and look down at the lake. The forest is dark but pretty shades of jade, juniper, and chestnut. I think it's going to electrocute me, but it doesn't. Gwen grabs my hand with both of hers. "Can we go a little further?" she asks. This makes me anxious, but her sensors are slack and she doesn't seem alarmed.

"Okay, but not too far."

Gwen lets me go and we walk down the hill towards the forest. I crush dandelions and tall grass under my feet. It's nice to walk on something other than concrete or steel. Gwen stops to watch two butterflies. They have blue and green wings. She puts her hand up and they dance over her. It's subtle, but I see a smile on the Ex Machina's face.

She leads me further into the dark woods than I'd like to be, but I am engrossed by the vast green tones and the glory of my creation. I see her kneel down. She is inspecting a beetle crawling across a pink rose. Her eyes are luminous gold in the dim forest.

"We should go back," I say.

"Can we stay out just a little longer? I sense nothing harmful near us," she begs.

The Ex Machina could do whatever she wanted, and I'd be helpless to stop her but she asks for permission. It's so childlike. I give in.

"Okay, just a little longer."

I smile, but I'm tense. Gwen isn't afraid. I shouldn't be either. She takes my hand and walks me to a small stream. It makes quiet bubbly noises. A bird sings and another joins in. Gwen's eyes are on the sky. They glow in the shadows of the pines.

"Was this what it was like before the Mantodea came?" she asks.

"Kind of. We could just be outside and not worry. I used to play baseball with my friends," I tell her.

She doesn't know much about me. I'm not sure if she cares, but maybe she does.

"Do you want to play baseball now?" she asks. It humors me and I laugh.

"I haven't really thought about it in a long time, but yeah. I miss it."

"I want you to be able to do whatever you want, Bellamy." Gwen seems to be expressive today.

"Thanks. I feel the same about you."

We sit in a patch of sun and admire the clouds through the canopy. Gwen reaches for my hand again. Her grip is gentle, but I have horrible visions of her ripping off my arm. I blink away the thought. Gwen stands up quickly. The wires are darting with wild movements. Something is nearing us. She grabs me and uses her ability to fly. I'm terrified, but I trust her. She finds a ditch surrounded by irises and tall grass.

"Stay here," she whispers. Gwen takes off into the sky and I can no longer see her. My stomach drops and I'm afraid I won't see her again. I lean up against the dirt wall and wait. She must be fighting a Mantodea. I hope there aren't many of them.

Gwen's been gone a while. I'm getting paranoid she's not coming back. Maybe she got hurt. No, Gwen is too strong. Nothing could hurt her. She could have taken off. She knows I have no real way of controlling her. I have been relying on our emotional bond.

The earth rumbles. The mud around me quakes. I hear the disgusting whirring noise the Mantodea's wings make. I'm in the shadows, but above me is an opening in the trees. In the patch of blue against the dark forest, I see a dozen Mantodea swarming around something. It's Gwen. She's using her wires to shock off their exoskeletons. After they are exposed, she zaps them to death. They are grotesque. Their oily black bodies fill the sky. It hurts my ears when they screech.

Pieces of the Mantodea's black exoskeleton rain down along with bits of their burnt flesh. They smell sickly. Their blood is greenish yellow. It hits the tops of the cedars and oak trees. The foul liquid drips from the branches and lands on the dirt. It scorches the earth it touches.

I cover my face as chunks of dead aliens fall from the sky. They land around the dike I'm in. They thud and make squishing sounds as they taint the grass. The black exoskeletons are heavy and leave indents where they hit the dirt. Fleshy bits of the Mantodea reek of sewage and evaporate in the sun. The aliens' naked bodies are meant for the darkness of space. Gwen shreds all the Mantodeans apart and returns to me.

"Are you okay?" she asks.

"I'm fine," I say.

"You're shaking." She helps me out of the ditch, and I see my hand is trembling.

"I'll be alright."

The Ex Machina analyzes my face. I think she knows I'm lying. Gwen's eyes catch the light of the sun. I love her, but she frightens me. She is a machine capable of murdering anything.

***

Hotaka and I are listening to music and going over our notes. I'm showing him Gwen's results from her tests. She is unbeatable. There is no match for her. Hotaka and I eye each other with understanding, but don't say it out loud. The glare on his glasses hides his true emotions, but I sense he is apprehensive as well. Gwen cares about us, but we are nothing compared to her. Humanity is fragile and fleeting. Gods have nothing to fear.

"You should have seen it," I say as I tell him about Gwen's recent battle with the army of Mantodea.

"She is impressive," he says. Hotaka bobs his head to the music and taps his pen. I slide my chair across the room. My father has a bookshelf of his theories, plans, and ideas. Now that Gwen has survived birth, passed all her tests, and shown emotional connection, I feel the need to reread some of my father's work.

"I see why my father was so obsessed with her," I say over my shoulder.

Hotaka stops tapping to the beat of the song.

"Do you think Gwen is falling in love with you?" he asks.

My tongue fumbles in my mouth. I can't get the words out.

"No. I think the Ex Machina would fall in love with someone a lot cooler than me," I joke.

Hotaka smiles with his teeth but doesn't laugh. He stares at the screen and then goes back to looking at the notepad.

"I think she is."

I slide my chair back so we are sitting next to each other. Hotaka is giving me a strange look. He appears quite young, a pale face with no harsh lines, but he has shadows under his eyes.

"What makes you say that?" I ask.

Hotaka and I are friends, but we are also avid scientists. I try to listen from the point of view of a professional and not from my own perspective.

"After her birth, she touched your face. She didn't show any emotion, but imprinting did take place. Gwen has chosen you over anyone else. She and I spend time together, but it's not the same. Gwen seeks you out. She follows you around. I see here in Nori's notes he wrote: The Ex Machina appears strong, healthy, and capable of defeating the Mantodea. Her abilities are numerous: strategic, formidable, and intelligent. Acts mostly robotic but has a strange infatuation with Dr. Krim. The Ex Machina was aware of the underwater cameras, which may have encouraged her to make provocative gestures. When Gwen approached the glass where Dr. Krim was, she didn't cover herself. She put her hand on the glass."

"She could be exploring her sexuality," I suggest.

Hotaka rests his chin in his hand and examines the notes.

"Gwen became agitated when she couldn't understand why she liked a song," he says.

"I think she is getting better at dealing with her feelings. She is still very new to the world. We have to be patient with her."

Hotaka nods to agree and flips through his notepad. He pauses on another observation.

"She prefers to read children's literature and books from the romance genre as opposed to complex scientific theories, history, or nonfiction."

"I think it's kind of cute. She is trying to be more than what she is," I state with conviction. Maybe it's because I truly want to believe.

"Besides you, the only other person she's touched physically is Shira. She is polite to everyone but shows no interest in being intimate with them," he announces.

I spin around in my chair. I'm in my thirties, but I can't help myself.

"She hugged me once," I admit.

Hotaka writes it down with blue ink. He leans back in his chair. Taking off his glasses, he smiles to himself. He doesn't make eye contact with me like he usually does.

"When you sprained your ankle, Gwen brought you back. She seemed upset. It was the first time I saw her express any deep emotion. She puts her hand on your heart. I think she is trying to understand it."

"All this time I've been trying to figure out the mind of the machine, she's been trying to understand me. Perhaps this is a good thing," I say.

Hotaka shakes his head at me.

"You shouldn't play with her emotions," he warns.

"I'm not going to."

Gwen is everything I've dreamed of. I wouldn't do anything to hurt her.

"I mean it. Women are already scary when they're pissed off. Don't lead the Ex Machina on," he says sternly.

"I wouldn't do that. She heard me tell her I loved her years ago when she was still in stasis. I think it's partially why she feels attached to me. I wouldn't do anything to ruin the bond I have with her."

"What do you think your dad would say?" he asks.

I rub the back of my head, trying to think of what my dad would have to say about his precious creation having a crush on me.

"He'd probably say I ruined the entire project," I laugh.

It's not funny, but it's true. My dad would probably be really upset if he were alive to see how Gwen favors me over everybody else. In a sinister way, I feel special. No one else can have what I have.

"Be cautious, Bell. We designed her to kill the Mantodea and save the world. She could fry us all in under two minutes if she wanted to. Gwen still has a human heart, and the heart holds darkness in it. We should be careful not to warrant any cruel intentions."

"I'll be careful," I say.

Hotaka and I go back to poring over our paperwork. I can't focus, though. Blonde hair and gold eyes keep distracting me. Her bubble kisses. The way she hid me in the ditch by the irises. How she held me when I was hurt.

Then I get another vision. The Ex Machina is angry with me. Gold and blue lights tell me I'm in trouble. She doesn't care about her purpose anymore. The aliens are meaningless to her. Gwen's hand is around my neck and her steel fingers are clawing out my heart because I broke hers.

CHAPTER SIX
ARDOR

I was happy when Eva's parents came to work with my father. Eva was a bit too young for me. She was nineteen; I was twenty-four. But nobody was going to tell us what to do. We were together for less than six months, but I loved her.

Eva had long, dark hair and sea-green eyes. She had olive skin and a beauty mark on the left side of her cheek, right below her eye. We were happy. Eva liked the same dorky stuff I liked. We geeked out over music and comic books. It was the end of the world, but we spent our days laughing about nothing.

Everyone knew I was Adam Krim's kid, so they let me goof off. They caught us making out in the halls and racing around the building. The scientists that worked for my dad were annoyed by me, but what could they do? We were stuck here. I was making the best of it.

One day, Eva asked me to show her Gwen. This made me hesitate. I don't know why. My dad hovered around the tank, but not as much. His colleagues were strict with him after he had a mental breakdown, where he threw a chair and broke the screen on one of the monitors. Thankfully, it wasn't in use. If he refused food or sleep, they just medicated him. It was the only way.

We waited until my dad had to be sedated. It felt like a criminal act sneaking into the forbidden part of the building. It wasn't technically against the rules. My dad made me feel weird about it for the past year. Eva and I were holding hands and creeping around the shadowy parts of the laboratory. I opened the steel door, and we were greeted by the blue glow of Gwen's tank.

Eva and I stood in awe. She was glorious. Her wires moved with the gentle sway of the amniotic fluid. Machines made a symphony of beeps, whooshing, and hums. Eva's deep green eyes were as big as saucers. Gwen took a slower breath and so did I. My girlfriend and I watched the child Ex Machina, humanity's savior, take rhythmic breaths through a respirator. Our eyes didn't leave her.

I spent three weeks sulking in my room after Eva and her family went back home. We didn't have the deepest relationship, but we were happy. I felt like I needed her. Sophia and I never clicked the way Eva, and I did. My dad didn't notice my absence. In fact, I think he enjoyed it.

I'm wandering around the all too familiar building in search of Hotaka. I find him and Gwen. He's reading a poem to her. She seems entranced by the words. To my surprise, Gwen gets up to sit next to him. I can tell Hotaka is sweating bullets from here. Gwen takes Hotaka's glasses off. Her gold eyes bore holes into his. I intervene.

"Hey. What are you two up to?" I ask as casually as I can.

"Oh, nothing. I was just reading Gwen some poems," says Hotaka.

Gwen gingerly places his glasses back on for him.

"Do you like poetry, Gwen?" I ask.

She considers my question.

"Yes. I don't understand a lot of it, but I like it for reasons I can't explain with words," she says.

Gwen realizes the limitations of verbal speech. The heart speaks a unique language.

"That's how art works. It's good to feel indescribable things," I say.

Hotaka is watching our interaction with curiosity and fear.

"Why is it good to feel indescribable things?" she asks.

It takes me several moments to find a way to convey an answer, but I do.

"It's part of being human," I say and sit across from her.

Hotaka is relieved her attention isn't on him anymore. Gwen's eyes cease to flicker gold and return to their natural hazel color.

"Part of being human," she repeats.

Hotaka has a wild expression. He has never seen her eyes without the gold glow of the device beneath them.

"Can you read me the poem?" I ask.

Gwen's mind fascinates me. I want to know what touches her heart.

"Made of metal/flow like water/soft as a petal/I am a daughter/there is no other," she recites the verses.

"I like it. It's really beautiful," I say.

Hotaka swallows and loosens his tie.

"It makes me feel...awake," says Gwen.

"It's one of my favorites," says Hotaka.

Gwen swishes around her wires and we both flinch. Does she do it on purpose to put us on edge? She seems at ease, but I am wary of her.

"I like how you are enjoying beautiful things," I say.

"Yes," she says it in a flat tone, but she reaches for my hand across the table. Hotaka stands up abruptly. He's nervous.

"I'll talk to you later, Bellamy. Bye Gwen," he says.

I see him jotting something down in his black notepad. Gwen looks at our hands with glowing eyes. Her racing mind can't stop for long. Why would she be infatuated with me? I'm not the most handsome, funny, or smart guy.

The Ex Machina's affection towards me is flattering but confusing. She could be attached to me because I was the one who was there when she reached out. I said I love you to her when she couldn't comprehend that combination of words. Because of our emotional connection, Gwen has protected me, agreed to help me, and stayed with me despite knowing she can do whatever she wants. She chooses me above everyone and everything. But why?

"What do you want to do now?" I ask.

Gwen doesn't meet my gaze. She keeps her eyes on our hands. She holds my right hand with both of hers. For some reason, it reminds me of praying.

"Will you show me something you like?" she asks.

Gwen wants me to share with her. This is a great opportunity to learn about her. I show her the comic books I like. She flips through the pages with delicate fingers. Her hands are small, but I remember the way she bent steel like it was nothing. I think of how she could fold a submarine or take down an aircraft.

"What do you think?" I ask.

Gwen doesn't stop reading.

"They make me happy," she says.

It's less flat this time. Gwen is surreal.

"You don't think they're silly?" I ask.

Gwen's taste in reading material is varied and unpredictable. Like her.

"Why would I think that?" she asks as she finishes another one about a female superhero.

"I don't know. I wasn't sure what things you would like."

"I like outside. I like flowers, butterflies, and birds. I like the forest. I like music and books that I don't understand. They make me feel impossible things," she says.

"What else do you like?" I ask.

"I like having my hair done. I like swimming. I like flying…" Gwen puts her hand on my chest and I feel it shock me with no electricity. "I like you," she says.

I'm worried my voice is going to shake. I put my hand over hers.

"I like you too, Gwen."

This makes her smile, which is what I wanted, but I hope I didn't encourage something I shouldn't.

***

Around the time I turned twenty-six, my father took a turn for the worse. Again. He became more paranoid. His colleagues had to restrain him a few times. He tried to attack me once. My father believed I was looking at Gwen in an "unscientific" and "inappropriate" way. He said he couldn't trust anyone around her except himself.

After we forced him to eat and rest, he went back to being his dorky self. It was like day and night. His moods would decline as his appetite and sleep varied and then became none. My father taught me everything I know, yet I knew nothing about him. He was known by the world but a stranger to his son and wife.

He knew so much, but didn't know how to keep his family together. Not even before the Mantodea. He was never around. I didn't let it bother me. My friends, baseball, and school filled my days. I loved my dad from afar. It didn't strike me as odd until much later in life. My dad was on the news, doing interviews, and producing technology that had only been seen in science fiction.

Our family received a lot of admiration, but also a lot of hate. People thought my dad was a good guy. Others thought he was a lunatic. Many benefited from his scientific achievements, but everyone had an opinion about him.

He wasn't like everybody else. At twenty-four, he had already started his company and created ripples in the field of futuristic transportation. My father wanted us to be able to travel anywhere in space. He wanted to see the crushing depths of the ocean. I wanted to be a normal kid with a normal dad. But my father was extraordinary, and the world knew it.

One evening when I was sitting with Gwen, I couldn't help but feel a pang of guilt. She was physically age twelve. I actually felt bad about what we were doing to her. It only lasted a millisecond, but it existed in my consciousness. I didn't want to notice it, but once I did, I couldn't stop. She wouldn't have been able to live a normal life with the Mantodea, but her innocent face and serene expression haunted me for several weeks.

If permitted, I would read to Gwen. I would play music and sit with her. I wanted to witness her development, too. If Gwen resented being an Ex Machina, I would be devastated. I put my hand to the tank again one day when my father was restrained. She twitched slightly and took a deeper breath through the respirator. I said it again: I love you. Maybe my attachment to her was unhealthy. In a way, I felt like I could understand my father if I understood her.

Gwen is following me around the lab. It's startling to my colleagues. I'm doing my rounds and checking on all the equipment. My team is analyzing their notes and watering crops. They're hanging out and drinking tea. Some are in their rooms reading or sleeping. Our lab is solar powered. We haven't had any issues with electricity or clean water. My father was methodical and planned for everything. I check on our systems periodically the way he would. His habits rubbed off on me.

I go into the room where Gwen was born. The tank is empty. Greatness was created in that glass. Suspended in blue liquid, weightless, for twenty years. Now here she is. Walking right beside me. Gwen has spoken little today, but she said she wanted to stay with me. My team tries not to show their apprehension. Hotaka is friendly to Gwen, and she is polite. Shira waves at her and she waves back.

Isamu, Katsuo, and Nori nod at me but have wide eyes as they gaze at the Ex Machina behind me. Katsuo pulls his son closer to him. We keep walking. Nori's notes were accurate. He observes Gwen as she follows at my heels like a pet. Her wires sway with slight jerky movements. It puts us all on edge. I don't think she is trying to intimidate us, but it's a possibility. The Ex Machina is a strategist.

"What's on your mind?" I ask her.

Gwen's eyes are lit up with gold flecks. She is thinking.

"You," she says the word in a feminine way.

Every day, she sounds more human.

"What about me?" I sit down and gesture for her to join me. It's been a while since we played chess. She lets me go first.

"It's hard for me to say."

She fiddles with her hair. Gwen moves her pawn, and I move mine. I think she is toying with me as she plans her victory.

"Take your time," I offer. We play in silence for a while. Gwen is subtle but flirty. The way she touches her hair and leans on the table.

"I want to be around you all the time, but I don't know why," she says.

I move my rook, and she moves her knight.

"I like that you want to be around me."

It's not a lie. I hope I'm not creating an unsavory dynamic, but I want Gwen to have room for her own feelings.

"Bellamy, can I ask you something?"

I move my bishop; she moves her king.

"What is it?"

She takes my queen. I lose. She arranges the board with swift, calculated movements.

"Am I pretty?"

This time, she looks at me. I take in her features. Defined eyebrows, full lips, gold eyes. She has a part in the middle and long blond hair tumbles down both sides. Her round nose has freckles on it. Gwen has a perfectly symmetrical face.

"You're beautiful," I say.

The Ex Machina gets up and stands next to me. I feel the hair on the back of my neck stand up as she touches my face.

"So are you," she says.

***

It's a bizarre phenomenon. To be related, to live in close quarters, and know nothing about the other. By the time I was twenty-eight, my father was dead to me. Dead to everybody. He lived for Gwen and nothing else. The blue glow of the tank reflected in his square glasses. Adam Krim was lost to his creation.

I sense she and I are bonded. She glances at the door leading outside but stays next to me. I catch her eying it when we pass. Gwen is loyal and doesn't abandon me. She follows me most of the time now. When offered other company she indulges them, but not for long. Shira brushed her hair and gave her red lipstick one day. Gwen seemed really happy. She reads poetry and listens to music with Hotaka. The older scientists are polite but cold to her. They are frightened by her capabilities.

Hikari shows interest in the Ex Machina. He told me he thinks she looks like an angel. I thought it was cute. It was so subtle it was barely noticeable, but I saw Gwen and Hikari make eye contact and smile at each other. Katsuo pulled him away from her and both their faces fell. Isamu and Nori keep their heads down if she passes them in the halls.

When Gwen began maturing into a woman, my father became intensely paranoid. He thought people would do bad things to her if he wasn't around. I remember offering to sit with her, and my father tried to choke me out. He was a loose cannon at this point. Never a violent man, but he grabbed the collar of my shirt. We wore the same lab coat, had the same eyes, but we were not the same. I shoved him off me.

He accused any male scientist of being inappropriate, even if nothing took place. Everyone was a threat. I tried to ask my father what he thought I did, but he wouldn't answer me. He most likely didn't have one. I cared about her. It hurt me to know he thought I was perverse. Gwen's long mermaid hair swirled in the tank. She was a siren. Her song did something to my dad, and he wasn't the same.

I'm showing Gwen more books. It's exciting to see what she picks. The gold glow beneath the hazel is bright as she scans her different options. She wears red lipstick and plays with her hair. The wings peek out from her shoulders. They illuminate the blonde a sapphire color. I think Hikari is right. Gwen does look like an angel.

Gwen picks another children's story. This one is about a mermaid who falls in love with a human. She chooses a book of poems with romantic themes. It makes me smile. She might be a killing machine, but she is still a cute girl. I think the novels are influencing her personality. She's sitting on her bed. I get up to sit with her. Gwen opens the book of poems and shows one to me.

Razor wire/around my heart/it hurts to admire/so don't let me start.

"What does this mean?" she asks.

I read it a few times over her winged shoulder. Blonde hair coils next to her.

"Poetry is up to interpretation. No one really knows what it means except the artist," I say.

"How odd."

"What's odd?"

"Artists make things I like, but I don't know why I like them. It must be nice being an artist. To make people feel things they don't understand," she says and runs her index finger over the page with the poem.

"It's what makes art fun. It's unique," I say and without thinking, I pick up her hair. It's astonishing how long it is.

"What did you feel when I read the poem to you?" she asks.

I mull it over. Poetry isn't really my thing. Not that I don't enjoy it. I'm not the kind of guy to analyze my feelings after reading them.

"It made me feel…" I try to find the words. "Hopeful but sad."

Gwen surprises me by touching my heart.

"I don't know how to describe how I feel," she says.

"That's okay. Most people can't express what they feel."

Gwen's touch isn't aggressive, but it's making me nervous. Images of her ripping out my heart come flooding in. No, she wouldn't do that. Gwen is emotionally attached to me. She was worried about me when I sprained my ankle.

"I think I want to be alone now," she says and withdraws her hand.

I take my leave. Gwen does this to me. She follows me around like a puppy but then sends me away. There are days I seek her out and she ignores me. Other times she has her hand on my heart. I think Hotaka is right. She wants to understand it. Gwen wishes to understand her own heart as well.

"Goodnight, Gwen."

"Goodnight."

I go into my room and rip off my lab coat. My button-up shirt is driving me nuts. I could wear whatever I want, but I try to be professional. It's the end of the world and I should try to look nice. Lying on my bed, I try to slow my heart. It's pounding a million miles a minute. I wonder if Gwen did something to it. There's a knock at my door. I expect it to be her, but it's not. It's Shira.

"Hey, what's up?" I ask.

"Bellamy, can I talk to you for a minute?" She looks worried.

Her black hair touches the tops of her shoulders. It sways as she looks down the hall towards Gwen's room.

"Sure," I let her in. Shira is wearing a shirt dress and her lab coat. She has a small frame and a delicate face. Wispy bangs, arched eyebrows, and a pouty bottom lip. "What's going on?" I ask.

"It's about the Ex Machina."

"What about her?"

"Gwen's behavior...it's different."

Her voice is hushed.

"I noticed she seems to enjoy wearing lipstick now. She touches her hair and acts flirtatiously," I state.

"She does it for you," says Shira.

"Gwen is exploring her personality."

I resist rolling my eyes at her. Shira and I have considered dating but decided against it. We respect each other as professionals. Shira is pretty, smart, and kind. It's never felt right, though.

"Nori notices it, too."

Shira is becoming agitated with me. Good thing she's not my girlfriend.

"I know. Gwen has developed feelings for me due to imprinting. She heard me tell her I loved her over thirteen years ago."

I'm a scientist and feel the need to state the facts.

"What are we going to do about it?" she asks like it's another simple problem solving game.

"I try not to encourage her crush on me. It's probably a phase. She's still very new to the world. I'm the first person she touched. I'm sure she'll get over it."

I brush it off. Shira doesn't want to let it go, though. She uncrosses her arms to shout at me in a hushed fashion.

"Your father's project, the savior of humanity, is putting on makeup and blowing kisses at you."

Shira saw the footage. She's done her homework.

"So what? She might be humanity's only hope, but she is still a person. I'm not going to tell her what to do."

"You're really going to just ignore this?"

Shira folds her arms again. She's tapping her foot with anxiety and irritation.

"What can I do? Tell her to stop liking me? It's part of how we're going to get her to help us."

I'm losing my temper. For the most part, I'm a mellow guy. Right now, I want to be left alone.

"I don't think it's a good idea to play with her heart," she states.

Shira picks up the strands of hair tickling her cheek and tucks it behind her ear.

"I'm not going to," I assure her.

It's getting late. I could sleep for twelve hours.

"Be ready," says Shira as she hurries out the door.

Ready for what?

CHAPTER SEVEN
TETHERED

Valerie came to work for my father when I was twenty-nine. She was two years older than me. We started dating within the week. Everyone rolled their eyes at me. I felt grateful to have any opportunity for an intimate relationship. My father was gone. He wasn't dead yet, but we didn't speak much. If we did, it was an awkward exchange of words.

My girlfriend experiences were never typical. Nothing in the world was normal. I was lucky to not be alone. Valerie had wavy auburn hair and brown eyes. We had a lot in common, but she was distant from me. Most of the time we would work together, eat together, sleep together. But then there were days where she brushed past me in the halls and didn't bother to look up at me. I think working for my dad was stressful, but I was hurt by it.

I remember finding her admiring Gwen by herself one time. Valerie stepped around the tank. She got so close she nearly pressed her nose to the glass. Gwen was physically age fifteen. Her brain showed massive amounts of activity. It was off the charts. Her vitals were stable. The machines hummed and sighed. Gwen's hair got longer and longer every year, adding to the voluminous tornado in a glass.

My father favored Valerie over me. I suspect it was because she was a woman. He still had paranoid ideas about the male scientists that worked in the lab. I don't recall anyone doing anything inappropriate. I think he was just crazy. Or did he see something? It burned when he allowed Valerie to sit with Gwen, but not me. I was jealous. Valerie could tell, but we tried not to talk about it.

We dated for two years. I never felt like she was fully mine. No matter what, she was out of my grasp, even if we were sleeping next to each other. I respected her as a scientist. I loved her as my girlfriend, yet I never truly knew how she felt about me. She would hold my shoulders and lean over me while I worked. I miss it.

After my father died, I fell apart. Then Valerie wanted to have a baby. It was all too much for me. I was incapable of dealing with my grief and supporting my girlfriend's desire to start a family. She left me. I was inconsolable, but couldn't explain why. My dad and I were strangers. That didn't matter, though. I couldn't stop thinking about him.

I'm searching the lab for Gwen. Isamu greets me in passing. I haven't seen Hotaka yet today. He might be in the infirmary or tending to the crops. My footsteps echo on the metal floor. Ever since Shira and Hotaka pointed out how Gwen is changing, I've been deep in thought. Reading and re-reading my father's notes.

The Ex Machina was female. My father theorized a male would become too interested in their own freedom or ego. Some people criticized him, saying he was a sexist. He wasn't a good husband or father, but he respected and admired many female scientists. My dad held them in high regard.

Rounding the corner, I see Gwen. Hikari is in her lap. They appear to be reading something together. The wires swish sleepily. Gwen is calm. I hear her telling Hikari the story in her breathy voice, humanistic. Hikari is listening but looking up at Gwen. I feel beads of sweat on the back of my neck.

"Hey, what are you two up to?" I ask in a neutral way. Hikari holds up the book and shows me the picture.

"Gwen is reading to me," he says.

"She is? Very sweet of her," I say.

Gwen is wearing red lipstick. Her hair is lustrous. She washed it and had Shira style it today. Hikari squirms in Gwen's arms so he can get a better look at her.

"I think Gwen is beautiful, like an angel. But she has long hair like a mermaid," he says as he grabs a handful of blond hair but doesn't pull.

Gwen not only smiles, but she lets out a small laugh. She's been awake for three months and this is the first time I've heard her laugh. I need to write this down, but I want to pay attention to every detail.

Hikari continues to stick his tiny hand in her hair, but he doesn't yank on it. He shows no fear. Gwen and him make intense eye contact and she smiles like a movie star. The gold behind the hazel dims and Hikari's eyes brighten. They are bonding. I'm so caught up in the moment I don't notice Katsuo approaching.

"Hikari, come here."

He says it with no inflection, but I know he doesn't trust Gwen. She knows it, too. Her face falls and the smile fades. Hikari kisses her on the cheek and hops off her lap. His father takes his hand and they walk down the hall. Katsuo nods at me but says nothing else. Hikari waves at Gwen and she waves back.

"It's nice you and Hikari have been spending time together."
I try to make light of the situation.
"I like Hikari. He's full of life," she says.
Her childlike innocence is present. I think he inspires something in her.
"Yes, he is. Most children are."
Gwen's eyes glow gold as she ponders what I said.
"He is the youngest one here, but he is the only one who isn't afraid of me," she states. Gwen is quite perceptive.
"Everyone knows how strong you are. They aren't trying to be inconsiderate," I say.
"They think I'm going to hurt them. Katsuo doesn't want me around Hikari but Hikari likes me," she says it like a regular girl.
"You can do incredible things, Gwen. I trust you."
Gwen gets up to sit next to me. She doesn't put her hand on my heart this time.
"What does that mean?" she asks.
Her gold eyes bore holes through me. They are amber bullets tearing me up.
"It means I don't think you'd ever do anything bad."

***

I was a complete mess. Thirty-one was painful. It was like I lost everything, but how could I lose something I didn't have? My father and I had no relationship towards the end. I kept thinking of my youth, though. He never came to my games or took me to practice, but the days I did see him, I remember him being loving. He was a kindhearted man back then. The Mantodea had not come yet. He wasn't lost in the darkness of his creation.

Nightmares never bothered me until that year. I had horrible dreams night after night. The only saving grace was Gwen. I could see her whenever I wanted. The nightmares left me hollow and fragmented. I would get up to stand in the blue light of her tank. It soothed me after the jarring and fitful rest I had.

I dreamed about all my girlfriends hating me. They would scream at me and throw everything I didn't do in my face. I dreamed about the Mantodea entering the lab and destroying all my father's work. Those gave me stomach aches. I dreamed about Gwen dying. Those nightmares haunted me the most. I would check her vitals and look at the monitors every hour.

One dream standing out is one I had about my dad. He was in his chair next to Gwen's tank. I tapped on his shoulder and he glared up at me with misty, grey eyes. He stood up from his chair and looked like he was going to hit me.

"You're not good enough," he said.

My father had his hands balled up into tight fists.

"Good enough for what?" I asked.

The dream was blurry and blue, illuminated everything. I felt like I was underwater. My dad tried to slug me on the shoulder, but I dodged him.

"Good enough for her," he snarled at me.

The machines started beeping. Gwen's respirator was leaking. She was drowning. I tried to save her, but my dad choked me out. That one left me in pieces. Rationally, I knew it was just a dream. I still got out of bed to check on Gwen, though. Nagging thoughts about her dying alone in the tank, choking on water, no longer existing, kept flooding in. I'd have to go see her serene and peaceful face. The only way to get my muscles to relax.

My father's notes mention Gwen having the potential of a god but the heart of a human. She would be unique. Most scientists believe in artificial intelligent machinery, but my father took it to the next level with his Ex Machina project. The human body infused with strength enhancing pieces and the human mind augmented by an increased amount of synapses was a game changer.

That's why we had to wait so long for her. She had to develop with the device in her head. It was necessary for Gwen to be in the tank for numerous years to absorb the liquid, giving her the exoskeleton and fortifying her bones. The chrome plates on her back have grown with her. Although made of metal, they were synthesized with human DNA. They couldn't be installed after birth. The plates fuse with her shoulder blades and into her spine. They use atmospheric pressure and electricity to power her through the sea and space.

Gwen has been hiding from me. She is attached to my hip one day and nowhere to be found the next. I see Katsuo and Hikari chatting with Hotaka. My friend waves at me, but Katsuo looks pissed. Hikari's face is forlorn. I smile at him, but he stares up at me with big sad eyes. I continue through the corridor.

Yui is busy as always. She is hurrying around the research room with all my father's notes. The young scientist copies my dad's words into her notebook. She opens binders, flips through loose leaf paper, and tears through hardback journals. Her shoes click as she scurries about. It's like watching a robot.

"Hey Yui, have you seen Gwen?" I ask.

Yui stops working for a millisecond to answer, but immediately returns to stacking binders and shuffling paper.

"I saw her early this morning, but not recently."

"Thank you." I go back to Gwen's room.

The children's book is on her bed. On the nightstand is another romance novel. I sit on her bed and look around. All our rooms are relatively empty. We all have a bed, nightstand, desk, chair, and lamp. Everyone has decorated theirs differently. Mine has band posters and baseball paraphernalia. Gwen's room has a small mirror, red lipstick, a wooden hairbrush, and books. Shira is passing the room and I grab her arm.

"Have you seen Gwen?" I ask her. Shira gives me an exasperated look and sighs.

"We had tea early this morning," she says.

"How was she?"

"She seemed fine."

"Thank you," I say and continue back towards the front of the building.

Where could she be? Gwen hides from me in playful ways, but today I feel like she's doing it to hurt me.

"Bellamy?"

It's Nori. I turn around. He seems flustered. His face is sweaty.

"What's wrong, Nori?" I ask. He loosens his tie.

"Come with me," he says.

Anxiety pours through my veins like toxic sludge. He leads me into the room with the security cameras. Nori runs his hand through his bangs, wet with perspiration. He rewinds footage from this afternoon. It's Gwen. She's walking out the front door. No one noticed.

"Bellamy, are you okay?" asks Nori.

No, I'm not. I find myself in a rage. Nori is talking to me, but I run out of the room. I head for the front door. He must have alerted my team because as I try to leave, Katsuo and Isamu grab me. I'm thrashing. Gwen is out there and I'm here. I need to get her back. It was ridiculous to believe she would never leave me.

"Let me go!" I shout. Casual, mellow, nice guy Bellamy is gone. I'm a loose cannon.

"Bellamy, calm down," says Katsuo. He is looking me in the eyes, but I'm not here.

"Let me go!" I shout again.

Isamu is frightened by my wildness. So am I.

"Don't do this, Dr. Krim." Isamu is trying to be rational, but I can't be that right now.

I need Gwen. I flail and try to escape. Shira walks up to me with a needle in her hand. She sticks it in my neck and I go limp.

***

I smell wildflowers. They're fragrant and dewy. Sunshine gives the leaves a warm green aroma. It mixes with the scent of harsh chemical cleaner. I have a killer headache. My throat is dry. I try to remember what happened. Shira had to sedate me. The way my father had to be sedated. Perhaps me and my old man have a lot more in common than I thought. I cough and turn to my side.

"Bellamy?"

It's Gwen's voice. I sit up right away. It feels like I got crushed by a Mantodea, but I want to see her. She's sitting next to me on the bed. Her blond hair is all over the place.

"Gwen, I thought you left me."

The Ex Machina seems hurt. She opens her arms and embraces me. Gwen doesn't understand her heart, but she tugs at the strings of mine daily.

"I wouldn't do that."

"Where did you go?" I ask.

She points to my nightstand. There's a vase full of flowers.

"I wanted to bring outside to you," she says.

Gwen is full of surprises. I didn't think she was capable of being affectionate, but Gwen has shown a range of protectiveness, sympathy and kindness. The hourglass vase is overflowing with pink, yellow, and orange flowers. They have hunter green leaves, round and glossy.

"Thank you," I say and lie back down.

Whatever Shira gave me has my head feeling full of rocks. I close my eyes and Gwen runs her hand through my hair. It eases the migraine. I hold her other hand in both of mine. The dreams of her dying come to mind. She is indestructible. The thought of her leaving me puts me in a mood. I refuse that reality.

"Bellamy?"

Gwen calls for me, so I open my eyes.

"Yes?"

"They said they had to sedate you because you were going to go out there by yourself," she says.

"I was," I cough.

My throat is scratchy. The side effects of the drug make my tongue swell and my mouth dry.

"You could die if you go outside without me."

The Ex Machina is factual and correct.

"I know."

I'm tired and start fading out. Gwen is worried about me. I want to keep talking, but my head is spinning.

"Hey Bell," it's Hotaka. I look up at him, defeated. He wears a sympathetic face, but there is something else behind it.

"Hey," I rasp.

"Gwen, can I talk to Bellamy alone for a minute?" asks Hotaka.

He gives me a glass of water. I drink it all in one gulp. Gwen gets up and walks out of the room. I don't like it. It's stupid, but I want Gwen where I can see her. I keep my neediness to myself.

"What is it, Hotaka?" I ask.

He waits until Gwen is further down the hall.

"It's about Gwen. I know without a doubt she loves you now," he says with a shit-eating grin.

"Shut up," I sigh and turn to my other side and face away from him.

The steel wall and I make eye contact.

"She brought you flowers to make you happy. When she saw what we were doing to you, she became upset. I told her we had to because you were going to go outside by yourself. She felt very guilty."

"Don't we want the Ex Machina to have human connections?"

I ask the question with irritation. It makes me feel awful. Hotaka is my friend.

"Of course. I didn't read anything in your father's notes about what to do if the Ex Machina falls in love."

My father would resent the fact she favors me. I'm glad he's not around to see it. I shouldn't think like that about the dead, but it's true. He wanted her all to himself, but she's mine.

"Gwen could fall in love with someone else. We don't know the scope of her personality yet," I offer as a scientist.

It's ridiculous, but I want Gwen to come back and sit with me.

"She might. But I don't think she will. The imprinting, hearing you say you loved her all those years ago, the bond, they were not variables expected in the project," he says while scratching his cheek.

"What do you think I should do?" I ask.

"How do you feel about her?" he asks his own question.

"I waited for her for twenty years. It's silly because I was just a kid back then, but I felt sort of like a father to her. I didn't enjoy leaving her alone. She's been the most important thing in my life."

"Gwen knows you care for her. Watch how she interprets that," he says and stands up.

Hotaka exits my room, and I am left alone. I toss and turn, trying to get comfortable. It's impossible. I can't sleep anymore. My body is weighed down with cinder blocks. I want to get out of bed, but it's too hard.

I'm frustrated. My behavior is surely being talked about. I know Hotaka won't take part in gossip, but the older scientists have always found me odd. After all, I'm Adam Krim's kid. It's one thing to know about someone. It's a whole new thing to actually work with that person. I lay on my stomach and try to disappear into my white pillowcase. The mattress dips. Someone is sitting next to me. I feel her hand on my shoulder and long fingers in my hair.

"Are you okay?" she asks.

I roll onto my back. My hair is sticking up in every direction. The sweat and Gwen playing with it have turned it into a mess.

"Yeah, I'm okay."

I smile at her. Gwen puts her hand on my heart for a minute. She is getting up to leave, but I grab her hand. "Gwen, wait. Will you sit with me for a little longer? I can't sleep," I admit.

"Okay," she comes back to me.

Gwen keeps her hand on my heart. I put my hand over hers. All the other scientists would disapprove, but they don't have what I have.

CHAPTER EIGHT
PERSUASION

Thirty-two was a better year, but not by much. I lost a lot of weight. My sleep was irregular. I had nightmares, but not as often. Valerie kept popping into my head, and I felt like I had made a huge mistake. I should have given her what she wanted.

I was in no condition to be a father, though. During this time, I was in an insomniac state and my memory was fragmented. It felt like I was in a fog. My work suffered. I barely got anything done. The other scientists hated me. I had all the power, but I couldn't do my job. The people working for my father couldn't stand me any longer and they left me, too. That's when I hired Isamu, Katsuo, Nori, Yui, Hotaka and Shira.

It was a struggle, but I cleaned up my act. I didn't want my precious project to go sideways because of neglect. All my energy was used for converting myself back up into a real person. I stopped lying around. Gwen seemed lonely. I felt like I had abandoned her. Putting my hand up to the glass, I watched her hair swirl. The tornado was getting bigger.

"I can't wait to meet you, Gwen." I said it out loud.

In two years, we'd finally see the results of my father's brilliant but outrageous mind. Her respirator was secure, no leaks. Dreams about her drowning plagued me for over a month. It threatened my sanity. I sat next to her for hours. My new team didn't arrive for several weeks. It was just me and her.

My hand was on the glass, but my mind was somewhere else. I kept thinking about my dad, past girlfriends, baseball. I missed my mom; I wished Gwen was here. Then I felt it. The reverberation in the tank. I looked up to see Gwen had her hand on the glass where mine was. It startled me and I fell over in my chair. The Ex Machina heard me, but I didn't know it at the time.

Once my new employees arrived, I eased myself back into the routine of working and functioning as an adult. I didn't starve myself or go days without eating. If I didn't want to eat, it didn't matter. I made myself a schedule to eat a certain amount of calories at specific times. It was the only way I could get myself to eat consistently. I drank tea with my colleagues. We laughed about what we liked and who we were before the Mantodea. Everyone thought I was a really nice guy. I am. At least I think I am.

I've been on edge. Gwen is supposed to save humanity, but I'm not sure I'm willing to part with her. What if something bad happens? She should be out killing off the aliens, but we've been playing chess and letting her read children's books. I know she is stronger than any being we have ever encountered, but I'm tense.

Gwen could bring the Titanic back up from the bottom of the sea. She can take down an army of Mantodea. I want Gwen to succeed, but I'm hesitant to let her out of my sight. When I was knocked out, she was worried about me. She said she wouldn't leave me, but I don't fully trust her. I sense she is playing a game with me.

I'm looking for her right now. We play hide and seek, but not really. She mostly follows me, but more and more she disappears to make me worry. Gwen and I enjoy the time we spend together. It's slight, but I can't help but feel she is putting on some kind of show. She's in her room. What I see surprises me. I act casual.

"Hey Gwen," I say.

Gwen is sitting at her desk. She is looking at herself in the mirror and brushing her hair. Her makeup is done. She's not wearing her white dress. Instead, she has on a red dress, it's much shorter. Her feet are bare. Gwen could have been a movie star or a model.

"Hi Bellamy," she says, but doesn't look at me.

I lean in the doorway and analyze my creation.

"You look nice."

I let myself in and sit on her bed. She continues to mess with her hair. It nearly touches the floor.

"Thank you."

She looks at herself in the mirror and tilts her head. It's like she isn't sure the person in the reflection is her or not.

"How are you today?" I ask.

She is in one of those moods where she wants to ignore me, but I keep pushing her until she sends me away.

"I'm not sure," she says as she runs her hand across her collarbone.

"That's okay. Can you try to explain it to me? Please?"

"I'm not really sad, but I'm not happy either. Hikari isn't allowed to play with me. I feel…" she struggles to find the word but lands on it, "…unwanted."

"I'm sorry you feel this way. But I want you. We need you. A lot of people are going to be happy when you save the world," I say, hoping to cheer her up. She frowns in the mirror. I get up and kneel next to her. "I don't want you to think you're unwanted. It's far from the truth."

"How do I save the world?" she asks.

This time, she faces me. I'm not ready for her piercing eyes.

"I'm not sure yet. We'll figure it out together," I say and stand up.

"Okay." She is distant.

I want to make her feel better and get an idea.

"I'll be right back," I say and go into my room.

It's been a while since I've looked at any of it, but I have my mom's jewelry. I take out the necklace my dad gave her when they first started dating. It's a simple chain with a diamond in the shape waning crescent moon. I go back into Gwen's room. "I want you to have this."

I reach behind her neck and clasp the necklace. She reaches up to touch it.

"Why?" she asks.

Gwen is perplexed by my gesture. It makes me want to laugh, but I keep it in.

"Because I want you to remember I care about you."

***

I fall asleep peacefully. No dreams, no nightmares. I'm sleeping, but not for long. Shira is slapping me awake.

"Bellamy," she shrieks at me.

I sit up and rub the back of my head where she's been hitting me.

"Shira, what are you doing?" I shout.

She is in a huffy mood. Her face is serious.

"We need to do something about Gwen," she hisses, and crosses her arms at me.

"About what? She hasn't done anything harmful."

I'm getting angry. This is not a good start to my day.

"Yet," says Shira and I want to say something hurtful but don't.

Shira is being practical and rational.

"What are you so worried about?" I sigh.

"Have you seen her new look?" she asks.

I can't tell if women are jealous by nature or if Shira sees something I don't.

"So she wants to wear makeup and a tight dress. Who cares?" I shrug.

Maybe I don't get it because I'm a guy.

"You don't think it's a little…" she pauses like she doesn't want to say it.

"A little what?" I snap.

"Inappropriate. Improper. Unsavory," she holds out her hands, palm up.

"Any woman who wants to be considered sexy is unsavory to you? I thought you were a feminist, Shira.”

“This is different.”

“How?”

I’m getting fed up with this conversation. It’s too early to be shouting. I haven’t had a cup of coffee yet.

“The Ex Machina project was never meant to be sexualized. You treat her like she’s innocent, but she’s not. She is a hundred times smarter than all of us combined. Have you forgotten she is strategic, analytical, and unbeatable?”

“What do you think she’s going to do? Has Gwen ever done anything to intimidate you? She has tea with you. You do her hair. You’re the one who gave her the lipstick, Shira.”

I’m sitting up because I can’t lay back down.

“I don’t know. That’s what scares me. Gwen isn’t what I thought she’d be. I figured she’d be interested in science, math, and theories. But she isn’t. She wants to read girlish books and play dress up. Don’t you think your father would be upset about the way this project is going?”

Shira has to be right about everything. I’m glad we never dated.

“Gwen is brilliant. You said so yourself. She is smarter than all of us. So what’s the big deal if she likes romance novels?”

“The Ex Machina should be focused on destroying the Mantodea.” Shira stomps at me.

“Gwen has protected me from the Mantodea twice. I’ve seen her kill them. She is undeniably strong. She can do this. Give her time,” I say.

“What if Gwen decides she doesn’t care for you anymore? She has free will. What will become of us if she suddenly becomes disinterested in helping us?”

“Gwen won’t abandon us,” I growl.

Shira notices the change in me and steps back towards the door.

“She won’t abandon you,” she emphasizes the word “you” as she spits the sentence out at me.

I cover my face with my blanket. Shira is only five feet, two inches tall, but she can cut down a forty story building. There is something gnawing at me. Something important. It’s Shira’s words. She thinks Gwen cares only for me. I want to believe Gwen’s heart is capable of caring for others. Hikari and she looked at each other with such love. The bond was visible. She laughed. The first time, Gwen laughed.

I’m upset Shira has put Gwen in this box. That she should like only intellectual games and literature. Gwen is more than I could have hoped for. She excels in all fields. I’m impressed with her growing humanity. The Ex Machina was never meant to be a lot of things, but I am not my father. I want Gwen to be who she wants to be.

When she was in the tank, I imagined her dreaming about deep sea fishing and snow. What she did see in her dreams? What do gods and angels think about? She heard me say, "I love you." What else did she hear? My father surely spoke to her. What did he say?

***

Gwen is pretty, but lethal. She isn't doing anything wrong, but her new look and swishing wires make us all nervous. Today she is a mix of affectionate and distant. This morning, she wanted to have tea and play chess. Now she's brushing past me in the hall and ignoring me. Maybe she'll want to talk later.

The Ex Machina said she will help me save humanity. I need to figure out how. The Mantodea spawn periodically from the maelstrom that forms in the sky. There is something up there. I should have Gwen take a trip to space and find out. Then why am I so reluctant to tell her what to do?

She wants to play with Hikari, but Katsuo won't allow it. Hikari is running down the hall. He has a toy in his hand he's making fly. Gwen stops when he nears her. He looks up at her and she touches his face for a moment. Katsuo eyes her and she gets the hint. Gwen walks away, saying nothing to Hikari. I think it hurts them both. It's a stinger in my chest. Yui is looking over her notes with fury. I step into the room she's in and stand by the door.

"Hey, can I talk to you for a minute?" I ask.

"What is it, Bellamy?" she continues to flip through loose paper and slam binders shut.

"I was curious about your opinion."

"Opinion about what?"

Yui is young but incredibly bright. I think she may be neutral about this matter.

"About Gwen," I say, and she stops working to look at me.

She leans on her elbow and ponders my inquiry. I appreciate how Yui is taking my question seriously. No one has taken me seriously for a while now.

"She is magnificent. Truly capable of anything. I admire her."

"Are you afraid of her?"

"I'm cautious around her. She could be dangerous. I think Gwen is rather mellow for an engineered robotic human hybrid. Of course, she is the first of her kind. We weren't sure what her personality would be like," she says.

Yui offers me her thoughts without judgement.

"Shira thinks Gwen behaves inappropriately."

I grimace, thinking about Shira yelling at me.

"Gwen isn't what any of us anticipated. She wants to beautify herself and read children's literature. I don't think those things matter though," she says with conviction.

"You don't?"

I'm surprised by the young scientist.

"No. Gwen is smarter than all of us. She is trying to unlock the parts of her brain that don't function as well, such as her emotional intelligence. I believe it's why she chooses romance novels and children's stories. She is tactful. There is nothing random about her."

"Thank you for your insight, Yui. I appreciate your candor," I say.

As I'm about to exit, Yui calls for me.

"Yes?" I ask.

"The only thing troubling me is…" Yui pauses. She stops flipping through one of my dad's notebooks with a serious face. "How she reacts to you. It's obvious she has a bond with you. Your emotional connection is the strongest. Although I think Gwen has become quite attached to Hikari. If Katsuo would allow it, I think we could see an intimate, perhaps sisterly or motherly, version of Gwen."

"What is so troubling about it?" I ask.

"I worry Gwen could change her mind about us, depending on how you feel about her."

"Gwen knows I care about her."

"Yes. But what if she wants more from you?"

"I don't think she does. Gwen could have anything, anybody. Why would she choose me?" I shrug.

"I saw the imprinting. It's not mentioned in your father's notes, but I believe he wanted to be the first one she saw so he could have this bond. He wanted her to want to help him."

"I want that as well."

"It's not a priority in your father's journal, but I think he believed Gwen wouldn't be interested in romantic love. He thought the heart of the machine would be difficult to penetrate. Turns out the Ex Machina feels more than she lets on."

"What do you think I should do?" I ask.

Yui is ten years younger than me and Shira, but is able to capture the essence of what's important. No bullshit.

"I think you should let things unfold organically. Don't force anything or be ingenuine. The Ex Machina will be able to tell."

"What do you think will happen if I accidentally break her heart?"

"We should plan for the worst," says Yui.

I want to keep talking but she is fanning papers and typing loudly. I leave the room Yui is working in and wander around the building in search of Gwen. Isamu and Nori nod at me in passing. I wish things weren't so awkward between me and Shira.

I can't find her. Why does she do this to me? She brings me flowers and holds my hand until I fall asleep, but avoids me when I want to talk to her. I should bring her outside. Something nice to cheer her up. Seeing Hikari's and Gwen's sad faces nag at me. Katsuo has every right to keep Hikari away from her, but it's not fair to either of them. I can't tell him what to do with his son, though.

I haven't checked the room with the water reservoir. Gwen said she enjoyed swimming. All the equipment is untouched. I survey the cameras. Nothing but black water. Sitting down, I rub my temples. I feel a migraine coming on. It's a flash, but I see something on the screen. Something light in the inky depths.

Waiting to see her again, I loosen my tie. I've been stressed. I don't want to be like my dad and lose my mind to my work. I feel like I already have, because I look up to see Gwen blow a bubbly kiss at me on the screen.

***

Compared to most of the population, I have a cushy lifestyle. Sure, we are isolated, but my father's laboratory is spacious, well equipped, and, to be frank–rather luxurious. When the Mantodea first arrived, I was stunned. It was like I was living in a movie. My life is a science fiction film. Adam Krim would have owned the world. He might be dead, but he still owns me. I think part of him owns Gwen, too.

I try to put it under a microscope. What would my father say to her? She hasn't mentioned hearing another voice. Maybe he said something about me to plant the seeds of mistrust. During that time, he didn't trust me. He didn't trust anybody.

The tiny window on the front door offers me a glimpse of the outside world. The moon is full. It's parked right in front of me. The stars are sprinkled across the sky like after thoughts. I remember being a kid and going camping with my mom. My dad didn't do stuff like that. He didn't like dirt, or trees, or anything other than sterile lab equipment and the brink of insanity creations.

My mom would take me camping at her favorite childhood spots. She enjoyed fishing and hiking. I miss her all the time. We have the same sandy brown hair. I like to think I have her heart. It was kind. My dad wasn't unkind, but he was cold without meaning to be. A faraway planet, frozen in outer space.

The Mantodea are unpredictable. They hunt in packs. Sometimes they are alone. Nymphs are smaller than the full grown aliens. Females tend to be solo hunters. It's like they are given orders to be erratic. Once we assume they are one way, they show us a different tactic.

The day I hurt my ankle, the female Mantodea was a lone hunter. When Gwen hid me in the ditch, they were hunting in a pack. The aliens have supreme staying power. They don't back down. Once they choose to engage in battle, they won't stop. It doesn't matter if they know they will lose, they will fight anyway.

I can't sleep. The halls are lit with dim blue lights. It's the middle of the night. I'm pacing around until I'm tired. The thing is, I'm tired, but my mind won't shut off. This happens to me from time to time. I have to run myself into the ground until I crash and burn.

Hotaka has been trying his best to help me, but I won't accept it. He tries to make me eat and sleep. I say I will, but I don't. He knows I'm lying, but is a friend who knows when to back off. I hope I'm not coming off like a jerk. Yui has been pleasant to discuss the Ex Machina project with, but I suspect everyone is turning against me.

I hate myself for saying it because I sound like my father. How did he ever have enough charm to win over my mom? She was the pretty girl next door. He was the geek. Not just any geek, though. Adam Krim changed the world before he was twenty-six.

My dad had me when he was thirty-three. I wonder if he wanted me at all or if it was to make my mom happy. My mom and I were close, but my father remained a faraway persona I saw on TV more than I saw at home.

I go into the room where Gwen was born. The tank is empty. She is here, but I feel a crater inside, looking at the empty glass. The tornado walks around in a short dress and wears red lipstick. I want to trust her. I want her to trust me. This is a dangerous game we play. I touch the tank where I first felt the vibration of her response.

In my room, I face the steel wall and let my thoughts race around. They bounce off my skull. It reverberates behind my eyes. Sleep won't happen for me tonight. It's all the same. Whether I rest and eat the appropriate amount doesn't matter. I feel exhausted. I get migraines lasting for two days. My door opens. I cringe, thinking it's Shira, about to smack my already tender head.

My mattress dips and I feel long fingers in my hair. A hand too big to be Shira's grips my shoulder. Gwen's gold eyes glow in the dark. They reflect off the metal. I get an intrusive thought of Gwen ripping my head off.

"Hey Gwen," I say.

"I saw you walking around. Are you okay?" she asks.

"I'm alright. I can't sleep, though."

"Me neither," says Gwen.

This makes me laugh like a maniac. I don't know if she meant to, but I think Gwen might have made her first joke. It's unnecessary for her to sleep unless her power source is low. Since she can be sustained by both human food and electricity, she will most likely never need to sleep. This humors me. I turn around so I can see her. She covers her mouth but lets out a small giggle. It's so human, almost innocent. I don't know why, but it chills me. I like it anyway.

"What do you do all night?" I ask.

"I walk around like you. Or I read. Sometimes I swim. I like to draw. Hotaka gave me a device so I can listen to music. I lay in bed and try to understand songs that make me feel impossible things."

She's holding the moon. The diamond sparkles in the gold glare of her eyes. Her head turns, and the device is visible. It reminds me of what I am dealing with.

"Gwen, can I ask you something?"

"What?"

"Would you protect someone else the way you protected me from that Mantodea?"

Gwen reaches for my heart. It startles me, but I'm becoming accustomed to it.

"What do you mean?"

"If you saw someone being attacked by one of the aliens, would you try to save them?"

"Is that what you want me to do, Bellamy?"

She sounds robotic this time. Calculating and cold.

"Yes," I say.

Gwen nods her head.

"Then I will do it," she says.

This should comfort me, but I'm upset. It's like she didn't pass this test. I wanted her to want to help us. Shira might be right. Gwen does what I tell her now, but what about later?

CHAPTER NINE

COMPULSION

"Gwen, do you want to go outside with me?" I ask.

She is laying on her bed reading a new romance novel. Her dress is too short, and she isn't being modest. I know she is doing it on purpose.

"Yes," she says and sits up.

She flips her hair and brushes past me as she walks out the door. Gwen likes to do this thing where she pretends I don't exist sometimes. I follow her to the front door. Her wires aren't swishing, but they are moving slightly. They are sensing. Gwen's hair keeps getting longer. She refuses to cut it. Hikari says she has mermaid hair.

Nori and Yui shudder as Gwen waves at them. They smile, but it's a tense grin. Both of them look at me and I nod my head and show them my teeth. They don't look convinced. Gwen waits for me at the front door. She's looking out the tiny window. I hit the button and the heavy steel moves. Gwen turns to me. She wants me to go first.

I step out into the sunlight. The shadows are long on the hillside. It's windy but I don't mind. Gwen seems to enjoy it. Her eyes are closed and her hair is dancing. She has her arms crossed over her chest. I watch her through the eyes of a scientist. What is she thinking? What is she experiencing? I look at her through the lens of something else, something familial. Is this making her happy?

Gwen's wires are active. They make calculated movements as they swish about. She is feeling the breeze on her skin, enjoying the sun on her face, but still very much aware. I'm afraid of her but at the same time I feel safe with her. Gwen has had faith in me. I have faith in her despite all she does to frighten me.

"Do you like the wind?" I ask.

She turns up the corners of her mouth covered in red lipstick. She is barefoot. Gwen doesn't want to wear shoes anymore. She doesn't need them.

"More than like it...I think I love it," she says in a breathy whisper.

This is the first time Gwen has used that term. I need to remember to write this down. Gwen loves the wind.

"It's invigorating," I say over the breeze.

"Bellamy, close your eyes."

"What?" I laugh.

"Please," she says.

I'm wary of her. The wires are sleepy. She is happy. I decide to play along.

"Okay," I say, and do as she asks. At first there is nothing but then Gwen's arms are around me and I feel us lift off the ground. "Gwen, what are you doing?" I haven't shouted at her, but I'm not prepared for this.

"I want to show you something beautiful," she says into my ear.

Gwen propels us through the sky at breakneck speed. I close my eyes so I don't get sick. She weaves through the tops of the trees. I feel her lowering us and open an eye. She slows her pace and flies me across the emerald and blue lake. We are about ten feet off the water.

There are moss-covered rocks and pines with ivy growing up them in the surrounding hills. It smells like clay and lilies. The sun is about to set. It's gold and pink. Gwen takes me higher up. I get the awful idea she might drop me into the emerald blue and kill me. It's rude of me to think such horrible things when she is trying to have a meaningful connection.

She holds me the way a child holds a toy as she shows me the landscape, the sunset, and the world. Her eyes aren't glowing at this moment. The hazel is visible, and she looks less like a god or an angel and like a normal girl. It doesn't last. The wires swish with rapid and jagged movement. Gwen's face tenses as she looks around.

"Gwen–" I say her name and she covers my eyes with her hand.

She flies us faster than before. I feel like I'm going to pass out. The adrenaline won't let me. I can hear the rumble of Mantodea wings. It sounds like there are at least ten. She stops and even though she is covering my eyes, I see the angel light of her electricity. I hear the gravel in a blender. They emit their sickly screech and smell like turpentine. Gwen takes off again. She is trying to evade them to keep me safe.

"We're almost back to the lab," she says. Then the energy changes. She uses her power again. Her hand is small and cool on my eyes. "Bellamy, there are more Mantodea following us. I have to hide you."

"Please, no–" I can't finish my sentence.

Gwen uses her infallible mind and vision to find a secluded place by the lake. There is an enormous wall of clay behind me. Tall grass is growing on both sides. Boulders obscure the view. She sets me down and leaves without a word.

"Gwen," I call her name.

It's useless for me to stop her. She should be fighting the Mantodea. So why am I upset she left me to fulfill the task she was designed to do? I press my back against the mud and clay wall. My hair is getting too long. I pull at it and feel myself going mad. The sound of grating metal and concrete is unbearable. I slump over and cover my ears. Loud splashing as pieces of their exoskeletons hit the water. I look up to see it raining dead alien carcasses. Gwen is tearing them to bits. There are so many of them. At least twenty. I can't see her, but I can hear her. She is fighting them in the shaded woods next to the lake. As she electrocutes them in the sky, they fall to the forest floor and bottom of the lake.

Extraterrestrial blood is foamy on the surface of the water. So many parts land in the emerald green and make it look like ocean waves. Gwen is relentless. The Mantodea stand no chance. It's getting darker. The sun is almost below the horizon. I have clay all over my lab coat and the bottom of my slacks. Gwen returns to me. She inspects my face and rubs my shoulders.

"Are you okay?" she asks.

"Yeah, are you?"

"I'm fine. I'm glad you're safe."

Gwen picks me up and we get back to the lab as it becomes night. My team is watching me with skeptical eyes as we enter. Katsuo and Shira glare at me and Gwen. The strangest thing happens. Gwen giggles and steps closer to me. This really pisses Shira off. I pretend I don't see her jaw dropping. Gwen grabs my elbow with both her hands. I have sweat building in my hairline.

"Thank you for showing me something beautiful," I say.

My clothes are filthy. I need a shower. This was a successful day. Gwen demonstrates great promise. She covered my eyes so I wouldn't pass out again. The Ex Machina acts coldhearted, but she is a gem.

"You're not mad?" she asks. The necklace I gave her shimmers in the dim lights of the hall. Gwen chooses to wear it all the time.

"No, I'm not mad." I smile to myself.

***

Today I'm looking over Nori's notes. I find him to be a neutral voice. Shira's opinion on the matter has become irrelevant to me. If she can't understand greatness, then I can't understand her. The low light of the lamp on the desk illuminates Nori's scratchy handwriting.

May 15th - Birth

The Ex Machina is awake. She appears healthy. Dr. Krim is the first person she sees. He lets her touch his face. Imprinting may be taking place. Her eyes scan the room with curiosity, a good sign. Intelligent and aware. The wires that harness electrical energy aren't presently showing any sign of aggression or alarm.

May 22nd - Mood

She is mild-mannered. Quiet, inquisitive, precise. Everything about her is pristine. The Ex Machina is promising. Gwen seems gentle. Has not shown any anger or mental health issues. The device has altered her brain. No present damage. Gwen's wires have sharp metal jacks at the end. She is careful not to touch anyone with them. We need her to be dangerous, but we also need her to care about us.

May 29th - Life

Gwen is learning how to adapt. She wears a dress and flats. It makes her seem more human. Her nakedness was uncomfortable for most of the staff. The Ex Machina has not shown emotions such as shame, embarrassment, or insecurity. Dr. Krim tries to increase her humanity by eating with her, showing her music, and giving her books. She chooses children's literature and romance novels over scientific theories, history, and nonfiction.

June 5th - Exploration

Dr. Krim took Gwen outside for the second time. She apparently ran off on him to chase an elk. He went after her, injuring himself in the process. Gwen protected him from a female Mantodea and brought him back to the lab. Showed great remorse. Was extremely worried. Kept asking if Bellamy would be okay. She wouldn't leave his side. First time deep emotions were shown by the Ex Machina.

June 12th - Attachment

She follows Dr. Krim around constantly. They play chess and spend a lot of time together. She is attached to his hip most days. But then there are periods where she acts like she doesn't see him. It is odd. Fellow colleagues speculate it could be a way for her to compartmentalize her feelings. They are new to her. She is trying to understand what it means to have a heart.

June 19th - Sexuality

The Ex Machina appears strong, healthy, and capable of defeating the Mantodea. Her abilities are numerous. Deliberate and formidable. Acts mostly robotic but has a strange infatuation with Dr. Krim. The Ex Machina was aware of the underwater cameras, which may have encouraged her to make provocative gestures. When Gwen approached the window where Dr. Krim was, she didn't cover herself. She put her hand on the glass.

June 26th - Savior

Dr. Krim took Gwen outside again. They were attacked by a group of

Mantodea. Gwen hid Bellamy and destroyed the aliens with no problem. She cares deeply for him. It is apparent she harbors no ill will towards the rest of the team, but she doesn't seem interested in any of us the way she is with Dr. Krim.

There's another two months' worth of notes, but I don't want to read anymore.

Laying down, I stare into the sheen of the metal wall. My bed is comfortable, but I can't stop tossing and turning. My muscles keep twitching. I'm on edge. It's bizarre because I want Gwen to sit with me, but I don't want to draw attention to myself. The entire team thinks I'm using the Ex Machina to fill the void. They don't know who I was after my dad died but they are finding out who I really am. I'm not the chill, casual, nice guy Bellamy all the time.

My neurosis is showing. I'm overly nice to everyone to make up for my peculiar behavior. When my new team first arrived, I faked it until it felt real. It became part of who I thought I was. The truth is, I never recovered from my mom's death. I definitely haven't recovered from my father's. It's never been my intention to make Gwen into somebody who needs me, so I can feel manly. No, that's never been my style. I've been complacent.

There is darkness in the human heart. I feel it. It's there when I want Gwen to pay attention to me. The lingering irritation I have in my gut after seeing Katsuo be rude to her leaves me seething, but I hold it in. I can't boss him around about his kid. If Gwen and Hikari had more time together, who knows the advances she could make? The places a child can take the spirit are limitless.

Shira is jealous. They're all jealous. If my father had this bond with Gwen, I would be devastated. I didn't think about it until now, but I would be. Adam Krim would probably drive her to madness. Then he'd bore her to death. Such ugly thoughts keep spilling out of my skull. I should be careful and not let myself think this way.

It's black in my soul as I enjoy her disinterest in everybody else. I pretend she isn't my shadow, that she doesn't hold my arm when I'm walking down the hall, or stare at me for too long. Everyone sees me for who I am. A fraud, a sick man. I'm becoming the person I swore I'd never become. I'm losing myself to the machine. Engrossed by my creation. I'm my father.

***

The year I turned thirty-three, I was not myself. I pretended to be confident. My work improved, and I had the help I needed, but I was an empty shell. Somehow, I compartmentalized all my traumas, my sufferings, and failures. But not that year.

I had become so accustomed to being grateful for my father's technological advances and wealth I forgot to notice what happened to me.

The earth was invaded by nefarious forces. I played my last game of baseball as the world ended. My mom died. I had no one until Sophia's father came to work for my dad. Sophia became my world. We kissed all the time. She hugged me when we were sitting next to each other. I told her I loved her. Neither of us knew what it meant.

I'm not sure if I've been in love or if anyone has truly been in love with me. My girlfriends have been convenient. I thought I loved them. But in hindsight, I know a lot of it was because we were trapped in this place together. Eva and I were the happiest. We drove everyone up the wall. Our love wasn't complicated. It was two kids having fun during the end of the world.

Valerie and I would have been a great couple if aliens didn't take over our planet and force us to live within this mountain. Gwen was the only thing keeping me going. I would stare at her serene face and pray for the day I got to meet her. The tornado in a glass was almost complete. My team admired her. When they first came to work with me, I showed them all at once. They were hand selected by me for their credentials and talents. I didn't trust just anybody to see her.

I opened the door to the room she was in. They followed me like baby ducks. I think they might have been afraid or perhaps nervous. No one has what I have. Yui was most interested. She had her notepad ready and an eager expression. Hotaka was friendly, but cautious. Katsuo was excited to show Hikari humanity's savior. Both their eyes never left Gwen. Isamu and Nori were intrigued, polite, and very skittish. They have been on the shy side.

Shira stood out to me. She was interested, but also detached. Like this wasn't the greatest moment in scientific history. I thought it would be impossible for anyone to resist Gwen's glory. Awe was absent from Shira's face. She looked like she was about to watch a movie or listen to a speech.

I thought Shira and I would fall in love, but she is a vicious little thing. Pretty, resourceful, and a brilliant scientist. She lacks the imagination I have. I think working for the Krim company is a novelty to her. Many people have wanted to see this lab. My father believed he would never get his work done if he didn't seclude himself. His eccentric personality garnered a lot of media hype before the Mantodea invaded.

Now I'm thirty-four and my reputation has dents in it. My staff has known of me for decades but has only worked for me for two years. I'm making a terrible impression. They think Gwen and I use each other as playthings. I'm not sure, but they might be right. I'm looking for her right now. She's been hiding from me.

"Bellamy, come quickly."

It's Isamu. He and I run down the hall towards the front of the building.

"What is it?" I ask.

"Katsuo is in a rage. He's yelling at Gwen," he says.

I pick up the pace. Katsuo's hoarse and demanding voice is echoing off the metal walls.

"Hikari, come here!" Katsuo shouts at his son, who is clinging to Gwen's waist.

"No, I want to play with Gwen!" cries Hikari.

Gwen remains neutral. She doesn't embrace Hikari or push him away. She does not try to attack or talk back.

"Dammit Hikari! Get over here right now!" Katsuo is continuing to chastise his son in front of the Ex Machina.

"Gwen didn't do anything. Why can't she play with me?" asks Hikari.

"I'm your father. You're supposed to listen to me. Not this thing," he hurls the word "thing" at Gwen and rips Hikari away from her.

Hikari turns and reaches for her. She kneels down and holds his hand for a moment, but Katsuo won't stand for it.

"Stay away from my son," says Katsuo.

He pushes her away with a stiff arm. Hikari is flailing in his other hand, but he keeps them apart. He walks off down the hall towards their room and I can hear Hikari sobbing. Isamu puts his hand on my shoulder. Gwen is still kneeling down, looking at the floor. I walk up beside her.

"Gwen, are you okay?" I ask.

She stands up but doesn't face me.

"No," she says.

As she heads for the front door, I see tears in her eyes. The Ex Machina hasn't cried until now.

"Wait! Please, don't go!" I shout, but she hits the button and flies off where I can't see her. My feet hit the steel floor and feel heavy. I can't reach the door because Nori and Isamu are restraining me. "Get off of me," I thrash until someone sticks a needle in my neck.

***

I try to rip out of the restraints as soon as I'm conscious. My shoes are still on. So is my lab coat. I'm kicking the wall and pulling so hard my wrists ache. The light is too bright, but it doesn't stop me. I keep kicking and thrashing.

"Gwen!" I call for her. Maybe she's back. She always comes back to me. "Gwen!"

I call her name over and over. It depresses me when Hotaka enters the room and not Gwen.

"Bell, please calm down. I can't let you go until you relax," he says in his gentle tone.

I stop kicking. My body lays limp on the bed in defeat.

"Is she back yet?" I ask.

"No," Hotaka puts his head down and takes off his glasses.

I'm so upset. Katsuo's protectiveness of his son is expected, but why did he have to hurt her feelings? What if she doesn't come back?

"Katsuo has been a real prick," I say.

Hotaka laughs, but I'm not in the mood to laugh with him.

"He's wary of yours and Gwen's relationship. Katsuo looks at Gwen like the killing machine she was designed to be. I don't think he anticipated Gwen taking an interest in his son," offers Hotaka.

He puts on his glasses and rubs the back of his neck. Our work causes a lot of body tension.

"Hikari loves her. Gwen loves him. Isn't that what we wanted? Meaningful human connection is part of the Ex Machina's progress," I say.

"Just give him time. He'll come around."

"What if she doesn't come back?" I ask with a shaky voice.

Hotaka scoots the chair closer and sighs.

"Gwen will come back. She won't abandon you."

"How do you know? Gwen can do anything, go anywhere. She doesn't need me."

"You're right, she doesn't need you. But she wants you," says Hotaka in a grave voice.

"Gwen could decide she wants to be outside," I grumble.

"The imprinting."

"What?"

"She may stray from you, but I believe the imprinting will make her come back."

"You're only saying that because you're my friend. It's okay, Hotaka."

"I'm your friend, but I say it as a scientist. I watched the imprinting take place. At the time it wasn't a major part of our work, but over the last few months I think that the imprinting is the major component to the Ex Machina saving the world."

"You do? Why?" I ask.

My friend is smiling at me.

"Love is powerful. When baby animals are born, they know nothing and they latch on to the first face they see. They feel love when they aren't sure what it is. Gwen isn't an infant or an animal, but she is attached to you. She knows it, too. I see her analyzing her heart with her mechanical mind. It perplexes her, but it's an instinct she hasn't been able to fight. Have faith, Bellamy. Gwen won't let you down," says Hotaka.

He exits my room. I am still tied up.

"Gwen, please come back." I say to myself.

Laying down is easier since I've exhausted myself with my thrashing. My arms are tight. When is someone going to let me out of these damn things? No one trusts me anymore. Not even my friend. I don't blame him; I don't trust myself. If I could, I would probably run out the front door in a heartbeat. My door opens, and to my surprise, it's Hikari.

"Hey Bellamy," he says.

His face is streaked with tears. I wish his father wouldn't do this to him.

"Hey kiddo, what's up?" I try to be pleasant, although I'm a crazed genius and currently restrained.

"I miss Gwen," he cries again.

Now I want to cry. I fight it.

"I miss her, too. She'll come back though. Don't worry," I lie through my teeth, hoping to make it true.

"My dad is so mean to her."

"He worries about you. But you're right. He's not very nice to Gwen."

"She's so pretty and smart and fun. I want to play with her all the time."

"Gwen loves you. She wishes you two could spend time together," I say.

Hikari steps closer to my bed and sits in the chair. His feet dangle. He is holding the book about a mermaid that Gwen was reading to him.

"Is Gwen an angel?" asks Hikari.

It makes me chuckle. Children are sweet. Hikari has chubby cheeks and long eyelashes sticking straight out.

"Technically, no, but I think she is."

"I think Gwen could be an angel, or a mermaid, or a princess."

"A princess?" I ask in mock disbelief.

Kids are fun to talk to. A lot more fun than adults.

"Don't you think she looks like a princess?"

I think about Scandinavian festivals with pale princesses with blonde hair.

"Yes. Gwen is very pretty," I say.

"More than pretty. Gwen is beautiful inside and out," says Hikari.

He holds the book close to his chest. There are big tears in his eyes. I can't stop them from falling.

"It's okay, Hikari. Gwen won't leave us."

My wrists have bruises on them. It hurts to move. I'm trying to stay engaged in our conversation, but I want to fade out until I feel Gwen's hands in my hair.

"This is her favorite book," he says and shows me a picture of a mermaid watching a human from behind a rock.

"Why is it her favorite?" I ask.

"Gwen said it reminds her of you."

"It does?" I ask with real disbelief.

"Yes. She said she wants to be like you, but she knows that she's not." The little boy's wisdom is worth more than what I pay my entire staff combined.

"Do you want to read it to me, Hikari?"

"Okay," he says, and he tells me the story of a mermaid who saw a human and wished to be closer to his heart.

CHAPTER TEN
SAVIOR

The Mantodea tore up the concrete streets and obliterated buildings. My mother was gripping my arm so tight I thought she might leave a hand print. We ran the seven blocks to my father's lab. Somehow we made it. I remember my mom running with her short heels and flowy green dress.

Other people were scrambling around us. They didn't know where to go, but we knew. My father may have been a maniac, but he was right about a lot of things. He knew something could turn the world upside down. They have exoskeletons heavy enough to leave cracks in the earth.

I saw one pick up a man and rip him to shreds. Another one landed on a car and crushed it completely. They fluttered their thick wings, kicking up dust and dirt. The Mantodea bit into necks, legs, and ripped off faces. They made guttural noises reverberating in my stomach. I watched people get murdered in slow motion as me and my mom kept jogging through the slaughtered city.

My baseball cleats gripped the ground and gave me leverage. I still had on my baseball cap. We maneuvered around panicking groups of people. Car alarms were going off and the sound of trumpets blared from the sky. I never heard anything like it before in my life.

When we got to my father's lab, he was waiting for us, standing at the door, ushering us inside. I remember looking at his worried face. He was showing more interest in us than in his work. This was as unusual as the alien invasion itself. His eyes were on me and my mother like we were the most important thing in the world to him.

We hid in the basement where my father had a small shelter. His team of four scientists at the time were also with us. We scraped by for several weeks until the military picked us up. My father tried to be humble, but his name got him special treatment from every entity. He created the most efficient cars in the world, revolutionized space travel, enhanced technology and made it faster, better, stronger.

My father designed humanity's savior. He was recognized as one of the world's greatest. It's difficult to live in someone of that stature's shadow. No one could do what he did. There wasn't another professional scientist willing to take on the task. He went where no one else would go.

China was excited to donate Nyx. People around the globe praised his intuitive mind and ingenuity. They praised him as much as they criticized his lack of compassion, grace, and empathy. Those were of no concern to my father. His only goal was to create the best. He wanted a legacy. His face was on the cover of dozens of magazines. He was immortalized.

Arriving in Japan was exciting to me—at first. I grew bored quickly though. There was no one my age. I couldn't go outside. Adjusting to living in quarantine was hard. My mom tried to make me happy, but I was restless and annoyed everyone with my constant running.

But no one could tell Adam Krim's son what to do. I ran through the halls. Every door was open to me. I didn't have boundaries. My father's lab was my lab. I touched everything. Sometimes I bounced off the metal walls with excitement. This would be mine someday. Chrome and blue everything. The nicest rooms to accommodate us. My father's fortune was unimaginable.

Then one day after Nyx had died, a new baby arrived. She was from Sandnes, Norway. My father cooed at her the way one would a regular baby. But she was different. I knew this one was going to be special. Her face was tiny. Barely noticeable fingernails on delicate fingers. She was precious.

"Look, Bellamy. This is going to be the new Ex Machina," said my dad.

He kept cooing at her and looking at me. She couldn't see him, but he made little pinching motions at the tank like he was playing with her.

"Is she okay in there?" I asked.

She was suspended in the blue liquid. The plates in her back were newly installed right before submersion. Her head was decorated with the floral device. Down her spine were the wires swishing like sleepy cat tails. The small respirator was covering the lower part of her face. She looked like she was sleeping, but I was concerned about her.

His glasses had a glare on them. They hid his misty, grey eyes. My dad often appeared to have no expression because of the way the light hit his round glasses. His mouth was a thin, straight line. Except when he looked at her. He grinned from ear to ear.

"She's fine, son. She's going to be fine," said my father with glee.

"When do we get to wake her up?" I asked. My dad pulled me to his side, and we admired the baby Ex Machina together.

"Not for a long time. You'll be in your thirties," he said, and I made a face. I thought thirty was really old back then. My dad laughed and so did I.

"What's her name?" I asked.

We returned our attention to the tank.

"I haven't decided yet. What do you think it should be?"

"It should be something that suits her," I said and shrugged. Names didn't really mean much to me. The first Ex Machina was named Nyx because she had black hair like a night sky swirling around in a glass.

"She is fair with light hair. I think I want to name her something wintery. Like Ivy," he said.

"No, she doesn't look like an Ivy."

This made my dad chuckle.

"What about...Alba?"

I shook my head. "No, that's not right either."

I was being stubborn, but I wanted her to have the right name.

"I like the name Gwen," he said and put his hand to the glass.

I put my hand next to his.

"That's the one." We smiled at each other. Then we stared into the blue liquid holding our salvation.

***

It's been three days. I'm destroyed emotionally and mentally. Physically, I'm not much better. Hotaka has had to force me to drink water because I'm on the brink of dehydration. He almost had to hook me up to an IV. I'm reverting back to the version of myself I despise. But Gwen hasn't come back.

I can't function. It's excruciating trying to get any work done. I do the best I can, which is pretty bad. Yui keeps glancing at me. Shira is huffy. The older scientists avoid me. Hikari is just as sad as I am, but we don't talk about it. It's too painful. Hotaka is the only one who treats me like a person.

They haven't restrained me, but I feel their eyes watching my every movement. I sit by the door but not too close and wait for her. Hours pass, the sky changes, and the sun begins to set. Another day. It's eating me up inside. Shira and Katsuo walk by but don't make eye contact. They pity me but they don't understand.

The dark takes over. I think about Nyx. She was midnight in a glass. I only saw her once. My father and I were both in awe. She was suspended in the bright light of the blue tank. Her long, long hair was swirling around. I studied her face. Nyx had a big nose and full lips. Pretty, but in a different way.

Hotaka wakes me up. He can't stand me sleeping by the door. I oblige, since he's my friend. We walk to my room in silence. He waits for me to lie down and sits in the chair. I loosen my tie and kick off my shoes.

"You need to take better care of yourself, Bellamy." He peeks at me over the rim of his glasses.

"I know. You're right," I say.

My lab coat is still on. I sit up and take it off. My shoulders are tense. I try to rub away the soreness.

"You say what I want to hear, but you don't do anything about your declining mental health, sleep, or appetite."

I've been called out.

"I'm sorry," I say and roll up my sleeves.

My back hurts. I lay on my side and rub my neck.

"It's okay. But I'm worried about you," he says and crosses his arms.

"I'll take better care of myself. I swear. I've just been having a really difficult time with Gwen being gone."

"Remember the bond," he says and stands up. Hotaka dims the light and nods at me. I get the hint. He wants me to get some rest. "I'm going to bring you food and check on you in a little bit, okay?"

"Thank you, Hotaka. You're a genuine friend."

"I am."

He takes echoing footsteps down the hall. My pillow is comfortable. I resent it, but I'm relaxed and drift off. It's nice to be in my own bed. I almost forget how upset I am.

My dreams are strange. I see my mom cheering for me at a baseball game. She has big Mantodea eyes. My dad is pushing me out of the room where Gwen was born. I dream about all my girlfriends yelling at me. They get in my face and storm off into the darkness where I can't see them. I wish they would stop.

There is the familiar pull of my hair. It's subtle. If I were in a deeper sleep, it would be undetectable, but I've been waiting for it. Gwen's fingers are in my hair. She has her hand on my shoulder. I'm so happy I can't talk. I enjoy her presence in silence. The glow of the device and her eyes illuminate the room.

"Gwen," I say her name, and she smiles. It's sudden, but I sit up and wrap my arms around her. She rests her head on my shoulder and keeps her hand in my hair. "I'm so happy to see you."

"I tried to stay away. But I can't," her voice is flat, robotic this time. Cold and calculated. It sends a shiver up my spine, bouncing in my skull.

"What?" I ask.

She talks into my neck. Her steel enforced jaw could kill me in a second.

"I can't be separated from you for long. I get too...sad."

"I'm glad you didn't stay away."

She massages my scalp but I have a horrible intrusive thought: she could peel off my skin with minimal effort.

"Why, though?"

"It makes me sad when we are apart," I say, and she pulls back.

The waning crescent diamond sparkles in the low light of the room. She touches my face like the day she woke up. Her gold eyes examine me. I let her run her hand along my cheek. Gwen puts her hand on my heart. She concentrates on it and the language it speaks.

"I'm sorry, Bellamy. I don't want to make you sad," she says.

I put my hand over hers.

"It's okay. I understand Katsuo hurt your feelings. I promise I'm going to talk to him about that."

"I would never hurt Hikari," she says.

"I know." I smile at her and move her hair to one side. "Where did you go?" I ask.

"Lots of places. I found a cave surrounded by oak trees. It had a pretty view. I spent a lot of time in the forest. I explored the bottom of the lake and followed a river."

"Wow, sounds like a really pleasant experience."

"I went to space, too."

My stomach is in my throat, but I act calm.

"What did you see up there?" I ask.

"Where the Mantodea come from," she says in a solemn voice.

"Where do they come from?"

"Their spaceship is hovering above the earth. I flew around it and these were my findings: The Mantodea have advanced tech but rely mostly on their bodily strength. They speak a language I can't decipher. From what I saw, they are ruled by a Queen. She gives birth to their armies. She gives the orders. The Mantodea are connected mentally through a telepathic link. I discovered this by analyzing a cluster of thirty. They were well strategized, like they had been planning this, but there was no way for them to calculate my moves in advance. I saw the way they make eye contact and their antennas move in specific rhythms," Gwen says in a matter-of-fact way.

I'm impressed but also worried. Gwen has been fighting dozens of them. She is still pristine.

"You're amazing."

This is the most information we've received on the Mantodea since the beginning of the invasion. Gwen tilts her head and flips her hair seductively at me.

"What do I do to save you?" she asks and touches my chin, turning my face from side to side.

"We'll find out soon." I'm not sure, but I think Gwen has made trips out of the lab I don't know about.

* * *

Gwen wants to spend every minute together. This is new. She isn't talkative but insists on following me. I don't mind. All my colleagues think we're being inappropriate, anyway. Might as well let her be happy. She holds onto my elbow, and I keep peeking behind me to see her swishing wires. I don't want to offend her, so I try to ignore them. The terrible intrusive thought of her using the deadly stinger on me seeps into my mind.

We've already had tea and breakfast. She wanted to play chess, so we did. I tried my best to beat her, but she wins every time. I'm checking on the equipment, peering in on my staff, and meandering about the building. I asked Gwen if she wants to go outside. She said "no." I think she wants to, but she doesn't want me to get hurt.

Shira and Yui have been distant, so I brushed her tangled hair. It's getting ridiculously long. I don't dare mention cutting it. That would upset her. I think Hikari is right. She has mermaid hair. The blonde locks smell vibrant, a flower in bloom. Like lily of the valley. Sweet but poisonous.

The Ex Machina has accumulated a wealth of knowledge about the Mantodea. It sends stabbing pains through my back, thinking about her leaving the lab. She may have recently taken an interest in the Mantodea, but I have this nagging sensation she's been sneaking out. I chide myself. It's not sneaking out. Gwen may do what she wants. I'm happy she came back. That was a dark time for me. Believing she had left me for good turned my body into an empty shell filled with rocks.

"What do you want to do?" I ask.

Gwen looks up at me and sways her wire tails back and forth.

"Stay with you," she says.

Gwen has already told me this. I laugh because Gwen has her own sense of humor.

"I know. But what should we do?"

"Will you show me something of yours?" she asks.

"Okay."

We go back towards my room. She hasn't seen photos of my life before the Mantodea so I decide to show her those. Gwen sits on my bed with the black leather photo album. It's a miracle it has survived. My mom took great care of it. She said memories were the most important thing in the end.

I sit next to Gwen and watch her analyze my past life. She is looking at me playing baseball when I was nine. She lands on a photo of me and my mom at the lake. She pauses on it. Her hair is wrapped around me. I'm leaning over her shoulder, watching her examine who I am.

Gwen keeps looking at pictures of a young me with messy hair making silly faces. My mom is wearing the necklace I gave to Gwen in a photo and she puts her finger on it. I see it incite something in her. She reaches up and touches the waning crescent diamond before turning another page.

There's a picture of me and my dad. We're in his lab in Boston. He was showing me around. The staff gave me a lab coat. It was too big, but it made my dad really happy. My mom showed up and thought we looked cute, so she snapped the photo. Neither of us looks prepared, but it's a pleasant memory and photo.

"Who is this man?" she asks. Gwen puts her delicate finger to his neck.

"My father, Adam Krim." Gwen doesn't continue through the album. She keeps staring at this version of me, but her eyes are locked on my dad's face. "What is it, Gwen?" I ask.

"I remember your voice. It sounds similar to how it sounds now. But I heard another voice. It was much older, hoarser. I think it was him," she says and taps on my dad's face.

"What did he say?" I ask, hoping I don't sound too eager or anxious.

"You will save the world. Then I will save you." Her breathy voice is hushed. I'm not sure what the words mean, but they are powerful. I feel them pump through my body like an electrical surge.

"Really?"

"Yes."

"It was my dad who created you. He died three years ago. I took over after he passed."

I rub the back of my neck. My body hurts all the time. I can't tell if it's the tension or the fact I treat myself like shit.

"Was he like you?" she asks. I'm not sure how to answer.

"We were similar, but very different. I wanted to play sports. He wanted me to be a scientist. He got his wish," I shrug.

Gwen stares at me and pierces my soul with her harsh gold glare.

"His eyes aren't kind the way yours are," she says and goes back to staring at the photo. The glare of his glasses plus his icy grey gaze is rather uninviting.

"You think I have kind eyes?" I ask.

Gwen perplexes me. She is evolving.

"I do," she says and reaches for my heart.

"You have the most mesmerizing eyes."

She's not wearing lipstick today. "Hikari says I have angel eyes," she giggles. But a wave of sadness overtakes her face.

"I'll make sure you and Hikari can play together again. I promise." Gwen keeps flipping through old photos. She sees me on my eleventh birthday with a paper party hat blowing out candles. Gwen is trying to understand me. She keeps her hand on my heart and fans through pieces of my old life. Moments that were captured.

She gets to the photos of me playing baseball. My tee shirt was stained in mud like it was a stamp of approval. Dirt streaked my cheeks. The whole team had missing teeth and wide grins. We were running, kicking up dust, and winning. I have my hands up in the air cheering. Gwen finds these ones amusing because she smiles with her titanium teeth.

CHAPTER ELEVEN
GAMES

My father and I used to enjoy watching Gwen grow together. Then everything changed. Something turned him against me. I never harbored romantic or lustful feelings towards the Ex Machina. That didn't stop my father from shoving me out of the room and choking me out with my shirt. Maybe he saw something I didn't. He was probably going nuts.

A certain amount of insanity goes hand in hand with genius. There can be no intellect without creativity. Intense, intuitive, creative ideas were what Adam Krim lived for. A once mellow man turned into an empty wineskin of a person. Nothing could fill him up. He wanted to be with Gwen.

To get to Japan, the military used one of the reinforced submarines my father's company made. It allowed us faster travel with immense space and the highest standards of safety. Flying was out of the question. The Mantodea roamed the skies and flocked together back then. They are spread out now but spawn periodically. Clusters are less common.

Other people remained in crumbling cities while we lived lavishly in the sea's blackness. We could hide, so we did. Not everyone was fortunate. The smaller, rural communities didn't attract as many Mantodea. There was a TV on board the submarine. The military officers would watch as the aliens ravaged the earth. We were tucked away in the indigo velvet, hidden from the enemy.

Cities like New York, Boston, and Philadelphia were decimated. The buildings were in ruins. Skyscrapers were toppled like plastic toys. The Mantodea were like a plague of locusts sent upon the earth. The gods weren't pleased with us. It was said we would pay for our sins. I've never been religious, but is this the rapture, the awakening, the return they were speaking of?

Religious leaders claimed the aliens were demons sent from Satan himself.

Then why would they come out of the sky and not rise from the mud? My naïve mind asked many questions back then. In a way, I was meant to be a scientist. It's my constant wondering. My unwavering interest.

Countries with cold temperatures year round like Canada, Russia, and Mongolia had better luck faring after the invasion. Tropic areas were hit the hardest. The Mantodea are attracted to hot and humid weather. Their ability to fly without needing rest allows them to haunt the earth endlessly. From what our studies and findings suggests, the Mantodea require little recuperation but are constantly hungry. It's what drives them the most. The need to feed. They will eat livestock and large animals, but for a while their diet consisted mostly of human flesh.

Animals in zoos around the world were ripped to bits. Lion fur, elephant tusks, and the hooves of gazelles sat in the sand of the exhibits. Cars were crushed and telephone poles were trashed. Communication is spotty, but there are still a few cell towers and the internet works in some parts of the world. We are civilized, but not.

I remember standing at the window looking into the black water. It was like night. Glow in the dark creatures passed by every so often. Whale songs and bubbling depths echoed in the steely structure. I wandered around the submarine and touched everything. My father's work was immaculate, impressive, but not appreciated until it was too late.

My mom tried to keep me happy and active. We raced around the open halls. She made up scary stories to tell me in a blanket fort. The officers and staff of the craft eyed us with disdain. It didn't matter, though. We were Adam Krim's wife and kid. We could do whatever we wanted. I don't think I ever abused the privilege. Until now.

I'm going through the cameras. It's embarrassing, but my mind won't let me relax until I look through the past few weeks. I need answers. No one else is around. Hopefully, the older scientists won't walk in on me. They would be the harshest judges. Nori not so much, but I know Katsuo and Isamu have lost their faith in me.

Rewinding back day after day, I scan the images. I'm walking around. Gwen is following. My staff is busy and going back and forth. Yui is like a flash flood. She is on screen and then gone in a blink of an eye. Hotaka is listening to music with headphones and nodding his head as he looks over some papers. Nothing out of the ordinary.

Then I see it on one of the screens. It's a sudden burst of red and blonde. A bombshell. Gwen is walking out the front door. The time stamp is eleven days ago. She's been sneaking out. My suspicions are right. I scold myself. It's not sneaking out. Gwen is allowed to come and go as she pleases. Then why am I agitated?

Watching Gwen follow me gives me a sinister pleasure. She looks at me like a puppy would, but I'm her toy. She is playing with me. The way she holds my elbow and leans into me when Shira is around makes it hard to swallow. Lately my throat feels like it's on the verge of closing up.

I keep rewinding. More fast motion movies of people working for me in this quarantined lab. It's a science fiction drama. I watch every screen and soak up all the details. Shira and Katsuo have been spending a lot of time together. Hikari and Gwen are playfully chasing each other. Yui continues to scurry all over the place with stacks of journals.

Another day, Gwen left without my knowledge. This one is time stamped twenty-one days ago. The Ex Machina is a femme fatale. Her face is mischievous. She is moving her hand across her collarbone. The most bizarre thing happens. Gwen looks up at the camera. She blows a kiss and winks. I've been a fool. She knew I would give in and spy on her.

***

She wants to play chess. Shira brings us tea and observes our interaction for a moment. Gwen doesn't glance away from the game. I give Shira the side eye. She huffs and stomps off. Gwen's wires swish in wide, sleepy motions. Her angel wings peek out from her shoulders and light up her platinum hair. Gwen is toying with me as well as beating me at the game.

Yui said we should plan for the worst. I hope for the best. It nags me, but I wonder: would Gwen murder us all or just me? Hotaka said to remember the bond. How can I forget? I'm not sure what everyone is driving at, but only I can convince the Ex Machina to be our savior.

"You seem quiet, Gwen. Everything alright?" I ask.

She leans on her elbow and rests her chin in her hand. The Ex Machina sighs. It's like watching an actress.

"I want us to be able to go outside all the time," she says as she takes my bishop.

"We will. All the information you brought to me is really helpful."

"The Mantodea are cunning creatures. They appear like beasts, but are extremely intelligent. The hive mind they share concerns me. I think they have alerted the others of my presence."

"How do you know that?" I ask and move my knight.

"The way the ones reacted to me on my way back to you. They acted like they were prepared for me."

"They can transfer information through their telepathetic link," I grumble and furrow my forehead. This might be why they switch their tactics and elude resolution.

"Yes. I can fight them, but more will spawn. It is possible for me to keep them at bay by using excessive force, but it is not a real solution. I believe I need to kill the Queen."

"Great, that shouldn't be difficult for you." I move a pawn.

"The Mantodea are protective of her. They swarmed me when I approached. I was able to get a glimpse into their ship and see the inner workings of their colony, but there were too many and they chased me away."

"We'll figure it out," I say casually.

"If I could plug into their ship, I could send a massive wave of electrical energy through the system and fry them."

"Is there a time when the Mantodea are distracted enough to allow you to do it?"

"I haven't observed them long enough. This will be the next thing for me to uncover about them." She takes my queen. I lose. "Don't worry. I won't leave for a long time like I did before," she says.

Her sincerity is flawless. Gwen really is smarter than all of us.

"I trust you," I say, and rearrange the board. Gwen reaches for my hand.

"Do you?" she asks.

The Ex Machina moves her head from side to side. The device is a sapphire star in her hair. Her wires make subtle whipping sounds as they slash the air.

"Yes." I smile at her. She focuses on me. There are beads of sweat forming at my hairline.

"What if I did something bad?"

Her inquisition is jarring.

"What do you mean?" Gwen is holding my hand with tenderness, but I have visions of her ripping it off or crushing it.

"If I did something bad, you wouldn't trust me anymore," she states flatly.

I knew she would be smarter than me. She is an apex predator. But I love her. I love her so much.

"Not necessarily. People do bad things and are forgiven," I offer.

She lets me go, and I fiddle with the pawns to calm my shaky hands.

"Would you forgive me if I did something bad?" Gwen leans back in her chair and crosses her legs. Her dress is revealing.

"No one is perfect. I would hope you'd forgive me if I did something." It's not a lie but I'm afraid of saying the wrong thing. The Ex Machina is playing a brutal game.

"Why would you forgive me?"

Gwen picks up the diamond moon with two fingers and bounces it on her chest. Her gold eyes scan me for threats, clues, and fears.

"Because I love you."

I blurt it out because it's true, but I wish I hadn't.

"You loved me when I was in stasis. We hadn't met yet, but I heard your voice. You didn't know who I was. I didn't know who I was. But I remember hearing those words. I love you. They are bold. I feel impossible things. Love is the hardest emotion for me to understand. Rage, hate, hurt, sadness, these feelings are easy to immerse yourself in. They make sense. Love is beyond my capabilities as an Ex Machina to decipher," she says.

"It will make sense eventually," I assure her.

Gwen gets out of her chair to stand next to me.

"My mind is altered, but my heart isn't. Why?" she asks.

Her hand is on my face. She runs her fingers down my neck and puts her palm on my shoulder. I try not to cringe.

"My father's theory. The heart of the machine. He believed you would want to help us if you got to know us."

"You could have used a control switch. A mechanism to stop me in case of an emergency. I have no limit to my power. Why did your father design me this way?"

"He wanted you to be free."

Gwen sits in my lap. My heart is beating in my ears. The fluorescent lights are harsh. She isn't shocking me with electricity.

"I want you to be free," she says and stares at the chessboard.

Her palm is on my face like the day she was born. Blonde hair is on my shoulder and sticking to the sweat on my cheek. I'm gripping my chair and letting her use me as her plaything.

***

There's a dip in the mattress. I expect to feel hands in my hair, but I get a slap. It's Shira.

"Bellamy," she shrieks at me.

I look at the clock. It's 3:30 am. The middle of the night.

"Dammit. What is it now, Shira?"

"Gwen is scaring me."

"How so?"

"She is wandering the halls, playing with her hair. I walked past her and she winked at me. Isamu and Nori were put off by her. She apparently reached out and touched their shoulders as she walked in between them. You need to do something."

"How is that harmful? If anything, it's just," I shrug and try to find the word as Shira glares at me with her arms crossed. "Unusual," I say.

"It's abnormal. Gwen is...different."

"We want her to be different. She can process logistics better than any machine, but she also feels human emotions. Sexuality, hurt, loss..." I'm about to continue, but she interrupts me.

"Love."

"She has shown me she loves Hikari. They want to play together. It's horrible to keep them apart!"

I shout at her. Shira and Katsuo are close. She shakes her head at me and grumbles.

"I'm worried about you."

"Why?"

I lay back down and turn away from her. Shira would have driven me crazy if she were my girlfriend. She seems like the kind of person to wake up a lot in the night and huff all the time.

"You let her walk all over you," she says and stands up.

"No, I don't."

"She hides from you. You look for her. If she wants to play chess, you play chess. If she wants to go outside, you take her outside. Whatever Gwen wants, you give it to her. I don't think it's healthy."

"I don't give her whatever she wants."

I scoff and pull the blanket over my shoulders.

"Keep telling yourself that," she says.

The clink of her boots is harsh but disappears. I think about mine and Gwen's relationship from the point of view of a scientist. Yes, a bit on the brink of inappropriate. She touches me frequently. I attempt to be distant and neutral. My lack of response doesn't deter her.

I don't encourage Gwen. It's not my intention to be her doormat, but what can I do? The Ex Machina is humanity's only hope. Shouldn't I try to be kind? Rejecting her outright would surely ruin this entire project. She isn't a project, though. I care about Gwen. If she is sad, I don't feel like I'm doing my job. I want Gwen to learn what it means to be human. Why can't I have a certain level of intimacy with her? I try to go back to sleep.

Nightmares of Gwen drowning stir me awake. I remember she's no longer in stasis. No need to sit by the tank and watch the stream of bubbles escape the respirator. I'm responsible for a tornado in a glass. Going back into a deep slumber, I dream about the Mantodea invading. They hiss and we all run in different directions. Thousands of people fleeing underground. Then the sun goes out. Black winter nothingness.

"Bell?"

It's Hotaka. He has a cup of tea for me.

"Thanks," I cough. The clock reads 7:42am. Time doesn't feel real in here. There are no windows.

"Are you alright? You were having a nightmare," he states.

I sip the hot tea. It calms me and soothes my scratchy throat.

"Yeah. I'm fine," I say and rub my face.

There are creases in my forehead.

"Can we talk about Gwen?" he asks in a non-accusatory way.

"Sure."

"I think she wants you to be jealous."

"What?"

I spit out a bit of the green tea he just handed me.

"She takes off my glasses and fixes my tie. Isamu and Nori said she brushes against their arms and hands when she walks by. She does it on purpose, so they claim. Yui said Gwen is gauging your reaction. Shira–"

"Shira has already scolded me about this."

"She is uneasy around Gwen. The Ex Machina makes her feel uncomfortable."

Hotaka is trying to be a detail oriented scientist. My chest is hot. I don't think it's the tea.

"Gwen hasn't done anything detrimental."

I lean against the wall.

"No. She is toying with us, Bellamy. You must see that," he declares it, and I know it's true.

"Yes."

"Gwen may be human, but her robotic brain separates her from the rest of us. She is attached to your hip. I read your notes. She says she doesn't understand why she can't stay away from you. The bond, it will be our salvation."

"What are you saying?" I ask.

The tea sloshes in the cup and burns my arm. I can't feel it though.

"Gwen would prefer to be free. She wants to explore and live her life for herself. But she can't. Something makes her come back. It makes her agree to help us. She protects you. Her loyalty is to you, but she can't comprehend it. Don't squander this," warns Hotaka.

"You're right. All this time, I believed she wanted to help. She does, but it's not the way I envisioned. It's like I'm forcing her."

I see the teacup shake and try to steady my hand.

"Gwen has a heart. She is like any new human. It's a long process trying to understand the complexities of one's self, especially matters of the heart."

"You don't get paid enough, Hotaka," I joke, and he chuckles.

"Has Gwen attempted to do more than be flirtatious?" he asks.

"No," I lie. For some reason, I can't admit I let her sit in my lap. I think it's because I know it was wrong.

"Don't be cruel, but don't be too inviting, either."

Hotaka heads for the door before I can say anything else. The hot tea in my hand helps me concentrate. I should get ready for the day. Gwen is probably waiting for me.

CHAPTER TWELVE
AMARE

I haven't smoked in five years, but I keep lighting up cigarette after cigarette as I go through the cameras. They are by the front door, the lobby, the corridor where the bedrooms are, and the hall leading to the room where Gwen was born. Surveillance is important but no need to be invasive. I thoroughly believe in privacy for myself and my staff. Yet here I am combing over the footage. It's undignified, but I keep smoking and rewinding.

Rewinding further and further, I see what I have been blind to. Gwen slinking out at night. Suggestively touching her stomach as she passes a camera. In the beginning, she'd only go out for thirty minutes. Now she goes out for up to four hours at a time. How have I been so careless? My father's creation has gotten away from me. She cares for me. But what if I mess this up?

Her knowledge of the Mantodea isn't from one or two days. No, she has been collecting this information for weeks. The Ex Machina is efficient. She wants to help. But she lies. I should have suspected she wouldn't be above petty traits. She is human underneath the exoskeleton. Her heart beats like mine. She touches it all the time.

Gwen paces around the building at night like an otherworldly being. The topaz lights illuminate her fair skin and hair. The glow of her wings enhances her angelic appearance. Gold eyes shine in the dark. Some nights she flies off and other times she remains in the building, wandering, perpetually restless.

She said she wants us to go outside all the time. Gwen can be sweet, but her severity and high voltage electricity make me fearful. I want her to defeat the Mantodea. Gwen is fully capable of doing such. After the earth is rid of the aliens, she said she wants to stay with me. I hope this isn't a fatal attraction. Is Gwen heroic or just doing what I say? She liked the female superhero comics. Or maybe she only liked them because I showed them to her.

I put out my cigarette and cough for ten minutes. There's at least half a pack in the ashtray. I throw them out and clean up my mess. Bits of ash are on the chair and floor. I don't want anyone to know I've been smoking or watching the cameras. They're already talking.

My head is spinning. I'm so tired I feel like I'm drunk. It's 4:13am. I stumble back to my room in my delirious state. Gold eyes greet me as I open the door. I almost fall on my ass. Gwen is laying on my bed.

"Gwen, what are you doing?" I ask.

"Looking for you," she says.

"It's late."

"You are awake late at night most of the time."

She shifts in my bed and rolls onto her stomach. Long blonde hair falls on the floor. I hold the doorway to steady myself.

"I need to get some rest. We'll spend time together in the morning."

I motion for her to leave. Gwen lifts her torso and flaunts her chest. The crescent diamond is in the middle. I keep my eyes in the hall and stand in the doorway.

"Can I stay?" she asks.

I feel my vocal cords give out on me.

"No, I need to be alone."

I refuse to sit down on my bed until she gets up. She doesn't for a moment. There's a tense energy in the room. She rises slowly and stands in front of me. Her gold eyes search my face for something. I'm not sure what she is looking for. She puts her hand on my chest. It jolts me. I try to act unbothered.

"I know you want me to stay," she says as she slips out the door.

I sit in my chair and rub my temples. I'm not sure what we are playing. There are no rules. The game is rigged. I can't win. She will win every time. I have to try, though.

My pillowcase is permeated with the scent of poisonous white blossoms, fresh but deadly. She's right. I want her to stay. It's unprofessional of me to be so selfish. If my dad were around, he'd be laughing in my face. This would please him. I'm more like my father than I thought. I rub my scalp and try to get the image of her laying in my bed out of my mind.

The Ex Machina is preying on my loneliness. She can sense it and not with her wires. My short list of convenient girlfriends makes me pensive. Who would I be if the Mantodea didn't come? Would I be married by now? What kind of life would I live? Sophia, Eva, Valerie, did we have anything or was it just pretend? The end of the world can make the wrong person the right one for a time.

I roll onto my side. That doesn't help. I lay on my back. The ceiling greets me. More metal. Everything in my world is shiny. I turn to my other side. My pillowcase smelled too much like her, so I changed it. I keep smelling flowers though. Where is it coming from? I sit up to inspect.

Nothing under my pillow. I pull back my sheet. There is nothing under the covers. Something is in here, though. Floral, white, fragrant. I put my hand in between the mattress and the wall. There is the cool rubbery texture of a petal against my index finger. I pull out a stem with white flowers. Lily of the Valley. Gwen went outside again. She wants to flaunt her power over me.

***

Blood swirling in my veins, the tension in my temples, and racing heart are all I hear. Everything else is muted. Nori is saying something to me, but I can't focus. Get it together. I need to focus on what's happening right now. I haven't been sleeping. My vision is hazy.

"I'm sorry, Nori. What were you saying?"

"Hikari is hysterical. He's locked us out of the room. Says he won't open the door for anyone but you or Gwen," says Nori. The sides of his head are salt and pepper. He looks uncomfortable telling me this. I look like shit.

"Let me talk to him," I say.

Gwen and Hikari should have time together. The two of us walk down the long echoing halls to the room Katsuo and Hikari share. Katsuo, Shira, and Isamu are outside. Katsuo is speaking through the door.

Hikari keeps screaming "No!"

"Please, son. Don't be like this," says his father.

"I want to play with Gwen!"

"Hikari–"

"No!" Hikari shrieks the word over and over again. It's shrill and is razor wire on my tender brain. Katsuo looks at me with disdain. His eyes take in my tired face, disheveled appearance, and fake smile. I kneel and speak to the door.

"Hikari, it's me. Can we talk?"

"Okay. But I'm not letting you in," says Hikari.

"That's fine. What's wrong? Why are you locking yourself in?" I ask in the fanciful way children ask questions.

"I want to play with Gwen," he says.

"I know. Maybe we can work something out."

I look at Katsuo and give him the eyes. He turns away and scoffs.

"I'm not coming out until Gwen comes for me."

Hikari is small, but quite robust in his tone.

"Hikari, please stop this!" shouts Katsuo.

"You stop it!" screams his son.

I put my hand to my forehead. It's warm but not feverish. My cool hand soothes my migraine.

"If I let you and Gwen see each other, will you stop this?" asks Katsuo.

"I'll do whatever you tell me to do, but I want to talk to Gwen," says

Hikari.

He's crying. Katsuo gives into his demand with a clenched fist and a tight jaw.

"Okay. But only when I'm around," he says and looks at me with shotgun barrels.

"I'll go find her for you," I say and excuse myself.

The other scientist watch me go. They are going to talk shit as soon as I'm out of earshot. I wander the halls and peek into different rooms with equipment, paperwork, journals, chrome, and fluorescent lights. But no Gwen. I search for her as she surely wants me to. Yui and Nori don't make eye contact as I walk past them. I remember Gwen saying she liked to swim.

The water reservoir is the deepest blue green, veering on black, but not quite. I think about looking at the camera and decide against it. I stand at the edge of the dark pool leading into the depths. She is in there. I sense it. Kneeling down, I peer closer. In the blackness, I see blue and gold. The Ex Machina is aware of me.

"Hey Gwen," I say as she surfaces.

She blows bubble kisses at me on camera but acts shy in my presence.

"Hi," she says.

"Katsuo said Hikari and you can play together. Want to go see him?" I ask. Gwen smiles, and this time I know it's not a facade. She is excited.

"Yes," she says and the gold beneath the hazel goes out for a second.

It barely flickers, but I notice it. This is important. I will write this down later.

"Come with me," I say and extend my hand to her.

She doesn't need me to, but I do it anyway. Gwen rises from the water. It cascades from her hair and over her wings. Gwen's nakedness never made me uncomfortable. Until now. She waits for me to look at her, but I keep eye contact. Ever so slightly, she turns up the corners of her mouth. Gwen wrings out her hair in a methodical, seductive way. She ignores me while she puts on her dress and I wait for her by the door.

Gwen leaves a trail of water behind her. Droplets splatter and fan out. They pool together and remind me of clouds. Her wires swish. They are moving with ferocity. At first I'm afraid she is sensing a threat, but I realize it's her deep need to find Hikari. We approach, and I avoid Shira's disapproval. Gwen's dress is practically see-through since she put it on wet. Isamu, Katsuo, and Shira all back up from her. Gwen puts her hand to the door.

"Hikari?" she says.

I hear Hikari jump up off the bed and run to the door. He opens it and runs into her arms. Gwen kneels down to be closer to him. Hikari and her are smiling. I take a photo of it in my mind. To remember when I doubt her.

"I missed you," says Hikari.

He touches the necklace I gave her. The little boy looks at the Ex Machina like the magnificent creature she is. His eyes are wide open.

"I missed you, too."

Gwen runs her hand through his hair. Katsuo winces as we make brutal eye contact. He looks down. Hikari laughs and all of us scientists turn to him. He won't stop laughing. This makes Gwen laugh. She has never laughed like this. It's an actual laugh. One that isn't forced or mocked. It isn't being emulated. Gwen is experiencing joy.

"Why are you laughing?" she asks when she catches her breath.

Hikari grabs two handfuls of hair but doesn't tug.

"I knew you were a mermaid. Or an angel. Or a princess," says Hikari.

Water is all around Gwen. It's a circle. Hikari is standing right outside it.

"I am..." Gwen pauses and studies Hikari. She looks for the right words with consideration, "whatever you want me to be."

"I want you to be you. Be Gwen," says Hikari as he puts his arms around her.

The other scientists and I watch something happen. Tears fall down the Ex Machina's face. I want to embrace her, to make her feel better, but as a scientist I choose to study my creation.

"What does that mean?" she asks.

I catch Shira covering her mouth. She must be stifling her vomit or shock. Isamu is writing something down. Katsuo has his arms crossed, but the creases of his forehead fade. This moment is melting his face off.

"I like you just the way you are," says Hikari.

Gwen lets him go. She stands and touches her face. It's as though she is using her intellect to put this feeling under the microscope. No matter how fast she can compute, she won't understand with her infallible mind. Gwen stares at her hand with fresh tears on it.

Hikari puts his palm over hers. "Will you read to me?"

"Of course," she says. Hikari pulls her into the room and she sits in the chair. The little boy lies on the bed. He hands her a children's book.

"You'll really like this one," he says. The other scientists and I stand outside the room but don't go in. We observe as professionals.

"Why's that?" she asks. Gwen opens the pink and gold book with thin metal laced fingers.

"It's about a princess put under a spell and only a kiss can wake her up," says Hikari. He pulls the blanket over himself. Katsuo dims the lights. Gwen's gold eyes illuminate the pages.

***

It happens so fast, I think it's a dream. A hand on my shoulder and fingers in my hair. I turn around in my bed and hear the door shutting. My heart is racing. I'm on high alert. Grabbing my lab coat and pants, I see a note by my bed.

* * *

I'll be back soon. Don't worry. I'll come back to you.
-Gwen

She's going outside. Gwen must want to find out about the Mantodea. I'm touched that she doesn't want me to worry, but I'm worried, anyway. Everything about Gwen has me on edge and grinding my teeth. I barely sleep. Hotaka has to bring me food or I forget to eat. My weight is low, one-hundred and fifty-nine pounds.

I act normal and do my rounds. The crops are flourishing. Equipment beeps and hums. I take my time wandering around. Wasting time is difficult when it's all I have. I want her to come back to me right now. My possessiveness alarms me. The darkness my father was consumed by is taking over.

Shira glares at me as I pass her in the lounge. She is going through a pile of journals. I'm sure she is judging me and my father through harsh lenses. Yui keeps her head down and scurries about with intensity. Hotaka is handing me a glass of the nutrition supplement and a bowl of leafy greens. I sit down on a couch and eat in a daze.

"Bellamy, what's wrong?" asks Hotaka.

"Gwen is outside. She left me a note not to worry," I say and take a bite of steamed kale.

Filling my mouth with food sounds better than talking.

"She'll come back."

"She said she would, but…" I sip on my drink and shake my head.

"You worry she'll break the bond and leave. I don't think she can. It's permanently ingrained. If she died, we could recover the device. Theoretically, we could grow another Gwen and she would still be bonded to you.

"What?" I ask.

The food makes me feel less sick. I don't think I've eaten since yesterday.

"The imprinting can only happen once. She is yours," he says with a smile.

"Why are you looking at me like that?"

"I think you love her more than you let on. Why won't you admit it?"

"That would be unprofessional," I say and continue to eat.

Hotaka is irritating me, but I don't want to be rude.

"No one like Gwen has ever existed. Your father made something miraculous. Something no one else can have. She will do anything for you and you love her. I can tell," says Hotaka.

I choke on my food.

"You're wrong," I say.

"How do you feel about her then?" he asks in an amused way.

"I don't know. It's like being on drugs," I admit.

"You don't call that love?" Hotaka takes off his glasses and stares at me without a filter.

"Maybe it is. I've never felt anything like it."

"Love can be...unexplainable."

"I thought I loved my girlfriends. They never drove me crazy like this though," I laugh desperately.

"We can love people in different ways."

"I love her, but I'm afraid of her. She does things to frighten me. It doesn't matter though because I so badly want her to like me."

It's pathetic.

"She likes you more than anyone," he says with a chuckle.

"I think Gwen could fall in love with being free."

"She might. But she won't be able to leave. Not for long."

He stands up and heads towards the kitchen area with my empty bowl and glass. I walk to the front door. Like a puppy, I pace around and wait for my master. The sun is setting. An orange square moves on the ground with the angle of the sun. I see dust flecks in the yellow light.

Katsuo and Hikari walk past me. Hikari seems happy. Katsuo looks at me with a hardened expression, but nods. We are cordial to one another. Gwen cried at Hikari's words. The little boy may be closer to the heart of the machine than I. Hikari disagrees with me. He says Gwen loves me the mostest.

Isamu is eating an apple and shuffling across the lobby. He looks sleepy but gives me a pleasant face and waves. I think he wants to trust me. Maybe the entire team doesn't hate me. It's hard to tell how I am coming off. I think I'm being rational, but really I'm losing it. The door opens.

"Gwen," I'm eager for her to approach me.

Gold eyes glow from her silhouette. The moon rises. Gwen opens her arms to me. I watch her wires swish as I bury my face in her hair as we embrace.

"I missed you," I say.

"You did?" she asks.

"Yes." I look behind her. Stars are lighting up the night sky. Gwen's angel wings glow. She belongs up there.

"I found out more about the Mantodea," she informs me.

We let each other go and walk towards the couch. She sits very close to me and presses her thigh against mine.

"What did you find out?" I ask.

"I can destroy the Mantodea if I use all of my electrical energy. If I harness enough of the atmosphere's power and exert every ounce of force, I can destroy the drones protecting the ship and fry the Queen."

"That's great news!" I grab her hand with excitement.

Gwen is doing this for me. She will save us all.

"The only thing is I'd have to die, Bellamy. When I plug into the ship, it will deplete my electrical energy. It will take all my power to annihilate them," she says without looking at me.

My heart drops.

"I don't want you to do that. We'll find another way."

"I thought you wanted me to save the world."

She looks up at me with glowing gold eyes. They flicker for a moment.

"I do, but I don't want to lose you in the process. You mean too much to me."

I stroke her hand. It's soft despite being covered in a thin titanium-like exoskeleton and laced with metal strands beneath the human flesh.

"If I have to die for you to go outside all the time, I will do it," she says.

It's an impulse, but I pull her closer to me. Gwen puts her arms around my neck. She says she feels impossible things. So do I.

"No, we'll find another way."

"If I die, will you always remember me?" she asks.

The scientists already don't trust me. I don't trust myself. It doesn't matter anymore. I break the boundary and pull Gwen onto my lap so she can be closer to my heart. Holding her is extraordinary. Real but not real.

"If you die, I'll have to bring you back," I say.

She presses her cheek against mine.

"Why?"

"Because I can't live without you."

CHAPTER THIRTEEN
PLAYERS

I remember being a kid and my parents fighting downstairs. If my dad was home, they were usually fighting. At least, that's what I remember the most. I think when I was really little things were okay, but by the time I was ten it was obvious my parents weren't truly happy but pretended to be. My mom was good at acting like everything was fine.

Laying in my bed with the covers over my head, I'd attempt to drown out their screaming. My dad would try to calm my mother, but she would be so beyond herself at this point. He was never home. She was raising me on her own. People took our picture and talked about us online and in the paper. There was no privacy being a Krim.

My friends were my friends until they realized who I was. Kids don't care about prestige. They don't care about money or fame. But then they do. Whoever has a better life is hated the most. Once everyone took notice of the Krim family name and everything it owned, my classmates started snubbing me. The baseball team felt like the only friends I had left. They were somewhat fake. We were friends, but they resented me.

Living in Mount Ontake isn't so different from my old life. I feel alone. People staring at me, talking about me. My girlfriend experiences have been unique, considering I didn't think I'd have any girlfriends after the alien invasion. Sophia loved me more than I loved her. I loved Eva more than she loved me. Valerie was perfect, but we could not connect the space between us. They were all pretty, but something was missing. My love life fulfilled me since I had little outside of my romances. During those years, I felt lucky to have someone.

Being alone felt like the worst thing that could happen to me. This feeling is something else. I don't know how Gwen feels about me. She doesn't comprehend it herself.

I'm trying to make up for my scatterbrained episodes. Today I'm going through my father's notes. Highlighting Nori's and reading over Yui's. I don't care about Shira's notepad. Sitting at my desk, I go over something my father wrote when Gwen was sixteen:

Vitals are normal. Cognitive signals are increasing. Ex Machina is healthy. Gwen is as lethal as she is beautiful.

I gulp and the saliva gets stuck in my throat. Adam Krim might have suspected all the male scientists because he was having unscientific thoughts. How did I never notice this? I have read over my father's theories, notes, and plans for years. Perhaps I read it, but it didn't resonate the way it does now. I feel guilty and shameful. Like an impostor. I flip through Nori's notes:

Gwen is becoming sensuous. Not sure if it is for stimulation, learning, or expression of sexuality. She touches my arms and shoulders. The Ex Machina sits in lewd positions on the couch in the lounge while she reads. Isamu dropped his pen, and she bent down to pick it up. It was peculiar.

I rub the back of my head. The tension headache is returning. Gwen is perplexing. What is she up to? She agrees to help and acts loyal, but wants me to be jealous. I hate myself because I am. What does she gain from making me feel this way? I get a pang in my chest. Gwen asked me why she was given a heart if she was to feel emotions like this. It stings and a scorpion enters.

Yui has never let me down. The young, brilliant, and diligent scientist. What does she have to say? I thumb through a couple of pages.

The Ex Machina is progressive and observant. Able to understand behaviors. Can act a certain way in front of one person to gain one thing while being something else to another.

I continue to flip through black and white. It's like shuffling cards. Soon I'm more than interested. I'm obsessed.

The Ex Machina is fond of Bellamy. She chooses to be with him most of the time. Is most animated in his presence. Flat affect in presence of others besides Bellamy and Hikari.

One more I tell myself...

Bellamy refuses to see what is most apparent. The Ex Machina obeys his orders. She is his to command. He treats her like his friend. Could enforce rules or give a stricter schedule.

"What are you doing?" Gwen's voice is in my ear.

Her hair is falling over my shoulder. She is leaning on me. It reminds me of Valerie. Can Gwen read minds? Does she know this is a distant memory of mine I've longed to experience again? Her hand is unbuttoning my shirt. She reaches in and touches my heart.

"Just looking over some notes," I say.

Closing the book slowly, so as to not seem suspicious, I turn to her. She keeps leaning on me. I reach up and touch her wrist.

"Did your father say anything about how to defeat the Mantodea?" she asks.

Gwen stands up. She is rubbing my shoulders. It gives me chills.

"I'm looking for an answer to our problem. He didn't seem to know much about them other than they were strong and we needed something stronger."

"What should I be doing?" she asks.

"Whatever you want. It's going to take me a while to come up with a plan."

"I want to stay with you."

"I'd like that," I say and pretend to go over notes not about her. Gwen isn't touching me anymore. She's walking away. "Gwen?" I call for her.

"Yes?" she asks.

"Do you want to play chess?"

"No."

"What about another game?" I ask.

"I'm fine," she says.

"Are you sure?"

"I want to be alone right now," she says and walks towards her room.

I'm put off by this. Gwen can be hot and cold. Who is winning this game? Gwen is programmed to be the victor.

***

Growing up as Adam Krim's son left little room for people to get to know me. They already had me figured out. Or so they thought. I remember my mom and I walking through a park one day and a man in a black suit took our picture. He had white hair and a lot of stubble. My father's work left little privacy for him or Bellamy and Bethany Krim.

I was on display. The days I played baseball made me forget my troubles. It felt normal. Something for me that was fleeting. I was an anachronism. My father made me such. People watched me, talked about me, and knew stuff about me. Whether I liked certain brands and what shoes I wore.

Adam was a distant father, but he was loving at times. We had days where we talked the way the average father and son would. He showed me nerdy stuff he liked. We both enjoyed comic books. He hated my music. We couldn't agree on any films. My father wasn't athletic and couldn't hit a ball or score a goal to save his life.

My mom wore the waning crescent my dad gave her every day. I think it reminded her of how he used to be. She could use it to fixate on a better time. Their past involved a lot of romantic gestures. My dad named a star after her. He bought her flowers, jewelry, and perfume. She really wanted a baby, though. Adam was hesitant, but he wanted his wife to have everything she desired.

It's mid-autumn. The leaves are falling. They drift and twirl in the wind. Flashes of gold and scarlet rain. I want to experience the changing season with her. She has been avoiding me. I think she wants me to seek her out. Gwen knows I've been unsure about her. I've always broken the rules. I'll break them all for her. As I stand outside her door, I am nervous, like I was twenty years ago.

"Hey," she lets me in.

Gwen sits on her bed and I take a seat in the chair.

"I was thinking we could go outside today," I say.

"You want to go outside with me?" she asks.

Gwen plays with her hair and doesn't make eye contact. I go along with her games.

"I do. I want us to look at the fall leaves together. Roses and cosmos are blooming. You'll like it."

"Okay."

The Ex Machina keeps me in my seat and doesn't allow me to rise. Gwen places a hand on my face and the other in my hair. Her stare has something sinister to it, almost predatory. Devious. I want to trust her. My leg is shaking. She walks out of the room and I follow.

The wires swish back and forth, back and forth. They are like a sleepy cat. Who knows how they will react once outside? Gwen will protect me. She doesn't know why she is attached to me, but she is. Hotaka's words bounce around in my tender skull. She is mine. Gwen is aware of it. But does she enjoy it? Does she resent me?

Yui styled her hair. It's in a long, intricate braid. Her face is youthful yet severe. Gwen has changed her appearance again. She's been wearing a strapless black dress with ruffles. It's longer than the red dress, but shorter than the white. It hits about mid-thigh. Shira glances at us as we walk by. She says "hi" and Gwen waves, but I don't say anything. We get to the door and I hit the button. Gwen waits for me to walk out first.

"I love this time of year," I say.

It's a mix of sunny with lots of clouds. Gold, mahogany, and scarlet leaves stand out against the gray sky.

"Everything is so..." Gwen searches for the word as she kneels. She sees a pink rose, "pretty," she says.

The Ex Machina picks the flower from the middle of the stem and hands it to me.

"Thank you."

I focus on the rose. It's a light shade of pink. An innocent color. It has thorns, but not many. They are still sharp and can draw blood. Gwen takes my other hand and we walk down the hill. In the tall grass are clusters of red spider lilies. Gwen's wires crack like whips as she senses, but her face is serene. There are no threats nearby.

We are holding hands. The Ex Machina is guiding me through red, white, and orange flowers. The cedars stand tall and we walk in their long shadows. Butterflies flutter above us. I've never believed in magic, but maybe Gwen really is putting a spell on me. Everything is flawless in her presence. Birds watch us from the lower branches. They have red bellies. The sun comes in through the oak leaves and Gwen's eyes shimmer.

"What are you thinking about?" I ask.

She looks into the forest in front of us. Purple and pink flowers line the edge of the treeline. Gwen holds onto my hand and doesn't let go.

"What I am to you," she says.

"You're the single most important thing in my life."

Gwen pulls me down to sit with her in the grass. It shines shades of emerald and jade. The wind moves across the top.

"What are you to me?" she asks.

Gwen wants to understand our bond. I don't understand it myself.

"I can't tell you that. Only you know."

"My ability to process complex theories, strategize, and use intuition hasn't helped me answer this specific question," she says as she plucks a cosmo.

Her gold eyes pierce the blossom. What is in the center of this flower attracting her? Does it remind her of the device in her head? The petals are a mix of orange and red.

"Are you happy when you're with me?" I ask.

The pink rose she gave me is in my hand. I won't let it go. Gwen scoots closer. Wires intimidate me as they wiggle and squirm like snakes behind her. She is Medusa, turning me to stone.

"It's complicated," she says.

Gwen is in front of me. Her unwavering gaze is making me uncomfortable.

"Try to explain. Please."

"I'm so happy when I'm with you it hurts. That's why I have to be alone sometimes. The days I separate myself from you are the times I want to be with you the most. It...confuses me," she says.

"I think I kind of understand."

I pick a purple cosmo. It has an orange center. There are grass stains on my khakis, but I don't care.

"You do?"

"Yes," I say. The Ex Machina reaches for my heart and turns me into a concrete statue.

***

It's criminal of me. The jealousy is driving me mad. I'm chain smoking in my room and pouring through my father's notes. There are clues I missed before. The ones he wrote the year Gwen turned sixteen don't disgust me, but they appall me in a way they didn't when I first read them. When Gwen was still asleep.

Entry 61: The Ex Machina is a perfect machine. A beautiful young woman. She is flawless.

Entry 74: A human mind infused with robotic technology. A body made with metal thread and covered in a thin exoskeleton. Her heart remains mostly untouched.

Entry 82: Is she a hybrid? No. She is something else.

Entry 99: Gwen is growing and so is my love for her.

I don't know what to make of my father's notes or my feelings for the Ex Machina. In the beginning, I was happy, as I always am when entering into a new relationship. We were safe with the space between us. Getting acquainted is exciting, but harmless.

Then we were curious. I thought we were just interacting, but the imprinting has affected our communication. Does imprinting work both ways? Gwen is bonded to me the way her veins are laced with steel threads. There is no removing them.

Did Adam Krim fall in love with his creation? Or was he simply intrigued by his progressive techniques? I'm his son, but that means little to me. It meant little to him. We are not the same, although I wear what he wore and I act more and more like him every day. I am losing myself. This reminds me to watch my health. I put out my half-smoked cigarette.

How long have I been ignoring these emotions? Surely they have been simmering below the surface. Beneath all my efforts to be scientific, I think I also felt something else. Gwen placed her electric palm to my heart and put a spell on it. It has felt like it's pumping in overdrive ever since. I thought maybe I was excited the project was a success. Is it possible to fall in love through the process of titration? It happened so slowly, gradually, over time, I didn't notice it until my behavior became unacceptable.

"Bell?"

Hotaka is standing next to me. I didn't hear him. My thoughts have been loud in my brain. The lights seem brighter than usual.

"Yes?" I rasp.

"I brought you some food. And water," he hands me a bowl of greens sauteed with root vegetables and a cup.

"Thank you."

I need to get my weight up. Hotaka sits on my bed and leans back on his elbows.

"What are you looking at?" he asks.

"My father's notes," I say in between bites of turnips and radishes.

"Is there something you're looking for?"

"Not exactly…" I trail off.

"I've read his journals forwards and backwards."

Hotaka sits up and rubs his lower back. We all ache from the tension.

"Do you think my father had…other intentions?" I ask.

This is it. Hotaka is going to call me a nutcase.

"Towards Gwen?"

Hotaka leans forward and removes his glasses. He rubs his eyes. Maybe the lights are getting brighter.

"I'm sorry. I sound ridiculous."

"I think your father was in love with his work," Hotaka starts, but pauses. My hair stands up from electrocution. "But you're in love with her," he finishes.

"I'm not sure what to do," I confess.

Hotaka smiles, exposing his small square teeth, but doesn't laugh.

"Neither do I. Neither does Gwen. We are all experiencing a milestone in humanity's existence."

Hotaka's declaration is said with certainty.

"Gwen says she feels impossible things."

"What is love, if not the very meaning of impossible?"

I don't want to accept this to be true, but it is. There are chemicals associated with love. Humans have written experiences of love transcending time, religion, and distance. But put under the microscope, nothing about it is logical. There are no words to describe what I'm feeling.

"If you asked me the probability of me falling in love with the Ex Machina, I'd say zero. But I've fallen in love with every pretty girl that has entered this lab. What does it say about me?"

I grimace at my romantic background. Who would I be if aliens didn't invade us?

"I think it says you can be vulnerable. It may be subconscious or unintentional," Hotaka stops himself. "I'm not trying to analyze you. You're my friend," he says.

I can trust him.

"All my girlfriends filled the void. I have too much space inside me. My thoughts echo. I pretend I'm content and busy with work. It's not my finest hour. I've been stupid." I look up to see Hotaka rubbing the back of his head. The edge is constantly giving us migraines.

"Remember what I said."

"What?"

I'm in outer space.

"Let's not do anything to warrant cruel intentions."

"Of course. I love her. She knows that."

I close my father's journal. My food and water have been consumed. I don't feel like death anymore.

"Her love may be dangerous."

"Don't we want her to feel connected to us?"

"Yes. I'm worried though...what if she becomes volatile?"

"Everyone's notes comment on her mild manner and mellowness," I shrug.

"I think we should still be careful," he says and rises.

Hotaka stretches his arms and rubs his back again.

"I'll get it together. Thank you, Hotaka. For being a true friend," I say.

He takes my dishes and nods.

"Get some rest, Bellamy. I'll check on you in a couple of hours."

He exits and I decide to move to my bed. It feels empty. I'm sleeping on one side the way I did when Sophia, Eva, and Valerie lived here. Gwen wanted to stay with me that one night. I can't let her. This is a game with serious consequences.

CHAPTER FOURTEEN
FIRSTS

During our military transport, I daydreamed. I blocked out what was happening to me. What was happening to planet earth was beyond my capabilities to understand. Being only twelve left me with few means of coping with such an epic event.

After the submarine, we had to be escorted by a small military vehicle to get to the lab hidden in Mount Ontake. There were small rectangular windows. I stared out through them. The sky was gray, but bright and blinding. I kept squinting my eyes, but wouldn't stop looking outside. Four soldiers were out there guarding the four corners of the vehicle.

My mother was stiff—eyes wide, lips tight. Her anxiety was heightened every time the vehicle bounced or stopped for a brief second. Adam Krim remained ever scientific, exuding a sense of calm, and observing the way a person who isn't worried about dying would. She kept trying to comfort me. I was looking at the plain gray sky. The seats had a musky, leathery scent to them. That smell would draw me from my thoughts because it kept making me car sick.

I could see the side of the driver's face. Black and gold aviator sunglasses covered his eyes. Buzzed brown hair and ears with big lobes. He had a five o'clock shadow and a goatee. It's all I could make out in the windshield's reflection. Just another guy who worked for my dad.

Suddenly, the military vehicle came to a halt. Soldiers outside communicated through hand motions. They readied themselves for something. A female Mantodea. We didn't know this at the time. But she was bigger than most of them. She was shiny black like plastic. Her eyes were dark red and full of otherworldly fury. They intrigued me as much as they frightened me. Her arms were folded and bent at an odd angle. As though she was praying.

Her loud hiss and guttural growl rumbled. It shook through the steel walls. She roared and reared up. The soldiers emptied their clips. Guns had no effect. The Mantodea was stunned and deterred but unharmed by human bullets. They died so we could live. The driver's expression was unreadable, but I think I saw tears escape from underneath the aviators.

I remained focused on the white and slate sky. My father took my mother's hand. She tried to comfort me. I didn't need it. Considering I was outcasted long before any of this happened, I felt a smug sense of self righteousness. My dad could pay for us to live lavishly after the world ended. He felt it, too. He was right all along.

Getting adjusted was difficult. My mother screamed all night one night. She couldn't get it together. I tried to be strong for her. My dad was useless when it came to these things. He was brilliant, but emotionally, he was retarded. She clutched the sheets of her bed and screamed. About nothing. No words. Just the echoing cries of a woman losing her sanity.

I walked a lot to calm my nerves. It's a habit I have to this day. I'm wandering the dim blue lit hallways right now. When I was a kid, I would walk around endlessly. I find there is this strange sense of control in meandering about in the night. Come here, monsters. I'm not afraid.

Shira has been huffier than usual. She glares at me daily. I suspect she finds my approach with Gwen unprofessional and, frankly, too intimate. She's right, but what choice do I have? The Ex Machina wants to understand my heart. She wants to know hers. I shouldn't be interfering with that. My father designed her this way.

It's not my favorite topic of discussion, but I worry about Gwen no longer caring for me. What if I piss her off? All my girlfriends have left me. My team hardly knows who I am. To them, I'm some playboy rich guy scientist. They do not know what it's like to be Adam Krim's son.

"Bellamy," she says my name in her airy way.

Her hand is latching onto the crook of my arm. Metallic enhanced fingers grip me. I feel each finger as it hits my arm, one by one.

"Hey Gwen."

She and I walk in the low light of the laboratory corridor.

"What are you doing up?" she asks.

"I can't sleep."

"Neither can I," she says, and it makes me crack up again. Gwen laughs when I laugh. I almost feel the blood in my heart rewind.

"I'm glad to have your company."

"You don't prefer to be with the others?" she asks.

Gwen gives me a side glance.

"No, I like being with you the most."

"Can we go outside?" she asks.

"Yes, that sounds nice." We walk back towards the front door. The moon is a waning crescent like the necklace. Gwen is staring up at it. Maybe she has already been there. I hit the button and we walk out together this time.

"I like the night," she says. We take a few steps away from the door, but not too far.

"Me too. It's tranquil," I say.

"It reminds me of before you woke me up."

"How so?"

"The empty potential, the comfort of it. Nothingness consumed me and held me in its womb. I heard vague noises. Then one day I heard your voice. And the older gentleman's. I couldn't see but the way the tone of your voice sounded, it was…" she searches for the word, "scintillating."

"Does it remind you of the stars?" I ask.

"Yes," she nods.

We look at the expansive night sky. It's black but also purple, gold, silver, blue, and yellow. A rainbow in the dark.

***

Hikari and Gwen are chasing each other around. Gwen lets him keep up with her. They dart across the lobby and run down the halls. The two of them circle back with happy faces. Katsuo is watching with his arms crossed. He's been smoking as well. Stress has us all indulging in bad habits. I'm leaning against the wall as a detached observer. At least that's what I tell myself.

Gwen's wires whip back and forth with her excitement. They make Katsuo's eyebrows raise and furrow. His forehead is filled with deep creases. Hikari and the Ex Machina play the way the innocent do. Their eyes are on each other while our eyes are on them. They do not take notice of us. She does something I've never seen before. She picks up the little boy and spins him around in her arms.

Her eyes cease glowing. The flicker happens and I see the hazel hidden by the gold light. It tells me she isn't thinking; she is using her heart. This is what I believe this phenomenon is. I've witnessed it on rare occasions, but it only happens when a deep emotion could be anticipated. Hikari's eyes go wide when Gwen looks like a normal girl. She is his angel, mermaid, and princess.

Katsuo lights up another cigarette and fidgets his foot. I don't want him to interfere. He seems tense enough. I decide to walk towards them, casually nodding at Katsuo, who holds his cigarette in his mouth and loosens his tie. His eyes are dark. The eyelashes that stick straight out. His flat nose causes him to resemble a woodland creature.

"Hey you two. Having fun?" I ask and kneel.

Hikari approaches me and claps his hands.

"Me and Gwen are having the best time," says the little boy.

His eyelashes are twice as long as his father's. Hikari has skinny legs. A tiny fawn.

"Good," I say.

Looking up, I see Gwen's glowing eyes on me. She is smiling. Her lips are red. Her dress is black. The Ex Machina looks like she's ready to attend a cocktail party. Gwen picks up Hikari and holds his small palm in hers. She dances around with him, which makes the little boy laugh. I peek over my shoulder and see Katsuo appear frazzled. Gwen isn't doing anything aggressive, but her hand is on his son's. He is in her steel-bending arms. The two of them love each other and it's a dangerous game to play.

"I know what else you are, Gwen," chimes Hikari.

Gwen stops dancing to look him in the eyes. She is curious to hear what he was to say.

"What am I to you, Hikari?" she asks.

"You are sunshine. You are the color yellow and you make me happy," he says.

Hikari runs his hand through the length of Gwen's hair. Her eyes are hazel and full of tears. The little boy reaches up and touches them. Are they also laced with metal? Do they smell like copper instead of salt?

"I'm sunshine?" she asks, confused.

The Ex Machina scans Hikari for clues, but will not find the logical answer she seeks.

"You are my sunshine," he says and wraps his arms around Gwen.

She reaches up slowly and places her graceful hand on the nape of his neck. Tears reach her dainty jaw and fall with care. They land on the floor with the faintest splash.

"I love you."

The little boy says the words into her neck and her red lips quiver. I haven't seen the Ex Machina at a loss for words. She looks at me. I was the first one who said those words to her. She didn't understand them then.

"I...love you," she says and hugs the little boy a bit tighter.

Over my shoulder, I see Katsuo has dropped his cigarette. The red cherry is lost to the floor. Smoke rises, but Katsuo doesn't pick it up. This moment is everything.

Gwen puts Hikari down. The little boy stares up at her and holds her hands. Her wings emit a low blue light. An aquamarine angel. The device in her head holds an entire universe. Her mind is expansive. Hikari puts his arms around her waist. He doesn't want to let go. Katsuo approaches them. Gwen nods at him and puts her head down.

"Let's go, son." Katsuo takes Hikari's hand.

The little boy waves goodbye to Gwen. She gives him a slight wave back.

"Bye Gwen," says Hikari as he and his dad walk towards the kitchen.

"Bye Hikari..." Gwen's voice is soft and lost to the open space of the lab. I step closer to her.

"You'll see each other again tomorrow," I say, trying to offer her consolation.

"I know, but I'm still so...sad. I miss him already," she says.

The Ex Machina is turned away from me.

"Love can make us feel like there is never enough time with a person," I say, but I don't think I know what I'm talking about.

Gwen surprises me by suddenly embracing me. She is digging into the cloth of my lab coat. My shoulders are tense where she is gripping the fabric. I'm hesitant, but I remember I shouldn't do anything to warrant cruel intentions. Her hair rustles my sleeves as I wrap my arms around her waist.

"Do you feel that way about me?" she asks.

Her arms are holding tight, but she pulls away. Instead of looking me in the eyes, she stares at my mouth. I feel my hairline getting damp and my hair frizzing. Gwen moves her hand over my shoulder and onto my chest. She keeps staring at my mouth. It feels like she is rummaging around inside the void with telepathy.

"Yes," I whisper.

The Ex Machina's eyes move over me. They are intelligent, strange, and cold. She reaches up and touches my face the way she did the day she was born. I'm glad she's not touching my heart anymore because she might rip it out of my rib cage. It feels bruised inside my bones from the constant thudding. Gwen kisses me gently at first, but nips me with titanium teeth, and I am frozen in place.

"I love you," she whispers as she gives me a softer kiss. I stand there and let her use me as her plaything. A steel infused canine hooks into my lip as she finishes her sentence, "But not the way I love Hikari," she throws me off her.

Gwen heads towards her room. I put my middle finger to my bottom lip. Blood. I wipe it away with my sleeve. When I look up, I see Shira staring at me. Her arms are crossed. Little black shoes tap on the steel floor. She saw the whole thing.

***

My first kiss was late, at twenty-one. I was overjoyed it happened at all. Sophia was more naïve than me. I didn't know at the time—I was clueless as well. The people working for my dad thought I was just some rich playboy. That's how they treated me.

Sophia initiated it because I was too shy to. She didn't seem to mind my awkwardness. I didn't notice hers. All I thought about was how pretty she was and how her hair smelled spicy, like cinnamon. Her dad hated me, but I thought it was typical. From what I gathered, watching movies and reading, all dads hated their daughter's boyfriends. I kind of liked how he hated me. It felt normal.

I sensed he resented when she slept in my room and followed me everywhere. I was polite to him. He was polite to me. But we knew he didn't approve of me. He thought my father was a lunatic, albeit a genius. I was the son who mooched off my father's lavish wealth and prosperous company. People died all the time from the Mantodea. My dad paid a lot of people a lot of money to protect us.

When Sophia kissed me, I kept my eyes open for a second. I was shocked. It was like I wanted to fully remember the moment. So I took a snapshot in my mind before I closed my eyes. She and I had something malleable. A tame sort of love. She was ordinary, but not in a bad way. When I think about first loves, I think about the Sophias of the world and how they make life bearable. Not that they are magic or all entrancing, but they offer a promise, a kiss, a hand to hold on to. She was safe to be in love with.

Pinky finger grazing the puncture wound on the left side of my bottom lip. I study my reflection and the hole in my mouth. Did she mean to draw blood? Or was it an accident? I want to believe the latter. I know it to be the first assumption. Gwen said she loved me. But not like Hikari. The way she shoved me off her like I was vile—it hurt. Gwen may be confused by her emotions, but her feelings towards me leave me with a lump in my throat and unable to relax my stiff shoulders. There's a knock on my door, startling me. It makes me jump.

"Come in," I say to whoever, and step away from the mirror. It's Hotaka.

"Hey," he says in his pliant tone.

"What's up?" I ask.

His eyes are on the tiny hole in my lip. It embarrasses me. I feel like I did when my dad saw the hickies on my neck Eva used to give me.

"I heard Gwen kissed you," he says, moving the focus to my forehead.

"She did," I admit.

Hotaka closes the door and sits in the chair. I lean against the wall. Sitting down might make me feel ill.

"It looks like she bit you, too."

"Yes. I'm not sure if it was an accident." I try to shrug it off.

My palms are sweaty. I wipe them on my slacks.

"I don't think Gwen does anything by accident," he says solemnly.

He is a fine scientist. Excellent friend. I know him to tell the truth.

"She said she loved me, but not the way she loves Hikari. Then she bit me and shoved me off of her like I disgusted her," I say and sit on my bed.

My elbows dig into my thighs as I bury my head in my hands. I don't know what's more feverish. My scorching hot palms or forehead. Hotaka sighs and taps his fingers on the desk.

"I think she is becoming frustrated with the imprinting," he says.

"What?" I ask.

This forces me to look up.

"She loves Hikari naturally. They formed an authentic attachment."

"What does that make me?"

"You're her keeper. You're unwilling to assume such a role, but you are. She knows it, too. Gwen can't leave you for very long. She worries about you. She misses you. The Ex Machina knows there is an unseen but powerful connection between you and her."

Hotaka massages his temple with two fingers. The bodily pain of being in mental agony.

"I don't want to upset her."

My limbs are vibrating with nervous energy. I try to calm myself down. A cold shower is what I need. That always gets me back to reality.

"Tread with caution. You may not be trying to piss her off, but she may begin to act hostile. Keep an eye on her. We need to be prepared for the worst."

"I don't know what I'm doing. My father was one of the greatest scientists in the world. Well renowned, innovative, and progressive. There was nothing he wouldn't try. He knew the answer to everything. What would he do with this bond?" I ask the floor.

My head is hanging and I try to rid myself of the knot at the base of my neck.

"I think your father would have given the Ex Machina the impression of self empowerment. His dream was to win, to conquer the Mantodea, and to restore earth back to its former glory. Your father's desire to change the world stopped him from engaging in it normally," says Hotaka with his chin in his hand.

"So you're saying I should let Gwen take the lead?"

"We have no other choice. You are our only hope, Bell. Gwen will do what you say. We are merely insects to her. A small colony."

"What if she wants more than I can give her?" I ask with my pulse in my throat, choking me out.

"Hopefully that doesn't happen," he says and stands up.
Hotaka exits my room. I'm alone. The power I have is bone crushing. I thought I'd be jealous of someone else having it. What an idiot I am to think I could control a project this massive. Now I'm about to blow it. Humanity's only chance rests in my hands. They are pruny from anxious sweating.

***

She has been avoiding me. I'm relieved but also disheartened. Gwen scares me. I miss her, though. She makes me feel like I'm on drugs. I haven't slept well the last few nights. My appetite is nonexistent again. I make myself eat an assortment of vegetables from the garden and take a handful of nutritional supplements. My weight is better, but not where it was, one-hundred and sixty-four pounds. I drink water even though it barely makes it past the lump in my throat.

Yui is working away as usual. She is a busy little bee. It fascinates me how she buzzes from this side of the room to the other with ferocity and grace. Her black hair is shiny blue under the fluorescent lights. The young scientist rifles through paperwork and breathes out her mouth loudly with her hands on her hips. I tap on the open door.

"Hey," I say.

She puts her hands down. I sense she knows what happened. Yui isn't buzzing anymore. She steps closer and looks up at me. Her nose is pointed at my mouth. I grimace, knowing she is examining the puncture. The mark of a steel canine.

"Be sure to put antibiotic ointment on that. We don't want you to suffer from infection," she says matter-of-factly.

She goes back to organizing loose papers and stacking journals.

"Yui, what do you make of all this?" I ask her the question in the bluntest form possible. I trust her to tell me her honest opinion.

"I'm...not sure. Gwen is valuable beyond comprehension," she speaks to the air and paces around, "But she is also unstable. Her turbulent personality may cause problems for us in the future. She is attached to Hikari. Capable of love and exudes a sisterly, perhaps motherly nature, is a positive sign. We should be most respectful of the Ex Machina's boundaries and wishes."

"What are you saying?"

"Do what she wants, Bellamy."

Yui goes back to working. Her ignoring me reminds me of Gwen. I watch her shoulders move rapidly as she turns pages and writes down notes. They are small but move with such momentum. I walk out of the room and wander around. My hands aren't as hot, but I feel my face flush.

Katsuo and Hikari are having tea. They watch me walk by. I keep pacing around the lab. Nori and Isamu make small talk with me. It's hard to pay attention. They stare at the hole in my mouth and I fall through the earth. Walking soothes me. I wish I could jog outside. Imagining hitting the ball and running to first base eases some of my anxiety. Finally, I feel a little better. Only then is it ruined by Shira.

"Hey," she hisses. Her voice is low. Arms crossed and agitated. Why are women always upset with me?

"Hey Shira." I try to be courteous.

"What are you doing?" she asks.

I keep walking, and she follows me.

"Trying to get some exercise," I say, and walk faster. Shira stays next to me.

"I saw Gwen kiss you," she almost shouts it, so I stop. I brace myself.

"I know."

"What do we do?"

"What do you mean we?" I snap.

"She might be bonded to you but if you fuck this up we all die," says Shira in her fine tuned voice.

I take a deep breath.

"I know."

"What's your plan?" Shira is practically laughing at me.

"To do whatever Gwen wants."

I say it like that to annoy her. It works. Shira uncrosses her arms and shakes her head at me.

"You can't be serious."

"I am."

I smile and keep walking. She stops in my shadow and doesn't stay at my side. Good. I don't want her to. Back in my room, I dim the lights and lay down. The fragrant scent of white flowers permeates my sheets. Gwen has been in here. I fumble around my blanket and the sides of the mattress. Nothing. She had to have been outside. Then she laid in my bed until it smelled like her.

I get up since it feels wrong. Changing my pillowcase assuages my guilt. I still smell her, but I don't want to change all my bedding right now. Falling asleep doesn't come easy, but it takes over the way night does during winter. It happens too fast to notice. I'm consumed by the dark. Indigo dreams of night skies and silver moons make me clench my teeth.

"Bellamy?"

It's Gwen. I shudder. Her hand is in my hair. The other is massaging the knot in my neck. I imagine her squeezing it out like the core out of a peach.

"Hi," I whisper.

My voice is weaker than I expected.

"Were you looking for me?" she asks.

"Yes," I say.

Partially because it's true and partially because I don't want her to rip my head off with steel laced fingers.

"I'm sorry. I was having one of those days," she says.

Gwen keeps rubbing my neck. Her white arc nail tips are massaging my scalp. I wish I could enjoy it.

"One of those days?" I ask.

"I wanted to be with you so badly it hurt."

"I'm sorry if I hurt you."

She keeps playing with my hair. My girlfriend experiences have never been average. This is entirely out of my league. The hand she is rubbing the knot with moves to my shoulder. She isn't being rough or harming me. It's actually kind of soothing.

"You don't hurt me, but it's..." she removes her hand from my shoulder and touches beneath the waning crescent. "This heart," says the Ex Machina.

"What do you want from me?" I ask.

Gwen can demand anything and I will do it. It startles me how corrupt I can become in such a negligible amount of time. Gwen reaches inside my shirt and puts her cool palm on my heart. It can be detected through the skin, muscles, and blood. She tries to read me.

"Can I stay?" she asks.

I want to say 'no.'

"Okay," I rasp.

She gets under the covers with me. The Ex Machina keeps caressing my hair. Gwen doesn't need to sleep. She says she can't, and it makes me laugh when she does. I can't sleep for real, though. It's like trying to sleep with something poisonous in the room. A deadly scorpion with a horrible sting. The hours tick by. I detach. Gwen leaves red lipstick on my neck. Gooey makeup stains the back of my shirt. Throughout the night I pretend to be asleep and all through the night Gwen touches my hair, rubs my shoulder, and holds me the way a child holds a toy.

CHAPTER FIFTEEN
DAMAGE

I initiated the kiss with Eva. Everything about her was intoxicating. We loved each other in the sick puppy dog way that makes everyone roll their eyes and gag. The end of the world was happening outside, but I got to spend every day, every moment, with my beautiful girlfriend who I loved very much. My girlfriend who was too young for me.

My dad never brought up mine and Eva's relationship. If I wasn't with her, I was helping him with the equipment and going over paperwork. We studied books forwards and backwards. I could recite them all for a time. My dad and I took notes on Gwen together. Back then, my work was shallow. I tried my best. All I ever thought about was Eva's beauty mark, though.

Eva's parents were nice to me, but it wasn't as though I was part of their family. They knew my dad's level of wealth and genius. He might have been a nice guy, but his mental prowess made him untouchable. Adam Krim's head was not in the clouds, it was in space, next to the moon and stars.

I remember how her mom and I would make small talk. Eva noticed nothing off-putting between me and her parents, but I did. Eva's mother was pretty. They had similar features. She would laugh at my jokes but then have an air of distrust about her. Eva's father was a tall and boisterous man. I was actually kind of intimidated by him. He was rough around the edges. I liked that about him. Everything in my world was perfect, but Eva's father was never interested in appearing whole, perfect, or complete.

We kissed all the time. In my room, up against the hallway walls, and in the shadows, where we were on the verge of getting caught. I would catch the scientists working for my dad glaring at me the times I opened my eyes. It gave me a sick surge. They didn't have what I had. I wasn't alone. My girlfriend loved me.

Eva and I loved each other too hard, too fast. She and her parents left before we could get into the part of our relationship holding tribulations, tests, and hurt. We never got to that part. My memories with her are flowy, tinted pink, and hazy. Probably because nothing could taint them. We were in love and forced apart. It felt really romantic and tragic.

My father didn't notice my absence. He was too enthralled by his creation. Gwen was spectacular, sure. But I was too distracted by my broken heart. It felt like it would never heal. In reality, it seemed like Eva took it with her. So there I was, a twenty-four-year-old love stoned fool, unable to get out of bed or turn the lights on for months, and my dad didn't give a shit. When I emerged from my room and back to work, all he said was "hey kiddo" and went back to staring at the Ex Machina.

"Hey." Hotaka is holding a cup of tea and a fig.

The smell draws me back to the present. I sit up in my bed, reeking of white flowers.

"Thank you," I say.

Hotaka sits on my bed next to me. I see his nose twitch. He notices the decadent floral scent.

"Gwen left this morning," he says.

I choke on my tea.

"What?" I cough.

"She blew me a kiss and then walked out the door."

Hotaka's voice is far away. He is in a fog.

"I let her sleep in here last night," I admit.

Hotaka nods his head and ponders this.

"There is no telling which way this project will go."

I set down my tea and try to eat. My weight is close to where it was. I don't want to lose control. Taking measured bites, I try to plan for the worst, the way a scientist would. It doesn't come to me. I plan what to do if my new hybrid supercharged girlfriend loses interest in me or decides she hates my guts.

"I would sacrifice myself. If Gwen becomes enraged, I want her to take it out on me. I don't want anybody to get hurt. Hopefully, I will be Gwen's only target. Like all the notes suggest, she is not interested in others the way she is interested in me."

"Maybe we can keep her happy."

Hotaka looks to the ceiling and pops his neck.

"She said she was willing to kill herself in order to destroy the Mantodea's ship. I know it is what we created her for. I should let her do what she is designed to do. But I can't, Hotaka."

I didn't realize I needed to say it out loud until now. My face stings from hot tears. Chemical burns from my toxic emotions streak my face.

"Gwen can fight them, but we need to find another way to obliterate their

Queen. She is the key to ending this war."

"I'm going to see if we can find a way to destroy the Queen without Gwen sacrificing herself. As much as she frightens me, I care for her. I don't want her to die. She means too much to me. I waited all these years for her. It's a cruel joke my dad died and left me his shoes to fill. I'll never be able to do it," I half joke and half cry.

"You're my friend, Bell. You're also the boss. The others may not like it, but it's the truth. This is your lab, your company, your project. You get to call the shots."

"Do you think my dad would have let her die so we can live?" I ask.

Hotaka is standing up and stretching his left arm out. His hand is a small fist that expands and opens. An audible pop is heard and Hotaka seems satisfied.

"I'm not sure. I never knew your father. I only know him through his notes. His journals are inconsistent, especially towards the end, but the constant remains: he loved Gwen. He loved her a lot."

"I'm going to get us out of this damn mountain," I say.

Hotaka chuckles with me.

"You are a Krim," he jokes and exits my room.

I finish my breakfast and tea. It doesn't bother me that it's cold. I can't taste anything. My hair is a mess. I run water through it to calm down the frizz and volume. Brushing it helps, but it's obvious I need to shower. I'll do it later. Right now, I need to go to the front door and wait for her.

***

She didn't come back for four days. Hotaka had to coax me away from the door. I'm less anxious when she's not around. It's no use though. She is my drug. I need my fix. Gwen came back like nothing happened. She put her arms around my neck. I saw her stare at the remaining mark on my lip from her bite.

"I'm sorry," she said and gave me a quick peck. It stunned me.

"It's fine," I said.

She has been at my side since. I haven't asked her about her departure. Did she seek out the Mantodea or was she searching for a way to get rid of her love for me? To dispose of me.

Gwen and I are eating. She is sitting across from me. Her canines sink into the flesh of an apple. I wince, watching her rip out a chunk and chomp down. It's hard to swallow, but I force myself to finish the piece of fruit. Yui walks by the table and bumps into it because she has her nose in a pile of books. She almost drops all of them, but Gwen stands up to catch them with impressive reflexes.

"Thank you," says Yui.

She bows her head to Gwen and scurries off. The Ex Machina's wires sway with restless movements. They make the swishing noise. I think it's an illusion in my fragmented mind, but I swear I hear them making the subtle sound of a rattlesnake.

Nori is passing us. I give him a wave. He nods, but keeps his hands in his pocket. Nori doesn't want to, but no one can resist taking a peek at Gwen. She is quite striking. Being aware of her sex appeal has her acting boldly. She winks at Nori and gives him a small wave with her fingers. Nori misses a beat and stumbles over himself. I offer him my hand to steady himself. He runs off with an embarrassed grin.

"The Mantodea have seasons," Gwen announces as she toys with the core of her apple.

"Seasons?" I inquire.

"Yes. When the Queen is Gestating the drones are most protective and plentiful. They move in formation around the ship. During Birth, some of the drones return to the ship. I assume their help is needed with the larva. Then they have a time of Procreation. This is the only time the army protecting the ship is absent."

"Does this mean you can fry them, Gwen?" I lean on the table.

Gwen is spinning the core by the stem, disinterested.

"I'm afraid I will still have to die. I tried to destroy the ship but I couldn't penetrate it completely. The ship has a thick exoskeleton like they do. It will require me to plug in and deplete myself of all my electrical energy, which means I won't be able to return to earth. I will die in space," she says.

"I don't want you to do that," I say.

Gwen gets up and looms over me. She traces my collarbone and down my ribs on the side where my heart is.

"I could annihilate them all, Bellamy. Then you would be able to go outside."

She continues to run her white tipped nails over me. I hope she doesn't scratch me.

"There has to be another way."

My body is heavy. It's like my brain is in an aquarium and the fish keep gnawing on it. Gwen moves swiftly. She is straddling me in the chair. I'm too tired and, quite frankly, too afraid to stop her.

"If you tell me to, I will do it."

Gwen has her metal jaw next to my ear. Her fingers run over my shoulder and down my back. The Ex Machina could reach in and rip my heart out without me ever seeing it.

"No," I say.

Gwen kisses my cheek and gets off of me.

"What do you want me to do?" she asks.

"Just wait. I'm sure I can figure out a way to kill the Mantodea without risking your life." Gwen points to her heart.

"You gave me my life," she says.

The Ex Machina speaks with cryptic wisdom. I wonder if the Nordic gods are watching as one of them ascends.

"It's your life."

"I don't feel like it's mine. I'm in an invisible cage."

"What?" I ask.

Gwen sits on the table in front of me and plays with her hair. Her thigh is exposed and next to my hand. On impulse, I reach out and rest it there.

"It is difficult for me to explain."

She gestures with her palms up.

"That's okay. I'm listening," I say.

Gwen searches inside her infallible mind for a way to tell me the impossible things she feels.

"I'm sure you have loved other women," she states.

Perspiration builds at my hairline.

"I have." I tell the truth.

A lie will piss her off. Gwen is thoughtful with her response. She takes her time.

"If only you could be damaged by this love like me," she says.

Gwen puts her hand on mine and the other in the hair at the nape of her neck.

"How do you know that I'm not?" I ask.

She doesn't know I feel strung out. How I can't eat. It's like being on drugs. Gwen hops off the table and moves behind me. It makes me nervous. I hear the wires whipping the air. Am I to pay for my sins? Is she going to strike one of them across my back? Gwen rubs my shoulders the way a loving girlfriend would. She leans down and puts her head on my right shoulder. The device is visible out of my peripheral. Gwen isn't like other women.

"You can't feel this the way I feel it," she says as she traces my collarbone again.

I keep getting vivid visions of her cutting me up with her razor-like nails.

"Why?"

"I'm not your first," she says in a harsh whisper.

Her hair is no longer spilling onto me, the scent of lily of the valley cloys the air, and Gwen is out of my sight when I turn around.

***

Abuse wasn't acknowledged in our household. It was never violent, so there was never any urgency. My father could play mind games with my mother without trying. She was desperate for his approval, his attention, his love. He was hardly around and when he was, he was somewhere else entirely. Adam Krim was often in deep space, in the recesses of his mind, and in my mother's heart. Dr. Krim was at work, in the lab, working tirelessly. He wrestled with mania and didn't sleep for days.

Bethany Krim enjoyed adventuring outdoors in jeans, shorts, and hiking boots, but was somewhat prim. She loved with a romantic Victorian era heart. I think my dad was the luckiest idiot I have ever seen. To this day, I don't know how he charmed her into marrying him. As a kid, I remember us spending a lot of time together, but by the time I was five, the image of my father faded and it's only my mother and I experiencing life's milestones together.

My dad neglected us, but not by withholding food or shelter. No, Adam Krim withheld himself. At times, I swore he had a second brain in that space between his rib cage. He never watched one of my games. Holidays were busy and full of family members but my dad was absent. He would pay someone to shop for us. I don't think he really got it.

My mom would go away sometimes as well. Not quite like my dad, but similar. Bethany Krim would drink white wine and zone out while watching a trashy movie. I could talk to her and she would smile and chat, but she was not really there. She would ruffle my hair and keep her eyes on the screen. Scenes of couples dramatically hugging or confessing their love filled the void inside.

No one ever hit me. My mom didn't yell at me. We never actively fought. It was silent brawls no one ever won. The house I grew up in was extravagant. Our lives were easy, but on a psychological level, we were in shambles. We ate expensive groceries, had a lot of nice things we didn't need, and yet we weren't happy. I had what I needed, but not what I wanted. A normal family.

All kids say stuff like that. But no kid was like me. No one had to live up to someone who was known worldwide. A person whose brand was on everything. Once a person does something great, then they are expected to do it over and over again. Adam Krim delivered every year. With each passing season, he made everything better, faster, stronger, and he was brutal about it. His forcefulness caused a lot of companies to disregard him, but it was fine. He didn't need them.

The thing about abuse, neglect, trauma, and love is that it makes everything hard to separate. Humans try to make things easy. Organize ourselves to get ahead. I can't compartmentalize my relationship with Gwen. She said she loves me. I find it to be up for debate. The imprinting keeps her bonded to me. There are so many variables here. What would my dad do? Would she love him this way? Gwen bit me. Her titanium canine purposely pierced a hole in my mouth. My lungs freeze and draw air in slow motion.

One time when I was eleven, I saw my mom slap my dad. They were arguing about him never being around. He claimed he gave her the world. She said just because he owned it doesn't mean she wanted it. There is no way to explain these emotions to someone like Dr. Krim. He was a glacial island isolated in a sea of normalcy. The world was changed because of his vision.

Who was the true abuser? The actual victim? I have so much sympathy for my mom. As much as I don't want to admit it, I understand my father better now. Not that it excuses his actions, but I'm able to see things through the lens of someone I barely know, but share half my DNA with. Because Gwen is tied to me, she can't leave. She wants to be free. Does she wish to free herself from me personally? Who is hurting who more? Am I neglecting her? Is she abusing me? I guess this would classify as mental and emotional abuse.

Can a human-robot hybrid abide by the same rules as humanity? What are the commandments for this new world? Since society has collapsed, I'm not sure what to make of it. We are living on a lawless planet. The Mantodea work together through their hive mind. This is their biggest advantage over us. People are difficult to coax into collaboration.

The Ex Machina is something else. Nothing like her has existed. There are no rules. I have to figure them out as I go. Gwen is a goddess with blonde hair and brilliant gold eyes. Hikari calls her sunshine. She is his angel. I hope she is a good angel and not the seraph of the end.

CHAPTER SIXTEEN
SACRIFICE

She seems bored. Not a good sign. Her wires swish and remind me of the way a restless cat would move its tail. Gwen is wearing her red dress. She is sprawled out on the couch in the lounge and reading another romance novel. Nori and Isamu pass by and flinch when they notice her short dress and long legs.

"Hey Gwen," I say.

She doesn't stop reading.

"Hey," she says.

I sit with her, and she puts her legs on me. The wires peeking out from her dress are in my lap and hanging off the arm of the couch.

"Do you want to go outside with me?" I ask.

"Okay."

She puts down her book. Sitting up, she kisses my cheek. I wait until she's not looking to touch my face. No bite marks, but my face hurts. I think it's from grinding my teeth. Gwen takes my hand and we walk to the front door together. Nori and Yui watch us with eyes that move, but their heads remain still. The Ex Machina is unbothered by other people's perceptions. Their opinions don't matter to her.

"Hey you two," says Hotaka.

He has a stack of journals in his left arm.

"Hi Hotaka. How are you?" I ask.

Hotaka hasn't had to baby me as much lately. I've been better about eating at set times. To aid in my recovery, I've been making myself rest daily instead of crashing and burning. I appreciate Hotaka as more than just a brilliant scientist. He is a true friend. I'm lucky to have someone like him taking care of me when I'm drowning in myself.

"I'm well. Thank you. What are you and Gwen up to?" he asks.

I see him glance at our hands, but he tries to keep eye contact and smile.

"We're going to go outside for a little bit," I say.

Gwen turns to embrace me. It startles Hotaka, and he backs up.

"I've been listening to the music you gave me. I like it," says Gwen.

Hotaka seems deeply touched but also frightened.

"I'm glad you've been enjoying it. I'll swap it out and get you new music soon," he says.

Hotaka has sweat dripping down his temple.

"You have excellent taste," I say, and he smiles.

"I'll see you later. Have fun," says Hotaka and he heads for the room where Nori and Yui are working.

Gwen drops her arms but keeps a firm hold on my hand. When we get to the front door, I hit the button to open it. The sky is blue with patches of clouds. We are greeted by ruby and orange leaves. She waits for me to take the first step. Gwen could fly past me. But she'd eventually have to come back.

I let the afternoon sun warm my face. It feels nice to experience the world. Plush grass, woodsy and floral notes, and Gwen's favorite, the wind. Its fingers pull through her hair. The arches of her eyebrows make her expression perpetually serious. Petite but fatal. Gwen and I meander through the field of flowers. Her wires extend and whip back and forth. Not sensing anything, she pulls me down into a cluster of cosmos.

We lay in the yellowing grass surrounded by purple, pink, and red cosmos. Our temples are touching and our legs point in opposite directions. We are Pisces, Yin and Yang. Gwen and I watch puffy clouds dissipate and swirl until they block the sun. The wind picks up, taking them away, scattering white cotton across the blue forever. Gwen sits up and lets the wind caress her skin. She closes her eyes and smiles. I have the urge to kiss her. So far, she has been the one to kiss me, touch me, hurt me. I lean in and put my lips to hers. She keeps her eyes closed and doesn't bite. Mine are wide open.

"What if I can't defeat the Mantodea?" she asks.

"I'll figure something out," I say and she stares at me. "What?" I ask.

"Will you think I'm useless if I can't do it?" she asks.

"No, of course not. Don't say that."

I take her shoulders and study her face. She has a flat affect.

"I was created to save humanity. If I fail, then I fail you. Won't you be upset with me?"

"You may have been made with a purpose in mind, but I think you are more than that. You are your own person," I say.

"My own person?" she asks.

"I know you think you have to help me save the world. I need your help, but I don't want you to make that your whole life. I want you to have some things for yourself."

"Like what?" Gwen is perplexed.

It's actually very cute. She wants so badly to please me. I chuckle.

"Like the music Hotaka gives you, or the books you like to read. It makes me happy to see you play with Hikari. Things that are special to you," I say and pick a purple cosmo with an orange center.

I hand it to her. She looks at it like it holds a secret.

"Or you?"

"Me?" I ask.

Gwen twirls the flower in her metal infused fingers.

"Yes. You are the most important thing to me. The most special. I can't explain why."

The imprinting. She is aware there is something there, but neither of us have the vocabulary to describe such a bond. I don't think there is a word for it.

***

Laying with her is like laying with a bomb. I can't say what I'm going through. All I can do is try to explain what it feels like. She eludes me and makes me miss her. Then her arm is around my waist in the middle of the night. Gwen doesn't ask anymore.

Her lips are touching the back of my neck. The wires move constantly. They rustle the crisp white sheets. I imagine one of them coming down on me like a stinger. She kisses my cheek and tells me she loves me. Her hand on my heart leaves me at a loss for words.

Everyone is appalled by how I am handling this. Yui and Hotaka told me I should do what she wants. Make her happy. I'm trying to do exactly that, but it also means sacrificing what little of my reputation I have left. It seems all I have is my dad's last name.

Nori tries to be professional in his findings. I dislike him casting dark stares in my direction. He is simply doing his job, but it vexes me. Isamu is polite, but I can tell he and Katsuo resent my relationship with her. But what do they know? They're not me. I'm not him. They wanted to work for my father. If only they knew me and him weren't so different.

Shira hasn't spoken to me in quite some time. I told her I was going to do whatever Gwen wants. She discredited my answer. After Shira took notice of mine and the Ex Machina's connection, she became withdrawn. I think she and Katsuo have something going on. Not that I really care. I saw them sitting close together in one of the research rooms. They were laughing. Neither of them ever laugh.

Gwen's wires make quiet rattlesnake noises. Maybe it's my imagination. She smells like flowers and the green notes of grass. She's been outside. What has she been doing? The Mantodea know her and communicate to one another over her presence. She said they are better prepared for her. That's why they are so difficult to strategize against. They change up their tactics depending on what they're fighting.

Steely fingers play with my hair. She rubs my scalp and gently pulls out tangles with long, slender fingers. The white tips of her nails graze my skin, and I try to block out the intrusive visions of her peeling me open like a piece of fruit. Gwen runs her palm over the back of my neck where I hold all my tension. Metal laced fingers massage my shoulder.

There are weeks where I don't sleep because my high voltage girlfriend keeps me up. I don't want her to go, though. Nights when I'm empty don't bother me if she is near. It's surreal. Gold and blue lights emit a soft glow in my dim room. Powerless against her, I shift to my other side so I can see her face.

"I love you," I say and I give her a kiss.

She puts my bottom lip in between hers but doesn't bite me. Cool fingertips trace my neck and collarbone. When she's done with me, she turns to her side. I wrap my arms around her.

"Are you mad at me?" I ask.

Gwen puts her hand over mine.

"No."

"I feel like you're not happy with me."

Gwen's hair cascades over both the pillows. Her skin is warm and sun kissed.

"I want us to go outside all the time, Bellamy."

"I know. We will. I promise," I say into the pile of gold thread.

"I thought I could defeat the Mantodea without killing myself. I went back up there. If I don't run out of air, I will run out of energy. I'm sorry," she says.

Gwen sneaks out, but it's to help me. At least I hope so.

"It's okay. I'll find another way. I can't let you do that."

"You're willing to live here in isolation and let everyone else out there fend for themselves," she states without emotion.

I don't know what she's feeling. What is she thinking?

"Yes," I blurt out the word, and my lips are on hers again.

***

My door is opening.

"Bellamy?" it's Hotaka.

I open my bleary eyes.

"Hey," I say.

My voice feels scratchy. Like I've been screaming.

"I need to talk to you," he says.

"About what?" I ask and rub my eyes. They are tired and watering. Hotaka is petrified, mouth agape, staring at me. "What?" I ask.

It's slight but palpable. Gwen is stirring behind me. She is sitting up with the blanket covering her. Bright gold eyes peer out from the shadow of the comforter. Hotaka falls over.

"I'm sorry. I'll come back later."

He fumbles as he attempts to get up. Hotaka runs out of my room. The tail of his white lab coat is ingrained in my memory. Gwen lays back down with me. This time, she rests her head on my chest. Perhaps listening to my heart is easier than trying to read it through touch.

"What do you want to do today, Gwen?" I ask.

"Can I play with Hikari?"

"I'll ask Katsuo when I see him."

"Katsuo thinks I'm dangerous."

The wires hang off the edge of the bed but curl up and twitch. They are alert.

"He's intimidated by your strength, but he knows you love Hikari."

I scoop up handfuls of blonde hair and let it fall through my fingers.

"Everyone is afraid of me. Including you," she says into my chest with her titanium teeth enunciating each word.

"To be honest, most women scare me," I joke.

"I'm not like other women," she says.

I stay in bed with her until she gets up. She disappears down the hall. I shower and brush my teeth. It feels like I'm losing my enamel and my mind. I should be overjoyed that this is how the project turned out. Yet I'm apprehensive. How will I control a godlike creature with a poisonous stinger?

I make myself drink a meal supplement and peck at a mix of berries and oats. My weight is back to one-hundred and seventy pounds. The hollows of my cheeks are fuller. The dark circles under my eyes are present, but less obvious. My hair is spiky and ridiculous. It sticks out in all directions from Gwen's constant playing with it. I think she likes my hair.

Sipping my tea, I ready myself to ask Katsuo if Gwen can play with Hikari. It's so juvenile. I hate asking for permission. Recoiling at the thought, I scold myself. My dad didn't enjoy asking for permission, either. He did what he wanted and fought lawsuits later. I find Katsuo reading in the lounge. He is also drinking tea.

"Hello Katsuo. How are you?" I ask, making friendly conversation.

"I'm okay. How about you, Bellamy?" he doesn't look up from his book.

"I'm well. Thanks. Can I sit with you?"

"Sure," he mumbles.

I take a seat but remain quiet. Maybe he will like me better if I'm forthcoming.

"I was wondering if it would be okay for Gwen and Hikari to spend time together today."

"When?" he asks.

"How about in an hour?"

"Fine," he spits.

I take the hint and get up. Now it's time to search for Gwen. To my surprise, she's in her room, sitting at her desk. She's wearing the black dress and brushing her hair. I swallow my tongue, trying to speak to her.

"Hi," I choke.

Gwen puts down her hairbrush to look at me.

"Hi Bellamy," she says. I kneel and take her hands in mine. They are tiny and cold. Steel ice.

"Want to go see Hikari in a little bit?" I ask. She lights up for me and nods her head. Gwen is excited. Her wires swish rapidly. She can tell I'm nervous and tries to control them.

"Yes," she says.

Gwen takes my face in her hands and kisses me.

Touched by an angel. Hikari is jubilant and lively. He and Gwen chase each other and play. They are mischievous little spirits. I'm glad she's smiling. She doesn't smile enough. I wish I had the effect Hikari has on her. Gwen said I was the most special, the most important. Why do I wish to be more when I can't handle what I already am?

Katsuo stands off to the side and observes with narrow eyes. Smoke floats in the air above him. He lights up another cigarette. The burn of the first drag is the loudest. Slicking back his hair, he sticks the match in the ashtray. It coats the air in a sulfuric bath. Like being in hell.

The two wild ones sing, dance, jump, and run. Gwen's wires with metal jack stingers do not deter Hikari. He doesn't even see them. Ruby red lipstick is painted on Gwen's pristine mouth. The arch of her eyebrows makes her appear fierce. Gwen and Hikari spin around and hold hands. An arctic heart melted by the soul of a child.

CHAPTER SEVENTEEN

TOYS

Sneaking a cigarette helps me go through my father's first promising, then confusing and irrational, to complete chaos and ramblings of a fractured mind. The notes are piled in front of me. Journals, notebooks, and loose leaf paper look at me like I am a joke. I guess I kind of am. Gwen doesn't hide her affection towards me. I kiss her in front of everyone now. It doesn't matter anymore.

I'm trying to understand his relationship with Nyx. Apparently, he treated her the way he treats everybody. Like they hardly exist. He may have not been aware of the bond until after she killed herself. I wonder if my father knew Nyx longed for him and only him. That would explain why he poured himself into Gwen. To make everything perfect for her. He read her bedtime stories, sat with her, talked to her, and put his hand to the glass, as I often did.

His notes about Nyx document a professional and cold view of her. He didn't talk about her with tenderness in the way he writes about Gwen. It makes my face hot. My father is an illusionist. He hasn't been around for years yet he haunts the place. I feel his ghost hover over my shoulder. I think I'm so jealous because I feel his envy as his spirit watches Gwen run her hands through my hair.

Nyx was lonely. He kept her away from everyone. The early stages of science projects are riddled with mishaps. None so violent or visceral as what happened to Nyx. A humongous project down the drain. Not just a project, a person. Nyx was a person like Gwen. My heart hurts thinking about Nyx missing my dad, and how he observed her from the glass. He never embraced her.

His mental health declined. It's obvious in the notes. But there is something else. He writes about Gwen in an intimate way I can't decipher. Is he being paternal? How could he feel something that strong towards the Ex

Machina but not me or my mom? He doesn't talk about her in a lustful way, but he mentions her beauty numerous times. When writing about Nyx, he calls her "unique," and "special," and "austere."

My father uses words sparingly. As the years go on, he writes more. Using more pieces of paper. Writing in the margins and inside the cardboard covers of the notebooks. The lack of organization is accompanied by the use of words I didn't think my father would write. Words like "sweet," and "peaceful," and "precious." These are not scientific, analytical, or necessary. They are excessive. I light up another cigarette.

"You shouldn't be smoking these. They're bad for you," says Gwen.

I didn't realize she was behind me. She takes my cigarette and puts it out. This is new. Gwen is showing interest in my health.

"I'm sorry. I've been kind of stressed," I say.

Gwen rubs my shoulders. Before I couldn't enjoy it because I was too afraid she was going to rip my limbs off. Lately, I've been letting my guard down. I hope it's not the wrong move. It feels right. Gwen has never done anything harmful towards me except the time she bit me. She kisses me throughout the day. No titanium teeth tearing out my tongue.

She doesn't sleep in my room, but she comes and goes as she pleases. I'm her toy. She picks up and puts me down at her leisure. Marveling at the device, I look into the center of the metal flower.

"What are you reading?" she asks.

"My father's notes. He was exceptional. A brilliant man but very enigmatic," I say.

I crave another cigarette, but Gwen doesn't want me to, so I resist. She keeps rubbing my shoulders. It's like she's softly digging out the pit of an avocado. If she wanted to, she could sink her whole fist into my chest.

"Like you?" she asks.

This makes me laugh. Gwen doesn't mean to, but she makes funny jokes a lot.

"I wouldn't say I'm any of those things."

Gwen sits in my lap. Her hair smells like rain. She's been outside. The wires peeking out from her dress are moving next to me. Medusa's rattlesnakes. I put my hand to the floral device. Everything that makes her who she is. She is recording every moment.

"But you are," she says and wraps her arms around my neck.

***

The Nymphs are as brutal as the adult Mantodea. They are smaller versions of the ruthless aliens plaguing our planet. In the early years of my family and I living here, I was allowed outside—with a wide range of rules. I had to be accompanied by the soldiers or in a military vehicle. My mother was to be notified. Be home before it gets dark. I wasn't permitted out after sunset.

My father's work offered us spectacular opulence. We were protected to the highest degree. Our family had access to luxury items and more than our fair share of necessities. While the rest of the world was scavenging in the woods and dwelling underground, we were living it up in style. It's so ridiculous. Adam Krim couldn't see beyond his own vision—costly as it may be.

One time, when I was thirteen, I accompanied four soldiers who were making a supply run. A truck was parked at the bottom of the steep hill. It wasn't far. A little less than two-hundred yards. We prowled through tall ferns and weaved around the pines. It didn't occur to me the insanity of the time or the place I was living in. As a young person, I had to decide for myself what was normal and what wasn't. Nothing could be considered average if the world was turned upside down, right?

As we snuck up to the truck, we were frozen in place by a ghastly sight. A Nymph was chasing a deer. It caught it, of course. The Mantodea eat only live prey. Hooves kicked, and it struggled the entire way down. I almost screamed. The soldier to my right grabbed me and covered my face, but it was too late. I saw everything.

The Nymph ran off after consuming its catch. We stayed completely still. Waiting, I watched the sun shift in the sky. No one said a word. I heard a bird chirp. It made me jump. When the soldiers were ready, we continued to our destination. I wasn't as afraid as I should have been, because I was invincible. It's how all kids feel.

I begged the soldiers not to tell my mom what we saw. She would worry relentlessly. I hated making her upset. My dad did that enough. The men varied in ages, but they all looked at each other and then at me. The younger one, about the age I am now, kneeled down to face me. He told me he wouldn't tell her but that I should. I never did.

The image of the small deer running in place as the Mantodea shoved it into its mouth lingers like mold on the windowsill. Impossible to get rid of the stain. The hooves cracked and split as the creature bit down with its iron jaw. I remember watching the head of the deer explode on impact.

"Bellamy?"

Hotaka calling my name brings me back.

"Hey, what's up? You said you wanted to talk about something a few days ago."

"I think I found something."

"What is it?"

"In your father's notes. I didn't know what it meant at the time, but I think I do now," he says with a thoughtful smile.

"I've been through them a thousand times. Half of them are written by a genius and the other half are written by a demented old man."

"What about this though: After she saves the world, I will have to save her from herself."

"He was crazy, Hotaka."

I shrug and lean back in my chair.

"I think he knew about the bond. He wanted her to do what he said. Then I think he wanted to set her free," he says in a serious tone.

Hotaka stands in front of me to make sure I'm paying attention.

"Why doesn't he mention anything about it? How to control her. What to do if she becomes erratic or dangerous? He left us in the dark," I huff.

"I think he wanted to leave you in the dark," he says.

I eye him for a moment. Pensive as I am, I never thought about how clever my dad could be. My suspicions were correct. He wanted Gwen for himself.

"Cruel as usual," I joke.

"I'm serious, Bellamy. Gwen will do what you say."

"Does anybody else know?" I ask in a hushed voice in my room.

"I haven't mentioned it to anyone. Yui doesn't seem to understand the nuances in the notes. She assumes he was losing his mind towards the end."

"I haven't told anyone she could destroy the ship and set us free," I confess.

The lump in my throat is back.

"That is up to you. This is your project."

"She isn't a project. Not anymore," I whisper.

Hotaka leans against the wall and rubs the back of his neck. The damn tension.

"She never was. We were too stupid to see it."

The words fall on the floor, and Gwen opens my door. She waves to Hotaka and smiles. This eases him, but the sweat is building at his temples again. Gwen makes herself comfortable in my lap. Hotaka wants to run out of the room. Good thing he is an excellent actor.

"What are you two talking about?" she asks.

Gwen kisses me harder than usual, but no teeth. She isn't wearing lipstick today. I think she wants to show off to Hotaka. He is like a tranquil body of water appearing still on the surface but has currents going all over the place.

"I'm thinking of ways to defeat the Mantodea," I half lie as I kiss her back.

She doesn't break eye contact with me. The wires undulate. Horrifying whoosh noises make it hard to concentrate. Does Hotaka hear the rattlesnakes?

"We'll figure it out," offers Hotaka with tight lips.

"I want to help you," says Gwen as she runs her hands over my face and shoulders.

Hotaka makes his way to leave.

"I know," I say and embrace her.

"I'll leave you two alone," he says.

The door clicks, and Gwen punishes my lie by playing with me.

CHAPTER EIGHTEEN
SURRENDER

I've fitted Gwen with an oxygen tank and respirator. This will give her more time in space. It's not my finest work, but I made her a weapon. It's a spear. I created it with aluminum and titanium alloys. Inside are copper wires and an array of magnets. These will help her harvest the atmosphere's electrical energy. Hopefully, she can destroy the ship with it.

My team looks at me like I'm a professional again for the first time in ages. They thought I was just fooling around but I have been working. I've been hoping to present this as the endgame so they wouldn't know she could do it before. Gwen and I are standing at the door. I don't want her to go.

"Be careful Gwen," I say.

She looks at everybody. I see her eyes land on Hikari. He gives her a tiny wave. She lights up and waves back. They are excited. This is a moment of many truths. I hope I'm not exposed as a fraud. Unbothered by how it appears anymore, I kiss her goodbye on the cheek in front of everyone.

She points to her heart and then to me, "I love you," she gestures.

Looking like a robotic angel, she goes out the door and flies up without me. I stay at the door, watching the sky. We don't know what season the Mantodea are in. This is only a test run, I tell myself. Then again, Gwen is her own person. She said she wants us to go outside all the time.

She has been running off on me and sneaking out as soon as she was born, but I'm worried now. I can't focus on anything else. Pacing by the door is all I can stand to do. Hotaka offers me tea and a smile, but I don't want company. I want Gwen to come back to me. This has to be a toxic relationship because I feel like I'm on drugs. I crave her, am afraid of her, but want her with me.

"She'll be fine," says Hotaka as he walks off. "She has been fine every time she's gone out."

I'm left alone with my cooling tea. The clouds pass over the tops of the oaks and pines. I sit down because my legs are shaking. The couch smells like white flowers. Gwen leaves her fingerprints up and down my mind.

Katsuo and Shira walk by hand in hand. Shira has a smug smirk she is trying to hide. Her new boyfriend refuses to cast a glance my way. I'm glad they're together. Now I don't have to expect her waking me up and smacking me. They are the perfect couple. I should have seen it all along.

They are both cold but privately insecure and full of desire. I have seen Katsuo's eyes narrow at Gwen, not in disapproval but with raptorial frustration. His annoyance with her infatuation with Hikari doesn't stem from parental concern. I can tell. He thinks he's so good at hiding it.

Hikari is holding Katsuo's other hand. Their eyes are all on the floor. I think Hikari is unhappy sharing his dad. I turn towards the door. She's still not back yet. It's been nearly an hour and a half. What is she doing? Is she okay? I need her to come back.

My head is resting in my palms. They are hot and dry. I hear the whirring of the air filter. There is the scent of someone making coffee. I want to smell white flowers and autumn rain. Someone is scurrying past me. From the sound of the tiny steps, it must be Yui. Then I hear it. The noise I've been waiting for. The door opening.

I leap up. Gwen's tank is smoking and the weapon I made her is bent and burnt at the top. She appears to be untouched except for grime on her face, arms, and legs. Tangled hair falls over her shoulders. It's messy and dusty. I run up and take off the broken equipment. Throwing it on the ground and knocking the weapon out of her hand, I embrace her. She puts her arms around me.

"You're okay," I say through heavy gold.

"I wasn't able to do it. I tried to penetrate the ship using the weapon you made me so I could preserve my energy to fry the spacecraft. They kept chasing me. I ran the spear through a majority of their ship. I damaged it extensively, but was unable to kill the Queen inside. I'm sorry," she says into my neck.

"It's okay. I'm happy you're back. We'll try something else."

I'm running my hands through her hair. The strands tickle my aching knuckles. Her floral scent is gone and replaced with the smell of space: ozone, carbon, and sulfur. "We should get you cleaned up," I say. We walk to her room and I draw her a bath. She smells the way I imagine hell would. It burns inside the bridge of my nose.

Her red dress is frayed at the bottom. Three long threads dangle in front of her left thigh. The wires are swishing like a sad puppy dog tail. Gwen is disappointed she wasn't able to execute the Queen. I kiss her cheek as she slips out of her dress. She seems disinterested in me. I think she's upset with herself.

I have her sit in the tub as I brush out pieces of space from her long, long hair. There are bits of meteor rock, black dust, and what looks like glitter. The water turns black, so I empty it and refill it. She says nothing as I wash her hair. The water sparkles from the fragments of stars Gwen brought back with her. We don't need to speak. I'm just happy she's here.

"I missed you," I say.

She stirs the space glitter in the water with her finger.

"You did?" she asks.

"I miss you when you're gone."

"I'll never be gone for long," she says and reaches for my hand.

***

Sleeping next to an apex predator is hardly sleeping at all. It's like astral projection. I go somewhere else but don't feel rested. Gwen is holding onto my waist and breathing onto my neck. I shiver as it passes over my ear. Her steel canines call upon images of vampires from horror movies.

She has been restless. A listless creature wandering the halls. She sprawls out on her bed and puts the crook of her arm over her eyes. I need to do something. Losing the connection could be fatal in countless ways. I lie to myself daily. Gwen and I are in love. I don't know what that means for humanity. What does it mean for me?

Hikari cheers her up. He calls her "sunshine." They play together like innocent beings. Gwen was created with metal, but she has a heart, a soul, she is a person. Hikari can see this. No one else seems to. The less I care about my reputation, the more they resent her. They think she is making me like this. I'd be lying if I blamed it all on her.

I've been in arrested development. Living in this mountain for the last twenty-two years hasn't helped me grow into who I was meant to be. I'm a grown boy pretending to be a man. Regardless of my circumstances, I have persevered. I'm not him, but I'm someone. Gwen chooses me over everyone else. I am that somebody.

Too bad I can't make her smile. She is the most lively around Hikari. Our time together is intense. Gwen isn't one for long conversations. Everything she says is stern, serious, and to the point. In the silence, I seek ways to unshackle us from this mountain, emancipate myself from her, and how Gwen may liberate herself from me.

I can't explain it. She haunts me. When she's not around, I'm lost and pacing. If she is pressed up against me at night, I can't sleep. She says I can't be damaged by this love the way she is. But I am. Every day that she pushes me away, I lean in closer until I'm invading her privacy. If she is holding onto me and following me around, I'm overwhelmed and want to be alone. She is nicotine. I crave her, but she makes me feel awful.

"Bellamy, are you awake?" she asks.

I turn to face her.

"Yes," I say and kiss the top of her head. Steely fingers reach into my shirt. "What are you thinking about?" I ask and touch the floral device on the side of her head.

"I don't want to tell you," she says.

"Why not?"

"It...doesn't make sense."

"That's okay. A lot about life doesn't make sense." I caress her face.

My hand on her back rests at the base of the plate in her shoulder blade. Half human, half robot, fully incomprehensible.

"I'll tell you later."

"Please, I really want to know."

"I want something," she whispers.

Her palm is cool on my chest. I'm going to let her rip my heart out.

"What is it?"

"It's ridiculous," she says and turns to face the wall.

"Not to me."

"Why do you want to know so bad?"

"I want you to be happy," I say.

Her gold eyes reflect off the steel wall. The wings are powered down but still emit a soft blue glow. I prop myself up on my elbow and toy with her blonde hair.

"What does my happiness have to do with saving you?" she asks in annoyance.

"I love you. Please, tell me what you want."

"I don't think you'd approve," she says and sits up.

"Try me," I joke.

I grab her hand.

"I want to have a baby," she says in her breathy but flat voice.

The memory of Valerie telling me the same thing moves across my mind like a motion picture. She and I were in bed. It was the middle of the night. I knew she was going to leave me, but I wasn't ready to be alone. She told me her wish and at first I said I'd think about it. I already had. Valerie was never going to get what she wanted from me.

Remembering Valerie packing up her room is a visceral wound. The steel, white, and fluorescent lab seemed unendurable once she left. That was my dark time. I couldn't deliver on my promises and I suffered the consequences. My immaturity has cost me. Because of my wealth, I figured I could get away with it. Not this time.

"Is that what you really want?" I ask.

Gwen's eyes cease to glow. They are hazel. Her humanity pops up in small ways, like daisies. I sit up and brush the hair off her shoulder so I can see the freckles on her neck. She reaches for me.

"Yes."

There are negative ions in the air like after a storm. Her skin is soft. She smells like rain and white flowers. Gwen is a goddess, bringing the lightning. The wires sway like dandelions in the breeze. They are quiet. This is unlike me, but I pull Gwen down on top of me. She wins. I'm sure it's all in my head, but I swear I hear rattlesnakes and taste rain in the dark where I try to give my girlfriend what she wants.

* * *

Standing at the door, I stare at the moon through the window. I'm pondering the complexities of life. How we can have everything and nothing, some have nothing but are content, and how one can be simultaneously lucky but also cursed. The stars are brighter without humanity's light pollution.

Tufts of pillowy clouds pass over for a moment. The moon is bright and eggshell white. It has cracks and craters in it. The fullness of it decreases my confidence. I look up at it and wonder what the fuck I'm doing. It can't answer me. Not the moon, not the Nordic gods, and definitely not my father could possess such wisdom.

Gwen hasn't been going outside. I can tell by the way her hair smells. No floral rain. She wants to be with me often. We've been having sex for four weeks. I'm going to give her an ultrasound in the morning. It's strange to be detached from something so intimate.

I've quit smoking. Gwen doesn't like when I do and I don't want to hurt my health in any way. She has started bringing me food and making sure I take care of myself. The Ex Machina could be carrying out her own selfish desires. Or maybe she is expressing genuine consideration. Gwen prefers to plug herself into the battery compared to eating, but since I told her, she should try eating more to increase her chances of getting pregnant. She eats whenever I tell her to. I'm not sure about this theory, but I figure the sustenance can't hurt.

I haven't told anyone. Hotaka knows I'm keeping a secret. Eventually it's going to come out, but for now I'd like to keep what little standing I have. Isamu and Nori saw Gwen stick her tongue in my mouth. She isn't concerned with how she appears. The Ex Machina doesn't have to be. I'm a house of cards. She is an iron fortress.

A nasty, guttural screech startles me. I blink to clear my head. A female Mantodea is outside. She is calling on the others. Two Nymphs join her. Their antennas twitch and their mouths vibrate. Chattering noises are emitted from their throats. The arms bend in prayer and are ready to tear anything and everything apart.

She is taking labored steps and screaming at the moon. The Nymphs join in and make rasping hisses. The sky sounds thunderous. More of them are coming from the ship. It rumbles and the steel of the door jiggles on the hinges. Katsuo, Hikari, Shira, and Hotaka step out from their rooms and stand around me. We watch with dread as the Mantodea's offspring pierce through the clouds.

Suddenly, I'm being pushed back. Gwen opens the door and flies out before I can stop her. Hotaka and Katsuo grab me so I can't run after her. Gwen takes to the sky and begins electrocuting the Nymphs. The female Mantodea keeps screeching and rearing up. Her antenna is twitching, and she is chirping profusely.

Gwen extends her wires and latches onto three Nymphs and shocks their exoskeletons. They bleed out green sludge. It turns the grass black and dissolves the dirt. We all cover our ears. That abhorrent sound of gravel in a blender. I get up and watch her annihilate them with her lightning like a Nordic goddess.

The Mantodea rain down on the earth. It's bright, like fireworks going off. She is ruthless in her strategy. Gwen flies circles around them as she zaps the newcomers and destroys the Nymphs three at a time. Black pieces of aliens fall from the sky and crumble. They hit the ground and make holes where they land.

She whips her wires through the female Mantodea, ripping off chunks of its protective layer. It lunges at her, but she sticks a jack in the alien's chest. She strikes lightning through its body and the shell falls off in a burning heap. Gwen digs the jack in before ripping it out. Green blood sprays everywhere. She sticks another jack in the creature and shocks it for good measure.

Hotaka's glasses capture the scene like a movie screen. Katsuo is impressed and alarmed. They don't know everything she is capable of. I've been hiding too much. Now they bear witness to who Gwen truly is. What she can do. She is a killing machine. As Gwen finishes off the last Nymph, the men let me go. Hikari and Shira are standing far off to the side. They don't need to see what we just saw.

Gwen comes back, and I open my arms to her. She kisses me with her eyes open. Her gold lights peer into the souls of the scientists behind me. Katsuo steps back and inches towards his son and Shira. Hotaka remains at my side. His breath changes slightly. I know when my friend is nervous. She lets me go. I watch her go into her room and shut me out. She said sometimes it hurts to be with me because she loves me so much.

"That was…" Hotaka starts and I finish for him.

"Riveting," I say.

"Vicious," he takes off his glasses to wipe them off on his shirt.

Hotaka's hair is damp with sweat. So is mine. The back of my shirt collar is sticking to my neck.

"Gwen was meant to be strong."

"What's been going on between you two?"

"Too much."

I look at him with a solemn face.

"She's powerful, but we need to find a way for her to defeat the Queen," says Hotaka.

He changes the subject like a polite person.

"I'll make her another weapon. Her own spacecraft. Whatever I have to do. I'll find a way." I clench my teeth.

"I know you will, Bell."

Hotaka slaps my back in a friendly way and heads back to his room. I go into mine and sleep for the first time in forever. No lily of the valley, no grassy green notes. No sound of rattlesnakes. I miss her.

CHAPTER NINETEEN
CATALYST

Sipping on my tea, I attempt to steady my hands. My back is tense. Muscle stiffness is common most days. As much as I love her, she stresses me out. We suffer from Stockholm Syndrome. The difference is we are both the captor and the hostage. The game has no set rules. I'm sure I've broken most of them if there were.

Isamu and Nori walk by me. They both nod, but the creases on their foreheads bunch up above their eyebrows. I make everybody uncomfortable. They can't fathom what it's like to be me. I am only a man. They expect me to be their hero. I'm not anybody. Just some crazed genius kid.

When he was creating technology to further the human race, I was playing baseball and wearing mud like a gold medal. The Ex Machina is full of surprises. Gwen isn't shy about her affection towards me. Yui walked in on her leaving lipstick stains on my neck. The young scientist apologized immediately and backed away like she saw a monster. Maybe she did. Which one would be classified as such?

"Hey," to my dismay, it's Shira. She invites herself to sit with me.

"Hi," the tea has made my voice less raspy, but it still sounds like I've been shouting.

"How are you, Bellamy?" she asks.

Shira picks up an apple and bites into it with fervor.

"I'm okay. A little disappointed Gwen couldn't defeat the Mantodea."

I try to make polite conversation.

"We all are."

"I assure you I'm trying my best. I want out of this mountain."

I rub my face and avoid looking at her. Shira is pretty but has an intensity about her. Who knew a ninety-pound female could be so draining?

"How is Gwen? You two seem happy together," she says it like she's my friend, but her rudeness is detectable.

I can tell she is studying my tiredness. Am I exhausted from being in love or fighting with my girlfriend? That's what she really wants to know.

"She's fine," I say in a hollow tone.

Shira gets the cue to back off. Toying with the chessboard, she picks up the queen.

"The Ex Machina fought the Mantodea with prowess." Shira eyes the piece of fruit. I can't eat red anything anymore. It makes me think of blood. My stomach has been sensitive. Shira continues with a hint of pretentiousness, "I can't wait to see what you come up with for us. The team is waiting," she says as she stands.

The apple crunches in her ruthless mouth.

I set down my tea and search for Gwen. Today is the day we find out. My throat closes on me. I loosen my tie, but it's not what's choking me out. Hotaka passes me in the hall and smiles. We bump knuckles like we're kids. It's nice to have someone to pretend to be average with. I find her in my room laying on my bed. The wires sensed me and she is sitting up.

"Hey, are you ready?" I ask.

She nods with enthusiasm. Gwen lights up for me the way she does for Hikari. I'm delirious from my insomnia. It's worth it though.

"Yes," she whispers.

I take her hand and we make our way to the infirmary. Nori watches us go in with glossy, dark eyes. I wave at him and he stumbles over his feet as he fast walks down the hall. We go into the room with white walls and bright lights. I have her undress and lay on the table. Covering her breasts with the sheet and using another to lay across her lap exposes her flat stomach. She has a small mole on her left side. My thumb grazes it and I turn on the machine.

"I'm nervous," I admit.

My shaky fingers cover under her navel area with petroleum jelly. Gwen grins and nods.

"Me too," she says.

I assumed the Ex Machina was incapable of such an insignificant emotion, but I learn more about her every day.

"Okay," I sigh and place the transducer on her belly.

Moving it around, a picture appears. At first, nothing is detectable, but then I notice it. A slight flicker. My heart jumps out of my chest. Gwen's eyes no longer glow. She puts her delicate finger to the screen.

"I'm pregnant," she says.

"Yeah."

More needs to be said, but I can't believe it. I'm speechless.

"I'm...excited." Gwen puts the tips of her fingers beneath her navel and touches her stomach with tenderness.

"Me too," my voice gets caught in my throat.

"Do you have other children?" she asks.

Gwen has shown a greater amount of interest in me as of late. She disappears on me, but not like she used to. Most days, she sticks to me like glue.

"No," I say and wipe away the petroleum jelly.

My hand covers her stomach. Knowing my baby is inside her causes me to pause. What have I done?

***

I started wondering if my father really wanted me around the time I turned ten. My mom was attentive, but my dad never being around made me feel like there was something wrong with me. It's a gruesome truth to admit, but my dad had me to make my mom happy.

Love, fear, hurt: these are three separate entities. So why do they seem so deeply intertwined? In movies, it appears love is sugary and forgiving. That it isn't harmful or scary. The pain described in most media is shallow. It's impossible to compare my life to anything other than films and my life before the Mantodea.

Valerie told me what she wanted. I declined, but I still think about her. Sometimes I see her auburn hair in my dreams and wake up to platinum blonde strands in my hands. Am I afraid of her and so I do what she wants? The Ex Machina is bonded to me. She has to do what I say. I test my control in small ways. So far I've gotten her to eat at regimented times and not go outside without me.

Gwen isn't like most women. She hasn't told anyone. The others do not show up on her radar. My other girlfriends would have told everyone in the laboratory by now. But not her. She has been docile. Her usually restless or bored demeanor has been replaced with an exuberant personality.

It's not a secret. Or is it? I don't know if I can take the judgemental stares of my colleagues. This is my lab, my company, my project—yet I'm losing my grip. The team of scientists have lost faith in me. I want them to believe in me. To believe in her.

The equipment I built for Gwen was a bust. I'll have to make her a stronger weapon. Now that she's pregnant, I don't want her fighting monsters. Just my luck. I've set myself up for failure.

A lie is like a grain of sand. One isn't noticeable. It's when the lies become endless, the pile grows and the grit against skin can't be ignored. In the beginning, I thought nothing could happen. Not like this. She is full of surprises.

I have loved her for years. Never in this capacity. They say 'fall in love' because there's no other terminology for it. No one seeking love finds it. A

132

person forcing or taking love is holding onto something that isn't theirs. No, love is pretty white flowers beyond quicksand. It draws in its prey and drags it down.

Being an only child was lonely. It seemed like everyone else had a sibling. It was probably a feat trying to convince my dad to give my mom one baby. Bethany Krim didn't want to spoil her luck. I was jealous of other kids who had a brother or sister. For a while, I wished I had a little brother. I thought it would be really cool.

Other kids had someone to joke with, to play with, another person to connect with. Siblings would walk home after school or a game and I would watch the way they never looked forgotten. I think I felt ignored even when my mom was talking to me. I would watch older brothers and sisters pick up their younger siblings with envy.

My dad was an only child. Bethany had three siblings. Two sisters and a brother. My aunts and uncle were fun like my mom. They didn't come around often. I think my dad's popularity made them skittish. It was exceptional being part of the Krim family. There was so much at stake. Over the years, my mom got good at ignoring people's stares and whispers. I don't think the rest of our family could get used to them, though.

I never wanted to be a parent. My mom was great. I don't resent her or blame her. I don't blame my dad either. Fatherhood hasn't appealed to me. Not that I find it unimportant. Aliens invading our planet and decades of isolation has caused me a plethora of emotional problems. In another world, one without vicious beasts plaguing the earth, perhaps my paternal instincts could kick in and I wouldn't live in survival mode.

I'm not trained or educated in how to do this. Somewhere deep in my animal brain, I sense my protective drive. I'm hoping this will be my guide. I've been noting Gwen's moods throughout the day. She seems less severe. I can sleep with her in the room. It's like the deadly stingers have been removed. I remind myself periodically they are still there, even if they're not as active.

Sleep isn't a necessity for her. The pregnancy doesn't affect that. If she isn't lying with me at night, she wanders the building. I appreciate her not running off. She must feel some kind of loyalty towards me. Maybe this is wishful thinking.

Gwen is reading to Hikari. He is sitting in her lap. In his arms is a stuffed animal. She is tickling him. The little boy squeals in delight. Once Gwen closes the book, he jumps off her lap and runs down the hall. I sit down with her. She embraces me.

"How are you feeling?" I ask.

She thinks about my question.

"I'm content," she says.

"Good." I put my hand over hers.

Gwen stares at my mouth. Titanium teeth intimidate me. I stay still as she kisses me. It fills me with lead and I fall through the earth.

***

Gold eyes take in her situation. She is methodical. The device strengthens her mind. Or has it warped it? I think about these things frequently. Gwen takes my queen and smiles.

"You could let me win one of these times," I joke as I set up the chessboard.

Rearranging the pieces and placing them in their proper spot gives me clarity.

"Maybe I will," she says and winks at me.

Flirtatious.

"Do you want to play again?"

"No," she sighs and twirls blond hair in her steel fingers. I'm uneasy when she becomes bored.

"What do you want to do?" I ask.

Gwen's wires hover above the floor, sensing, twitching. She has a new dress. This one is a unique shade of dusty pink. It makes her look youthful and sweet. Her face is slightly flushed, bringing out the caramel colored freckles on her nose.

"Can we go outside? Please?"

"Of course. Let's go before it gets dark," I say.

As soon as I'm standing, Gwen is at my side holding onto my elbow. We make our way to the front door. Everyone tries not to stare. I'm their boss, I give them shelter, and a lucrative job. Gwen could murder us all in ninety-seconds flat. They don't dare tell us what to do.

Their eyes peek over the rims of their glasses. Nori nods at me but shies away from Gwen. She waves to the older scientists. Isamu gives her a tight smile. Katsuo moves his head to gesture that he sees us, but does not try to be courteous. Out of the corner of my eye I see him look my girlfriend up and down.

Men aren't afraid when they should be. They think they can take on anything. Fight a bear, win against the strongest guy they know, and treat the Ex Machina with disrespect. Katsuo hides Hikari from her. He keeps them apart. Yet he likes to look at her. It's a common but confusing occurrence. To distrust something, or dislike it, but also be strangely attracted to it.

I hit the button. Gwen waits for me to go out first. She sneaks out when I'm not looking. If I'm around, she is on her best behavior. She doesn't touch the other male scientists anymore. No brushing up against their arms or picking up their pens. Her hands no longer graze their shoulders as she passes by. She hasn't tried to take off Hotaka's glasses. Gwen got her desired results. She lured me in and she's got me where she wants me now.

134

Fall is nearly over. The maroon leaves have turned brown and splotchy. The shades of yellow and orange are tinged with mold. It rained earlier. The grass is wet. Grey clouds veil the earth from the sun. We walk in the grass and patches of moss. Hunter green foliage lines the path. Gwen swishes the wires. Her hand slips into mine. Cedars and pines leave long shadows in the mud.

The jacks at the ends of the wire vibrate. I turn around and so does Gwen. It's a large elk, a bull. His fur is umber with a red sheen to it. He is massive in stature and spirit. The two mystic creatures lock eyes. They sense each other in a way I'm not familiar with. The bull exhales through his nose. His breath is visible in the cool weather. Gwen's eyes cease to glow. They both have hazel eyes.

"The elk and you seem fond of each other," I say.

He walks through the hydrangeas and ferns away from us.

"I was thinking about what it's like to be him," she says.

"What do you mean?"

"What it's like to be free."

A breeze moves through Gwen's hair. She smiles to herself. I remember her saying she loved the wind. This moment stains my memory. Gwen's hair is being picked up. She's smiling without me prompting her to. I don't have to wait for it. She is smiling because she is experiencing joy. I lean down and kiss her with my eyes closed.

The sun is about to set. Blood orange clouds swirl with the darkening indigo sky. A blackbird flies above me. The fluttering of its wings is palpable in the air. The wind is blowing on the sweat of my neck. It sends a chill through me. My lab coat rustles like a sail on a boat. She lets me go and we make our way back.

"Bellamy, how old are you?" she asks.

"I'm thirty-four," I say. She looks at me and then at the ground. We pass by ferns and lily of the valley. The aquatic ozone scent outside is intoxicating.

"When's your birthday?" she asks.

I laugh, but not very hard.

"The first of the year."

"When's my birthday?"

"May fifteenth." We are outside the door, but she stops. Her hand is on her stomach. "Is something wrong?" I ask.

"I was just thinking about our baby's birthday," she says.

Medusa has turned me to stone. I can't lift my feet. The weight of her words is heavy, leaving a crater inside me.

CHAPTER TWENTY
THINGS

The others disregard us. That doesn't stop them from staring. Slowly and subtly, Gwen and I have become a somewhat normal couple. We eat breakfast and play chess together. She still disappears to do her own thing during the day. At night, she stays with me. I trust her and can sleep next to a deadly scorpion, but the baby keeps me up. She and I wander the halls when I can't lay down.

Bile hits the back of my throat when I think about what I'm doing. How I have veered off the path? This is no longer scientific. It is very, very personal. I need to tell Hotaka. He will be the friend I need. I have had my chances, but haven been able to bring myself to say it out loud. He already knows how I feel about her. She's a little more than a month along. The shame lingers like the acid eroding the lining of my throat.

Gwen's wires swish in a docile fashion. No longer threatening whipping back and forth. She doesn't wear lipstick these days. Her face is constantly flushed and has a slight sheen to it. I check on her all the time. The pregnancy has been causing sporadic low-grade fevers. Shouldn't be anything to worry about. She seems to trust me.

"Bellamy, do you have a minute?"

Nori brings me out of my thoughts.

"Yes, what is it?" I ask.

"We have been designing a weapon for Gwen," he says.

I nod and follow him into one of the sterile rooms. Isamu and Katsuo are sitting at the wide table sketching something on a large piece of paper.

"This one will store additional atmospheric energy. Gwen should be able to charge it completely before entering space. Its precision tip is sharper and should penetrate the shell of the ship," says Nori as I stand over the drawing of a sizable spear.

It resembles an ancient Nordic weapon mixed with futuristic technology.

"What about her respirator and tank?" I ask, trying not to sound too protective.

"We anticipate making her those as well. They proved to be efficient," says Isamu.

Katsuo gives me an annoyed glare.

"Thank you," I say under my breath.

"She fought them with impressive strength," says Katsuo in a gruff tone.

His eyes don't leave the paper, his hand stays steady as he makes lines and tick marks.

"She is remarkable," I say.

My temples get hit with stinging pain. The migraines are back. I rub the side of my head and squint. The fluorescent lights are too bright in this place.

"I hope this works," says Nori. His hands are in the pocket of his lab coat. It makes him look like a little boy.

"Me too," I say and rub my fingers through my hair to ease the headache. "When will it be ready?" I ask.

"Give us three weeks," says Isamu.

His face is smiling, but I think he is disgusted by me. I heard him once call Gwen a "thing." It made me grit my teeth. I think I'm wearing down the enamel from my constant apprehension. Gwen massages my shoulders to try and make me feel better. I can't explain what it's like to be tortured with joy and terror at the same time.

"I look forward to seeing the finished product, gentlemen."

I walk out to hide my horror. Gwen will be close to eight weeks along by the time she is expected to fight. Nothing has come close to touching her. I can't bear the thought of her in space, fighting aliens, in her condition. What's wrong with me? I pray for redemption. It's futile. I never pray except for when I really fuck up.

It's midday but I want to see her. She is hiding. Gwen likes her time to herself. It's selfish, but I need her. I want her soul crushing focus. It's maddening to need her but feel on edge in her presence. I throw caution to the wind and seek out my girlfriend. She isn't in her room. Not in mine either. I can't seem to find her. It's cheating, but I check the cameras. She's not wandering around anywhere. Did she go outside?

Paranoid and emotionally fragile, I rewind and look for her. I'm waiting to see a blonde tornado. It takes a while, but I see what she is up to. It warms my heart to see she didn't go outside. She hasn't left me since her ultrasound. Gwen is in the testing room with the water reservoir. I bet she's swimming.

I'm tempted to smoke. My heart is racing, my breaths are shallow, and my forehead is sweaty. I have that incomplete feeling in my chest. A quick smoke would fill this hollowness. I decide against it. Gwen has kept her promises to me. I should start keeping mine. The Ex Machina is not one to be trifled with.

As I make my way down the dim hall, I see Hotaka in his room with headphones on. He is rocking out to a song. On his desk is a cup of tea. Hotaka is good at taking care of himself and others. Thinking about his kindness towards me during my stagnation reminds me to tell him the truth. I want to confide in him. He seems to be having a good time and I don't want to bother him. It's not an excuse. I will tell him later. Right now, I need to be with her.

The visions of the weapon in her hand and the Mantodea chasing after her stop me in my tracks. Time doesn't move. Water outside isn't flowing. The damn migraine is catching up to me. I shake it away with gentle movements. In the testing room, I find no one. It's silent and cool. The aquatic scent is refreshing. I think of the flowers Gwen brought me that time she said she wanted to bring outside to me.

I stand at the ledge of the reservoir. Inky water greets me. I see nothing in the depths, but I know she is there. So I wait. In the black liquid is the glow of blue and gold. I stick my hand in the water. She knows I'm here from her wires, but I reach for her. I rolled up my sleeves, but they still got wet. Her fingers are intertwined with mine. I pull her out of the darkness.

"Gwen," I say her name as I embrace her.

My button up and lab coat become cold and damp as she wraps her lethal arms around me.

***

"You look happy, Bell," says Hotaka as he sits across from me.

I'm drinking ginger tea, hoping to settle my stomach. It feels weak all the time. My weight is good despite my anxious gut. I'm excited, but the joy makes me suspicious. I know it can't last for long. Eventually, this will all turn on me. Blissful dreamy days tangled in blond hair, I'm sure can turn into a nightmare in a minute. No, in a second.

"Really? Thanks," I say and smile at my chagrin.

"I'm serious. You both look really happy," he says.

Picking up a grapefruit, he eyes it for a moment. His index and middle finger rip into the rind and reveal the flesh. It makes me nauseous. I keep my head down and sip my tea.

"We are," I say. Hotaka bites into the pink fruit.

I swallow my tongue.

"Gwen has been in a generous mood."

"What?"

I look up.

"She fixed my speakers when she saw they weren't working properly. Yui dropped an enormous stack of notes in the hall, and Gwen helped her pick up every piece of paper. Hikari was having a fit the other day. Katsuo and Shira could not get him to put away his toys. Gwen intervened and Hikari listened to her right away," he says, keeping his eyes on the rind he's tearing apart.

"I'm glad to hear she's showing more interest in the others."

"Now that she has what she wants, she has room for other relationships," he says.

I spit out my tea.

"I suppose she has me where she wants me," I joke.

Hotaka deserves to know. I contemplate telling him. The courage I had dissipates, and I keep my secret.

"The bond is the single most telling thing about this project. The key to our mission."

"Gwen doesn't do what I say. She anticipates what I want, and acts accordingly."

I give him a piece of the puzzle, since I'm too much of a coward to admit what I've done.

"The new weapon looks compelling. I hope she is able to destroy their Queen with it," he says and tosses the remains of the pink rind in the garbage.

"I want that, too. But I worry about her safety. I love her so much. I don't want her to get hurt."

They fall over themselves like dominoes. Hotaka covers his heart and grins.

"Her love for you drives her determination. I believe she can do it."

"Gwen is capable of anything and everything."

I tap my fingers on the teacup.

"So are you. You are a Krim," says my friend.

He leaves me alone to digest what's happening. I sip on my lukewarm tea. It's midday. What could Gwen be up to?

I fall asleep to the scent of dew on petals but wake up alone. At midnight I smell white blossoms and taste rain. I hear my name. When I wake, my palm finds the other side of the bed empty. She doesn't leave me for long, but she never stays. Twisted is the man who falls in love with a god.

This is a dangerous game. She has bested me. I'm grateful, but cursed to be the one she saw first. Woken from her slumber, where I wondered if she had dreamed about ice fishing and snow. I thought her eyes would be blue, but they're hazel. She has caramel freckles on her nose and shoulders.

Soon everyone will know. That word echoes in my migraine riddled skull, soon. It won't be long until I'm exposed. Our love is questionable. Undiscovered chemicals mixing together to create something no one has ever witnessed. It's beyond the spectrum of acid and alkaline.

I should eat. This means Gwen should eat as well. She made me laugh harder than ever last week. The crops were ready. This round yielded us broccoli, carrots, and bell peppers. Gwen took a bite of the textured floret and spit it out. She said it was "vile." I told her it would be good for her and healthy for the baby, but she shook her head "no" at me like a chastised child. Thankfully, she likes spinach, tomatoes, and radishes.

Being with Gwen is like an experiment. I try certain tactics on different days. Most of the time, I let her do as she pleases. Occasionally, I'm curious about the extent of my control. I don't want to make a habit of it, but I'll slip in a request and see if she does it. For instance, I said she could go outside if she would like, but I'd prefer if she waited for me. Then I checked the cameras at the end of the week. She didn't go outside. Her hair never smelled like rain.

Another time, she was in a distant mood, but I wanted her to acknowledge me. She was in her own world. I was laying in her bed. She was at her desk, brushing her hair. I kept looking at her girlish face. Gwen's eyes glow gold and she is in outer space. They are menacing in their splendor. I said "come here," and to my surprise she got up and sat with me.

"Gwen," I call for her as I open my door.

She's not here. I look at the cameras for the water reservoir. She's not swimming. I assume she is in her room. My feet sound louder than usual as they hit the metal floor. The clinking is making me jumpy. I turn the corner to the hall with Gwen's room.

"Gwen," I say her name and try to open the door. It's locked. "Gwen?" I ask. This time, I pull on the handle with force.

"Gwen, open the door right now!" I shout.

My yelling has caused Nori, Yui, and Isamu to step out of their rooms. Nori and Yui have concerned expressions, but Isamu looks annoyed. His hair is sticking up and his face is rumpled. He must have been napping. I have the access code allowing me into every room. I've never had to use it until today.

The tremor in my hand makes it hard to punch in the six digits with accuracy. The dim blue lights of the hall distort my panicking vision. I think about Nyx and how she killed herself.

The door opens too slowly for my liking. In my peripheral vision, I see Nori, Yui, and Isamu watch me lose it. I'm clawing my way in. The scene in front of me plays out. Gwen's grey blanket is covered in blood. She is wrapped in her white sheets, crying on the ground. A red puddle pools between her legs. The sheet is drenched. Her tan thighs are covered in maroon splotches.

"Bellamy," she sobs my name.

I get on my knees and bring her to my chest. Looking up, I'm met with six eyes. All of which see through me.

***

She is lost to me, and I am lost without her. After her miscarriage, she promptly flew off. It's been five days. The longest she's disappeared. I'm convinced Gwen won't be coming back. I tried to be there for her. She was obviously distraught. I stayed with her all night. The Ex Machina is a cold and ruthless killing machine but she is human and her heart being broken caused her to cry for hours.

I wake up alone as I often do. Feeling morose and agitated, I went immediately for the cameras. I'm not playing hide and seek anymore. That's when I saw her take off before the sun bothered to rise. I sulk in my room and hide in the crook of my arm. My door opens. I sit up with a swiftness I didn't know I could muster. It's Hotaka.

"What's been going on?" he asks in a gentle voice meant for a pious conversation.

I lay on my back and stare up at the ceiling.

"I've been trying to give her what she wants," I say.

"Gwen wanted to be pregnant." He says it the way a scientist would. No emotion, just the simple truth.

"Yes," I whisper and turn to my side. Everyone thinks I'm a monster of different proportions. I got her pregnant. I wasn't careful, I'm gambling with everyone's lives.

"Why didn't you tell me?" he asks.

Hotaka sounds hurt. He rubs his hands together with nervousness. I can hear the discomfort building between his palms.

"I couldn't handle the judgment. I know what I'm doing goes against all professional conduct and probably certain laws. The scary thing is I stopped caring about that," I admit.

"I can't speak for the others, but I'm not judging you. We are living during strange times in the strangest of predicaments. Who is to say it is wrong or unjust for you and Gwen to be together?"

"I'm sure Katsuo and Shira are going to give me an earful," I groan.

Hotaka takes off his glasses and laughs. He sits in the chair by my bed and rests his elbows on his knees.

"The probability of the Ex Machina falling in love or wanting to be human was slim, but it's revealing the extent of our knowledge," he says.

I massage my temples. The headache is recurring. I wish Gwen was here to play with my hair.

"How so?" I ask.

"It's proving we know very little about the human heart. It is unpredictable. We thought her formidable intelligence was the key to our salvation. It turns out you are the one she holds in her heart. The reason she will do anything to save us all."

"I don't know if that's true anymore. We lost our baby. She might not want anything to do with me."

I breathe a sad boy sigh into my crisp pillowcase. Hotaka scoots the chair closer. His hand is on my shoulder. My jaw aches from clenching my teeth.

"She will come back," he says and squeezes my shoulder in a brotherly fashion.

"How do you know?" I ask.

"The imprinting, the bond. It's irreplaceable. Love can't be imitated."

"I don't know if she is in love with me or if it's that stupid thing in her head," I snap.

Hotaka releases his grip on me. I'm barking like a disobedient dog.

"Gwen is happy with you. That's not the device."

"She told me she loves me so much it hurts. It's why she runs off on me. Does that sound healthy to you?"

"Sounds like most impossible romances," he says and exits my room.

Was he joking or not? I can't tell. Instead of doing my rounds and working, I sleep. What use is saving the world if she's not in mine? It's selfish, but I can't bring myself to get out of bed. Nori, Yui, and Isamu saw the terrible sight of my girlfriend miscarrying all over the shiny metal floor. They've surely alerted the other scientists.

Yui's face stood out to me. Perhaps because she is a woman, I looked at her for some kind of reassurance. She was frightened. There was a hint of hurt. Like I hit her in the face. I think knowing what Gwen was going through gave me her sympathy. The men's faces were perplexed, then horrified. Nori appeared serious, but the lines around his mouth from his frown and his demeanor made me think he was sorry for me. Isamu looked like he ate something disagreeing with him and like he was going to vomit.

"Thing," that's what he called her.

What are they calling our baby? Called our baby. Too soon to say goodbye, but already a past tense. I didn't think I wanted to be a father. It was a chore unlike any other. So why am I so wholeheartedly depressed? I want Gwen. It's more than that. I want a family of my own, this is why the feeling is intolerable. Miraculously, I fall asleep and dream about angels, white flowers, and endless rain.

"Bellamy," she whispers my name and I'm wide awake.

"Gwen–"

I grab her and breathe in her white gold hair. She smells like the pines and floral notes of peonies. Winter is arriving little by little. Gwen's skin is icy but flawless.

"I thought you might not come back," I say.

"I'm sorry. I was scared."

"I know you were," I say.

She combs through my hair with her delicate but intimidating fingers. The Ex Machina can annihilate an army of aliens but experiences fear and loss the way a human does. I should write this down. It doesn't matter. What for? I don't need scientific theories to explain that she may be robotically engineered, but she is the love of my life.

CHAPTER TWENTY-ONE
ANIMALS

I expected Gwen to push me away, but the miscarriage has brought her closer to me. The image of her bleeding out on the floor floats at the front of my thoughts. I try to ignore them and stay in the moment. Gwen is holding my elbow and accompanying me on my rounds.

Shira, Katsuo, and Hikari give us three sets of gazes: alarmed, annoyed, and longing. I know Gwen and the little boy want to play, but I'm waiting for things to settle down a bit. If Katsuo says something rude to upset her, I might cut his tongue out. Best to keep to ourselves.

It's a despicable secret. Gwen and I have been trying again. I didn't think she'd be up to it since she was so upset. She told me it's what she wants. I don't say "no." I give myself away until there's nothing left.

She's wearing a new dress. It's mint green. The fabric clings to her hips. I'm glad she doesn't wear red lipstick or red dresses anymore. The color red makes me feel ill. I can't watch anyone eat an apple or a strawberry. It churns my stomach. I don't even like to think about it. Scarlet wines, ruby fruits, and cherry scented anything causes my stomach to contract.

I'm in a despondent mood. Tonight, Gwen is to test our new weapon. She said she was ready, but I'm not. What if she's pregnant? It's only been three weeks. I don't want her to get hurt. The Mantodea are pitiless. How can I say I love her and let her do this? The team stares me down with ruthless eyes marked with crow's feet and dark circles.

No one apologized to me or said they were sorry for my loss. I didn't think they would. Hotaka holds empathy and space for me, but I don't know if he agrees with my choices. Regardless, he is my friend. I respect him. Yui has been kinder to me. She goes out of her way to bring me a cup of tea or ask my opinion on my father's notes and theories. The young scientist is clever. She tries to be sweet without trying too hard. I think she may have experienced a loss like this. When she handed me a cup of ginger citrus tea she looked different.

Nori puts on her tank and fits her with the respirator. He checks the oxygen levels. His hands are all over her, but not in a lustful way. Still, I wince at his rough knuckles grazing her cheekbone and his fingertips touching her waist. Isamu steps up and hands her the weapon. Gwen has the likeness of a Nordic goddess.

"This spear will harness the electrical energy from the atmosphere until you reach space. It should give you enough power to destroy the ship and the Queen inside. The weapon should be strong enough to ward off the drones and soldiers," says Isamu.

His hands are on the spear and are very close to Gwen's. He uncurls chubby fingers with care and steps back.

"The tank will give you one hour and fifteen minutes in space. After that, your lungs will only have the eleven minute reservoir. Be sure you have oxygen stored," says Nori.

Gwen nods. She is a mermaid in outer space. Hikari runs up and grips onto my khakis.

"I don't want Gwen to fight them. I love her," says the little boy in a small voice fit for a mouse.

"I love Gwen, too. We have to believe in her, okay, kiddo?"

I kneel down so Hikari can see how much she means to me. We have the saddest eyes in the group.

"Gwen is an angel," he says.

His big eyes have tears forming in them. Katsuo is frowning at me. I ignore him.

"She is," I say and stand up.

Gwen hits the button for the front door. The moon is full. She's gone without a trace. Everyone stares up at the sky through the tiny window. We count stars and hope for her to defeat the Mantodea. All of us long to lie under the night sky and not worry about being murdered by aliens.

One by one, they go back to their rooms. I should go back to mine. Gwen should be back in about an hour. If she's not, well, then I know the answer. I can't accept that as an outcome. Hotaka comes up to my side. He keeps his gaze on the moon. It reflects in his glasses.

"You should try to relax," he says.

"I can't. It's disgustingly possessive, but I want her where I can see her. I can't focus unless she's right there by my side," I say it and feel my tongue swell.

Hotaka nods his head. He grins at me, which is a surprise.

"Love is beautiful, but it can be all-consuming," he says.

I know what he is insinuating.

"I'm sorry. I'm worried about her. It makes me not myself."

I shake my head. That twinge of a headache is coming on.

"She'll be okay."

"I shouldn't be so protective of the Ex Machina," I joke.

Hotaka and I chuckle. He walks me to my room.

"Maybe you should be. She is the one who will bring us deliverance."

"Thank you, Hotaka. For being a true friend."

"See you in the morning, Bell."

I shut my door and lay down. It's no use. I can't stop tossing and turning. My bed smells like her. I wait like a lovesick puppy. The clock ticks by in slow motion. Ten minutes feels like an hour. Twenty minutes is maddening. I stop looking at the forty-minute mark. I'll throw the clock across the room and set this lab on fire.

It's past midnight. I want to feel her hand on my chest. Gwen is up there in the heavens, fighting evil. The war of the noble and wicked has lasted an eternity. I thought it was a concept only seen in movies. My life is that of science fiction. For all any of us know, the Mantodea could take over our planet. Hopefully Gwen can decimate them. The electrically charged super spear seemed promising.

I get out of bed and wait by the front door. The moon has shifted in the sky. If I didn't know any better, I would say nothing was happening up there. No war, no armies, no angels. I pull at my hair and fidget on the couch. The stars shimmer but offer little comfort. It seems too good to be true. Gold eyes glow outside the door. I rush to get up and let her in. The tank is dented and mangled. Her weapon is missing the sharp tip. It's smoking and a thin current of electrical energy is circling it. Gwen is holding it with white knuckles.

I didn't hear his steps, but Nori is behind me. He is wearing rubber gloves. With care, he takes the dangerous and broken weapon from her tight grip. With swift and calculated motions, he removes the damaged oxygen tank. He doesn't rip out her respirator. Nori is kind and treats her like a person. She takes in a raspy breath. I want to embrace her, but Nori puts his hand up for me to stop. She falls to the ground and I envision us cutting the earth in half from our weight.

***

The monitor beeps and hums. Her wires move, but not with precision. They are listless and exhausted. I have her in the infirmary. Sitting next to her in the chair, I wait for her to wake up. I've never seen Gwen deplete her power source. She must have put up quite a fight.

Nori might not trust me, but he is a good man. I was out of my mind seeing her in such a state. He helped me when we were both powerless. After I hooked her up to everything, he brought me dinner but didn't stay to eat with me or say anything. I think he cares.

Shira, Katsuo, and Yui watched me run to the infirmary with horrified faces. If Gwen needs medical attention, then we have a problem. They are thinking about how the Mantodea may be stronger and more strategic than Gwen. All I can think about is that Gwen is hurt. She did something up there. I know she used everything, not just the weapon given to her.

"Hey," says Hotaka.

He pulls up a chair next to me.

"Hey," I say.

Gwen's face is as serene as it was when she was in stasis. I take her hand in mine. The wires twitch but hardly detect what is happening around her. This is the first time since birth Gwen has been vulnerable. It sickens me how glorious it feels to be the one watching over her.

"I thought I'd come check on you both," he says.

I rub my collarbone. My acid reflux is acting up.

"I'm glad she came back to me. I worry she'll fall victim to the Mantodea like everyone else," I say, but Hotaka hushes me.

"Don't say that. Gwen is more than what we made. More than we could ever fathom."

Hotaka reaches for her necklace. He turns the crescent moon over in between his long fingers.

"I never thought it would end up like this," I say through clenched teeth.

It's painful to admit. I could free us from this mountain, but I can't ask her to sacrifice her whole life for me. I love her too much. She is my world.

"Anything can happen."

Hotaka drops the moon and sits back. He is admiring Gwen but not in a lascivious way. I think he feels friendly or brotherly towards her.

"I'm sorry I'm such a selfish coward."

It happens too fast. A stream of tears falls, but only for a second.

"I don't think you are either of those things, Bellamy."

"Then what am I?" I ask.

Gwen stirs and squeezes my hand. It jump starts my heart.

"You two are in love," he says and exits the sterile room.

The Ex Machina can save us all if I let her. Yet I don't. I could unleash her upon the army of aliens like a souped up kamikaze. Never. If being with Gwen means never seeing outside and eliminating the opportunity for humans to reign supreme, then I choose her. Everything holds little value if the one person who touches my heart can't be alive. I would rather die than ask her to kill herself for my benefit.

"Gwen, can you hear me?" I whisper. The wires move with tired motions. One of them loosely wraps itself around my ankle. I think Gwen is trying to tell me she's okay. "I love you," I say the three words and the monitor keeping track of her heart spikes. Finally, I stand after I can't take it anymore. It happens like I'm a puppet. I watch myself get up and get the necessary equipment. It's like I'm floating across the floor. I can't hear my footsteps.

She looks like she's having a painful dream. I put my hand on her face. Leaning down, I kiss her. Titanium canines peek out at me. They don't induce anxiety like they once did. I pull back the sheets. They crinkle as I bunch them up to the side. Standing up, I put the petroleum jelly on her stomach. The mole on her side attracts me and my fingers graze it. My breath gets caught in my throat. It's only been three weeks. I shouldn't expect anything for another two or three weeks. Her miscarriage has most likely messed with her hormones, and who knows if her ovulation cycle is regular or not?

Gwen's blonde hair envelops her. She has it all over the bed and hanging off the side. If Hikari could see her, he would say she looks like a princess because she does. Sleeping Beauty with metal wings and wires. I put the transducer below her navel. The screen is fuzzy black and white. Static moves up and down as I search her uterus. I assume there is nothing. In the abyss is a flicker. Something small but alive. Gwen is pregnant again.

***

"Bellamy?" I wake up to her breathy voice. She tries to sit up, but I push her back down with a soft touch. I have fallen asleep in the chair.

"Hey Beautiful, how are you feeling?" I ask.

The eyes light up. She has a pouty face.

"I'm...tired."

"You must have fought the Mantodea with ferocity. I was really worried about you," I say.

She takes my hand in hers.

"I wasn't able to kill them. I'm sorry," she says in a sad whisper.

"It's okay. I'm just happy you're back."

"I almost did it. I contemplated using the rest of my stored energy, but I didn't want to die alone in space," she announces.

"That's why you fell after you arrived. You depleted your electrical power."

The sentence is sticky in my mouth. Gwen came close to killing herself to save us.

"I hope you're not upset with me."

She reads my face with accuracy. I smile at her.

"No, I'm not upset."

"Are you sure?" she asks.

Gwen shifts in the infirmary bed.

"Of course. Hey, I have exciting news."

I change the topic. My girlfriend examines my expression.

"What is it?" she asks. I put my hand on her stomach. She knows exactly what I'm saying. We grin with our teeth at each other. If anyone saw us, it could be mistaken as threatening. She is bearing titanium canines. I'm hardly intimidating. "Really?" She puts her hand on mine. The realization she could have died with my baby inside her feeds a dark shadow in the illuminated eyes.

"Yes. I found out when I was checking on you," I say.

Not a lie, but not the truth, either. I'm happy I was overly protective. My gut has proven useful a handful of times.

"I'm glad they're okay."

"You should get some rest."

Gwen spent an hour in space fighting vicious aliens. I'm relieved she's safe. The revelation of our new pregnancy has me scolding myself for letting her act as our guardian. I can tell Gwen wants to get out of bed, but I shake my head at her.

"Just for a little while longer, please."

"If you insist," she says.

I comb through her white blonde locks. The strands are silky in my palm. The monitors show stable vital signs. She is breathing deeply. Satisfied she is alright for the moment, I get up to walk around the lab. I should shower and eat something. Be a person.

I clean myself up and change my clothes. My face is fuller, but I have dark circles under my eyes. It's kind of distinguishing though. Not totally unattractive. I go into the kitchen to make myself and Gwen a cup of tea. While I'm in there, I cut up a pear and grab a small bunch of arugula. I still can't eat anything red. The strawberries and cherries in the fridge make me gag. Only at my most unpleasant moment do I hear her voice.

"Hey," says Shira.

She has an apple in her hand. I hope she doesn't bite into it in front of me.

"Hey," I say.

The tea kettle screeches. I pick chamomile tea for us since it's soothing and mild. The nutritional powder meant to enhance our diets has a nutty flavor. I put a tablespoon in each cup. The floral tea is mellow and so is the meal supplement. It shouldn't be detectable.

"I didn't think you wanted kids," she says with blatant disregard for tact.

"I changed my mind," I growl.

This is proving to be a dreadful conversation.

"Why her?" she asks.

To my chagrin, Shira sinks her tiny teeth into the flesh of the apple. I wince and look away.

"It's none of your business. Not that I can explain it, anyway."

I grab my items and make my way to the door.

"You and I would have never worked out."

"What makes you say that?"

I know it to be true, but ask the question anyway.

"I'm not extraordinary," she says.

I have no words for her. She has nothing else to say. We part ways, but I know the conversation isn't over. I wanted her to be my girlfriend. That was before Gwen. That was before everything changed in my world.

I walk back to her and don't hear my feet. My brain has been scattered. The senses mix until they are useless. I can't hear, taste, or smell with individuality anymore. They blur into an indecipherable puzzle. I pass by the rooms where the artificial wombs are. To think we entertained the idea of growing three Ex Machina at a time humors me. We can't handle one. Knowing about the bond puts the brakes on any new projects until we further understand it. Not anyone can be trusted with this power. I'm not sure if I should have it.

"I brought you something," I say to her as I enter her room in the infirmary.

She sits up, and I don't stop her. Gwen takes her tea. She sips on it and slides her palm down her stomach. At first I think she is being flirtatious, but remember her pregnancy.

"Thank you," she says.

I sit on the bed next to her. Her lips are on my neck and this time I don't flinch. Having what she wants makes her affectionate and docile. I don't have to worry about her sneaking off or injuring me with steel kisses. The bitter greens are satisfying. Most food has little flavor or interest for me. I eat because I have to. It's not that I hate food. It's another task. There are a limited number of foods piquing my tastebuds. Gwen seems to enjoy bitter greens as well. I hold a piece of pear in my hand. Giving it to her reminds me of zookeepers feeding tigers and bears.

CHAPTER TWENTY-TWO
GENESIS

Snow is coming down in swirling strands resembling the double helix of DNA. Gwen walks up and hugs my waist. She seems fascinated.

"Do you want to go outside?" I ask.

"Yes," she says into my shoulder.

We walk through the heavy door that keeps the Mantodea out but locks us in. The burst of cool air makes me shiver, but I enjoy it. The vibration in my body is like when animals shake off a trauma. Gwen is staring into her hand as she catches the snowflakes but they melt within seconds. She doesn't get to truly enjoy them because they are gone in an instant.

I got Gwen an absinthe green dress. Shades of red, orange, or magenta have been making me queasy. She was delighted I gave her a gift. I want to give her whatever she wants. She gives me everything. Together we walk through the powdery snow and hold hands. Gwen's wires are alert, but she is smiling.

"What do you think?" I ask as I gesture to the winter wonderland.

"It's amazing," she says with her eyes on the sky.

"Do you like the snow?"

I pick up a handful of it and let it fall through my hands. Gwen kneels down to feel the cold crunch of snowflakes.

"It's...exciting. I enjoy seeing the seasons change."

She stands up and stares up at me.

"Yeah," I say and reach for her stomach.

The seasons have new meaning. Passing time will result in something.

The word "season" reminds me of the Mantodea. Gwen has tried to fight them during their season of Birth but not Procreation. She is expected to attempt the decimation of the ship again. I know that is why she is here. The whole reason she exists. Part of me is with her, and I don't want her to take it to outer space. I love her. I love them both.

A slinky stoat runs across our path. Its beady eyes stare up at us. It makes a small chirp and runs off. Gwen giggles, covering her mouth like a real person. Her mannerisms are less severe, not as robotic, and quite becoming. It's nice to see the spark in her heart. She lights up when she thinks something is cute or sweet.

Gwen guides me closer to the black pines and cedars. I let her drag me into the shadow filled forest. Snowy owls call down to me. They have piercing yellow eyes. A twinge in my left temple interrupts my pace. I put my fingertips to the pain pulsing in my head.

"Are you okay?" she asks.

Her hand is on my heart. Glowing gold beams into my soul.

"I'm fine. Just a headache," I say and smile at her.

She walks slowly but keeps taking me further and further. Another stoat rustles the ferns to my right. He watches Gwen hold my fingertips the way a child holds onto a teddy bear or doll, right at the knuckle of the toy's hand. She is delighted by the wild roses, peonies, and daffodils. She picks a pink flower and puts it in the pocket of my lab coat.

It has stopped snowing, but it coats everything. The tops of the trees, boulders, and Gwen's head. It makes her appear angelic but also like a Norse goddess. She could be Freya, a warrior, pregnant, and in love with me. Gwen also resembles Ran, the goddess of the sea. She sometimes appeared as a mermaid. Hikari said Gwen has mermaid hair. It's an accurate description. It's such a light blonde, it's almost white.

The wires swish low to the ground. They aren't threatened. Nothing to be afraid of. Not really, anyway. From behind a hydrangea, I see two eyes peeking out at me. They belong to a fox. She is wary of us and stays in her hiding place. Gwen glances in her direction but doesn't bother her. There's a white daffodil with orange in the middle. It stands out against the bleached woods. Gwen picks it and puts it in my pocket next to the peony.

"Thank you," I say.

Gwen puts her lips on mine. They are hot against the winter weather. I know she's kissing me, but I feel covered in cold and apprehension. The headache has me feeling out of it. I kiss her back. My senses are dulled.

"I want you to see beautiful things all the time," she says and points to the flowers covering my heart.

"I get to see you every day."

My words feel syrupy in my mouth, but they are true. Gwen runs her fingers through my bangs. I've let them grow out.

"That's not what I mean."

"I know."

I can't help but let a small laugh escape me.

"The Mantodea's season of Procreation is approaching," she announces.

It jars me. Knowing it and hearing it are two separate things.

"When?" I choke.

"In four weeks," she announces. Gwen will be seven weeks along at that point. Not too far, but far enough that it worries me. I conceal my anxiety. She doesn't need me upsetting her.

"The team will have another weapon ready for you by then."

My voice is hollow, and the ache in my temple has spread to my forehead. Gwen pulls me closer and has me face her.

"I can do it. I'll be fine."

She puts her palm to her stomach and says she won't let anything happen.

"I know you can."

I let myself lie through my teeth. She is powerful and I believe her, but my baby inside her is in a situation no parent wants to see their child in.

"If I don't do this, you and our baby will be forced to stay secluded. I can't allow that."

"Does it upset you how our baby will be like me?" I ask.

We haven't really talked about this. She knows she is different.

"No. I want them to be like you," she says and reaches for my heart again.

It snows but very lightly. The adrenaline has my face on fire and the coolness of snowflakes is welcomed.

"Why is that?"

"I wish I was like you," she says.

Gwen's admission is bittersweet. I remember Hikari saying Gwen wanted to be like me.

"You're exceptional, Gwen. Don't forget it," I say and smooth her hair.

An owl sits in the tree above her. He has yellow eyes analyzing my every move. Its talons let go of the branch. They take off with fury, flinging powdery snow onto the ground.

"I love you," she says with sincerity before pushing me up against a cedar.

A wire wraps around the tree so she can hold me in place better. She's pulling at my belt buckle. Razor-sharp teeth graze my mouth and neck. Gwen has her wires, arms, and leg around me. The snow comes down in thin, steady strands. She keeps kissing my lips as she has her way with me, but it's like I'm not even there.

***

"No!"

"Hikari! Knock it off!" shouts his father.

The little boy is having a tantrum. Why? I have no idea.

"No! No!"

Hikari has large tears running down his face. He cannot process whatever emotions he is going through. Katsuo continues to be harsh with his son.

"You're too old to be acting like this," Katsuo says in a huff.

He grabs his son's shirt to try and control him.

"Let me go! You're mean. I hate you!" The little boy's words startle me. I know he doesn't mean it, but those words stop me in time. "I hate you."

The most vulgar string of words I can think of. Gwen comes walking down the hall. She is wearing a lemon yellow dress. I still can't look at the color red.

Gwen is studying the family affair with caution. Katsuo is being too rough with Hikari and Hikari is breaking down. I haven't been noticed yet. Gwen takes small steps towards the little boy. The wires are docile. Her face is flushed and her caramel freckles are darker. The Ex Machina nears the father and son. Katsuo turns to her, wide eyed, and on guard.

"Hikari, you shouldn't say that." Gwen's voice is authoritative.

"Why? I do."

Hikari is pulling away from Katsuo, who won't let him go. The little boy is sobbing and flailing like a fish.

"No, you don't."

Gwen says it very seriously and kneels down. Katsuo seems aggravated but allows her to speak with his son.

"He's mean. I'm running away!" screams the little boy.

His minuscule fists are punching invisible monsters. Gwen wraps her arms around him like a trapdoor spider. It makes Katsuo flinch and let go of his son's shirt.

"Listen to your father," she says and kisses him on top of the head.

The Ex Machina stands and continues down the hall towards the room with the water reservoir. Hikari calms down and sits on the ground. His knees are to his chest. Katsuo picks him up and carries him to their room. I duck into one of the rooms where no one is working. My lungs are brittle. The air is drying them out. I wheeze, trying to push my heart back into my chest.

"I hate you."

Why did the sentiment disturb me so much? I know why. My child may say the same thing to me. What if they feel the way I feel about my father? I want to be a good dad. Seeing the little boy's breakdown makes me realize how unequipped I am for such a feat. Then my stomach drops. What if one day Gwen says it to me?

Isamu and Nori have left their blueprints out. I examine the weapon they have designed. It is similar to the spear they made her, but it has three prongs, like a trident. It appears to have the same technology that absorbs the atmosphere's electrical energy and stores it as Gwen leaves earth. The three prongs should be able to hold more power. My temple stings like it's been set on fire. The migraine is setting in.

I thumb through their paperwork. Well calculated, educated, and professional. At least my team is able to live up to the standard. While they've been crafting tangible solutions, I've been battling an invisible war of love and death. Nori drew a diagram of the weapon and oxygen tank on Gwen. I slam down the pencil smudged paper. Exiting the room in frustration, I run into Katsuo.

"Hey," I say in a friendly way.

Katsuo takes a long drag off of his cigarette. His son isn't with him.

"Bellamy, can I talk to you for a minute?"

"Sure."

"Do you know what it means to be a father?" he asks with cigarette smoke in his teeth.

"It means a lot of things," I shrug.

Katsuo smirks and crosses his arms at me.

"Adam Krim was a remarkable scientist," starts Katsuo. He takes another drag, long and smooth. He holds it in his mouth before blowing it towards the ceiling. "That didn't make him a great father," he finishes.

"My father and I are not the same person."

"The same person, no. Similar in personality and habit, yes."

"You never met him. How do you know?"

"No one has to meet someone with status like your father to fill in the skeletal parts of them," he says and narrows his eyes.

"I'm not him."

"Like father, like son," he says.

Katsuo shoulder checks me as he walks down the hall. This unnerves me. I'm unsettled. Rushing towards the water reservoir, I wait to see the tornado that's too big to fit in a glass. Instead of reaching my hand into the ink black darkness, I sit in the chair by the cameras.

They capture the dark water. Bubbles float by in a dreamy fashion. The fluorescent light overhead glows like a white orb. An artificial sun. I know she is in there. She hides from me. I sit and wait. Her wires tell her I'm watching. They know where I am. I can't escape her. She can't escape me.

I contemplate lighting up a cigarette, but don't. Gwen would be displeased to taste tobacco on me. I don't want to get the sticky scent of tar in her pretty hair. Wishing for golden eyes to appear, they do. She waves to the camera. Her smile is wide. Bubble kisses fill the screen. They are numerous. It must make her feel like she's winning the game. I used to try and beat her. Now I let her win.

***

Hotaka and I are having breakfast together. It's nice. He and I are listening to some of our favorite electronic-pop songs. It makes us laugh. We pretend to be normal. The other scientists are polite but disengaged. They work for me, but

I'm far removed from their vision. My pregnant robotic hybrid girlfriend is our only hope. She is our savior. Gwen is my salvation. Does willing her into existence make me a god?

"I love that song," says Hotaka. He sips his tea with contentment and a childish smile.

"You have great taste in music," I joke.

We have listened to the same bands for over twenty years. We eat and drum our chopsticks at certain parts of the song. I've been making a point of watching my health. Hotaka and I are having salads with an assortment of vegetables. The leafy greens, carrots, and cucumbers are fine by me, but watching Hotaka stab into a piece of tomato makes me want to gag. The squish of the flesh as it separates from the skin is sickening. I look away.

"You two must be excited," he announces. I shake my head up and down.

"Very much so," I say.

"It's amazing to see such a union."

"You're not disgusted by us like everyone else?" I ask.

Hotaka would never admit it if we did. He isn't like the rest of my team.

"Nobody is disgusted," he says as he peeks at me over the rims of his glasses.

"That's how they act."

I shrug and keep eating. It's not of interest to me to entertain them.

"I think everyone is a little nervous. But to see such a bond, a connection, a merging of worlds. It's incredible, Bell."

"Thank you. Everyone thinks I'm just some playboy loser, but I really didn't expect this. I have to say that I'm happy with the way things turned out. If it makes me a pariah, then so be it. I love her," I say.

Hotaka is eying me with an expression I can't read. I put on a song I would listen to before I played a game. When I hear it, I smell fresh cut grass and feel dirt on my knees and face. I remember wearing it like war paint.

"Love is…" Hotaka is careful with his words. He seeks out the right one. In his mind is a labyrinth of words like a library. He finds the one he is looking for, "incalculable."

It's a million dollar word. He wins this time.

"It is," I whisper to myself.

Hotaka grins at me.

"I'm glad it's you who she saw and not your father."

"Why's that?" I ask.

My friend's words seep in. I'm touched, but also curious.

"You love her the way she should be loved," he says and stands up.

I'm left with my thoughts. The low lights make it seem late, but it's daytime. I get up and walk around to wake myself from the dazed state.

Gwen has only been awake for eight months, yet we've gone through all the phases. Meeting, getting acquainted, curiosity, and now we're already at the point where she's pregnant. I'm not complaining. It's going fast enough to knock me out of orbit.

The heart of the machine wants to be close to mine. Has the device changed her heart? Thoughts and feelings are intertwined. We altered her mind drastically. She is human but also very much something else.

She probably wants her space, but I crave her. If she isn't going to let me smoke, then I need reassurance. The constant jitters have me refusing anything with caffeine. I look okay but feel panicky. Being an actual adult is terrifying. Gwen isn't in her room. Her bed is unmade and a romance novel sits on the covers. I put my hand to it but can't pick it up. The grey blanket is staring at me.

I linger at her desk that she treats as a vanity. The red lipstick sits off to the side on the right. I grimace at it. The morbid shade of deep crimson makes my throat close. I shift my attention to her trinkets. A dried purple cosmo, a quartz, an acorn, and a maple leaf. The Ex Machina wishes for us to be outside all the time.

Leaving her room, I run into Yui. She puts her head down and scurries past me. She mumbles "hello" but keeps fast walking with her tiny rushed footsteps. I head towards the room with the water reservoir. No bubble kisses on the screen. I wait. Nothing. She's not swimming. I check by the front door. Only Isamu and Nori are sitting on the couch out here. She must be in my room.

I loosen my tie. Talking to Gwen chokes me out some days. She is worth missing breaths. My lungs can't seem to fully inhale. I try to breathe deeply but am met with resistance. The adrenaline is fighting me. I arrive at my room. My door is ajar.

"Gwen?" I call her name. She's not in my bed or at my desk. I knock on my bathroom door. "Gwen, are you in there?"

No response. I open the door to find a miserable situation. Gwen is naked, crying in the tub with blood between her legs. It's all over her. Sheer scarlet splotches are on her arms and thighs. There are streaks of red on the sides of the tub. It's everywhere. I try not to stand there dumbfounded and help her. "Gwen," I say her name into her ear as I put my arms around her shoulders. She's not making much noise, but endless streams of tears pour out.

"Why is this happening?" she sobs into my neck.

I stroke her hair and rub her back to soothe her.

"I don't know. I'll run some tests. I'm sorry," I tell her.

The smell of blood is strong. It's immature, but I don't want to look at it. Apples, strawberries, and plums have been making me ill. It's because they remind me too much of the color of miscarriage. Tomatoes resemble the sickening texture of aborted flesh. I don't know what to do to comfort my girlfriend. Shit, I don't know how to handle this myself.

"Please, help me."

She is pulling at my lab coat. I have her use me to steady herself and stand. Guiding her to the shower, I gesture for her to get in. She is clinging to me and shakes her head "no." I take off my tie. She won't let go of my neck. I tear off my lab coat, shirt, and pants. The steam from the shower eases my growing headache. I get in and she follows. There's blood caked on her hands and in the bottom of her hair.

I clean her hands as she sobs. This is painful for me too, but I try to be strong since she has to do everything. I'm on the sidelines. I wash her hair and when I rinse it out, it tints the white foamy bubbles the color of Cabernet. Looking down gives me vertigo. My girlfriend is miscarrying again. It brings our dreams down the drain with the bubbles. I hold Gwen close and look out the distorted glass at the red massacre that took place in my bathtub.

CHAPTER TWENTY-THREE
CATASTROPHE

She doesn't need to sleep but is laying down. I dimmed the lights, but it's late morning. Gold reflects off the shiny metal wall. We haven't spoken much, but we are closer than before. Gwen isn't the same. Where I was once met with cool detachment has been replaced by an intimacy neither of us has experienced.

Her hair spills onto my lap and over the bed. I'm brushing out the tangles. Her romance novels and children's books are next to me. I look at their covers and titles to better see inside the heart of the machine. Hikari wanted to visit Gwen last night, but she wasn't in the mood for company. The little boy was sad but said he understood Gwen was sad. He isn't aware of what happened to her, only that something is missing from her life.

"How are you today, Beautiful?" I ask. With great care, I brush the hair around the device.

"I'm okay," she says into her pillow. I cleaned up the blood in the tub a week ago, but I still don't like going in there. .

"Hey you two," says Hotaka.

He smiles at me, and I can tell it's real. Gwen sits up to greet him.

"Hi Hotaka," she says.

"Are you ready, Gwen?" he asks.

She nods her head. Hotaka guides us into one of the exam rooms in the infirmary. It's bright in here. White walls, white lights, white coats. Hotaka said he would help me run some tests on her. I'm curious why she keeps miscarrying. Her body is perfectly healthy. Energy levels are good. She doesn't plug into the battery at all. Gwen has been consuming the necessary nutrients to sustain a pregnancy.

Hotaka and I have already spoken about this. He offered to assist me. I'm pretty smart when it comes to engineering something, but at a loss of what to do with the health of my girlfriend. Thankfully, Hotaka is a medical doctor with advanced certifications.

I feel awkward laying Gwen down on the table. She is nervous. Hotaka is professional and calm. He covers her with the sheet to keep her modesty. Gwen is holding my hand and staring at me with sad, glowing eyes with tears in them. I kiss her cheek. This cheers her up, but barely.

"It's okay. I'm right here," I say.

Gwen grips my hand with both of hers.

"This won't take long," Hotaka says with confidence.

He is washing his hands and putting on gloves. He grabs the instruments and begins setting up. I can tell Gwen is scared. The Ex Machina can fight armies in space but is just as human as any other person.

"Tell me what you think of the snow," I say, trying to distract her.

"It's amazing," she says.

"You're from Norway, where there are heavy winters and lots of snow," I tell her. "I used to think you were dreaming about snow when you were in stasis," I say.

The gold eyes cease to glow. She is smiling.

"Really?" she asks.

"Yes, that's why you have a wintery name. Gwen means 'white'."

"Did you pick my name?" she asks.

Hotaka is sanitizing everything and humming one of his favorite songs.

"Yes," I say.

My dad and I chose it together, but I don't want to talk about him.

"Are you ready?" asks Hotaka, who brings us back to the present.

I take a painful breath. My inhale is deeper, but it still doesn't seem like enough air.

"Yes," says Gwen.

Hotaka sits in the chair across from me on the other side. He instructs Gwen to put her legs up. She seems embarrassed. I look at her and then at Hotaka. She does as she's told and closes her eyes.

"You're going to feel a little pressure but it's nothing to worry about, okay?" says Hotaka in his reassuring way.

He peeks at me over the rim of his glasses to see how I'm doing. I'm sure I look like I'm freaking out.

"I'm scared," she whispers to me.

It rips my heart out.

"Don't be. Hotaka is going to take good care of you, and I'm right here. I'm not going anywhere," I say.

Hotaka turns on the screen and hits a few buttons.

"I'm going to insert the hysteroscope now," he says.

Gwen tightens her grip on me. I grit my teeth. Gwen's eyes are shut, and she's grimacing. Hotaka's attention is on his work and on the screen. I watch the Ex Machina cower from the medical device. Looking up, I see the instrument is passing through her cervix into the uterus. The shades of red, pink, and violet churn my stomach. I stay in place, though. Gwen needs me here with her.

I turn my gaze to her. The cutest little freckled nose. Her mermaid hair falls onto my lap. Fluorescent lights make it shine like a halo around the crown of her skull.

Hotaka says my name. I look up at the screen. It takes a minute. I can't tell what I'm seeing. Then I realize within her womb are the tiny splinters of the metallic strands. I cough. Gwen doesn't look at the screen, but stares up at me.

* * *

In our most defeated hour, I've been alone. Gwen flew somewhere. To space, to the lake, through the forest, where she goes, I'm not sure. All I know is the emptiness I feel can't compare to what she is experiencing. Hotaka was kind about it, but there is no way to console someone with a matter like this. Miscarriage is common but to be caused by robotic threads meant to connect the synapses, strengthen the bones, and fortify the organs—I would have never guessed it would compromise living tissue not belonging to her. Not that pregnancy was ever theorized or contemplated for the Ex Machina.

There are numerous journals and notes, but nothing to explain what's been happening to me. To us. Our fatal romance. The imprinting may have done something to me as well. My father left me in the dark. He surely did this on purpose. I shouldn't speak ill of the dead, but I resent him for what he did to my mom and Nyx. What were his true intentions with Gwen?

I'm getting distracted. I pace around the laboratory at least twenty times a day. If I stay in motion, then I feel less sick. I feel bile come up at the thought of red fruit. The scent of anything scarlet: cherries, lipstick, and blood nauseates me. I pass by Nori in the hall. He looks at the breast pocket of my lab coat. Staring down, I notice a copper stain. Gwen's blood. Our baby's blood. It's been on my coat, my jacket, my tub, and sheets.

"I apologize, Dr. Krim," he says into his sternum and rushes past me.

I make everyone skittish. Shira and Katsuo cast judgemental glances in my direction. They've never had what I have. It's incomprehensible to anyone other than me. Hotaka has a vague idea, but admits being unable to truly understand. This makes him the most valuable scientist, not because he is my friend. Anyone who thinks they know everything knows nothing. I'm reconsidering how smart Katsuo and Isamu may be.

I told Gwen we could conceive in other ways, but she wouldn't have it. She told me it wasn't the same. I said the end product would be. She said I could never be destroyed by this the way she is. That's not true. I am

160

devastated. She told me what she wants and I'm trying to give it to her. I asked her why she was against it and she said it was because she wanted the real thing. To feel our baby inside her. The closeness. Gwen said she didn't want our child growing in a tank like her. She wants them to be like me. To be normal.

That's when she ran off on me again. I try so hard to be a good guy. Maybe trying this hard means I'm just not. I love her, but I might not be good for her. Remembering my youth and how I felt like I raised her brings on the awful migraine. Pudgy goldfish swim in my brain. They die and bloat. It presses against my skull.

I go into the room where she was born. Putting my hand to the glass calms me. I sit in the chair and admire the blue glow of the tank. A tornado was created here. History was made. She's not in here anymore, but I keep my hand to the glass. It makes me feel like she knows I'm there for her. My insomnia catches up with me and I fall asleep leaning against the tank where my fate was made.

"Bellamy?" says Yui.

She is holding a cup of hot tea. It smells gingery with a hint of citrus.

"Yes, sorry. I fell asleep," I say in embarrassment.

Rubbing my temples and running my fingers through my hair, I look up at the young scientist.

"Here," she says and holds out the drink to me.

"Thank you."

"That day was exhilarating," she says as she stares at the artificial womb.

"The best day of my life."

"I wanted to meet your father. I became a scientist because I was so inspired by him. The work he did. When I came to work for you, it was a dream come true," she states.

It stuns me momentarily. Yui has never been personal with me.

"I was impressed by your dedication and credentials."

I smile sheepishly, unsure of what else to say.

"I think it's best Gwen saw you first."

"Why?" I ask.

Yui looks at the steam coming off my tea. I take a sip.

"You are the better choice. Your father, as genius as he was, would not be able to take the necessary measures to keep the Ex Machina happy."

I know what she is implying.

"I really love her, Yui."

The young scientist examines my face.

"This is why I said what I said."

With that, she saunters off.

***

Gwen comes back to me like nothing happened. She hasn't brought it up. I haven't either. It didn't hurt too bad at first. A mild sting followed by an annoying ache. The pain of knowing what's happening to her, what's happening to me, starts shutting down my organs. I smile at her, though. If I don't smile, she doesn't smile.

She is leaning against my left side with her arms around my shoulder while I go over my notes on the Mantodea. Her new weapon, the trident, will be ready tonight. I don't want her to go, but if I don't let her, the whole team will surely dog pile and rip me to shreds. Then Gwen will murder them all. Not the outcome I want.

"What are you looking for?" she asks and kisses my neck.

The titanium teeth no longer put me on edge. I've become accustomed to them grazing the artery in my throat.

"Seeing if I can find anything useful to help you," I say.

Gwen wants to win. Maybe she didn't before, but she does now. She has something to fight for.

"The Mantodea are unpredictable. They know me, but I think I can destroy the ship this time."

"I know you can."

Her eyes are glowing bright gold and searing me from the inside. The hazel beneath is barely visible. Gwen is strategic. She is planning in a relentless manner. For the past three days, she's refused to eat and only accepts electricity as her source of energy. My girlfriend's behavior has been bizarre, but ever since we saw the tiny steel threads in her uterus, she has been icy and robotic.

I thumb through the notes. Nothing I don't already know. The Mantodea are seasonal breeders; they have a hive mind, and they are much more intelligent than they appear. Nymphs are smaller than the adult male and females, but just as ruthless. They are tactical fighters. The exoskeleton seems to be the biggest issue. Gwen can zap them off the individual aliens, but the ship is covered in the same material. I hope the three-pronged electrical weapon we made can be enough to annihilate the ship and the army of aliens inside.

Blond hair scented like snow keeps distracting me. I continue to focus on my work. Gwen hasn't seemed angry with me, but I am tense. I said something that upset her enough to take off and leave me wondering if she'll ever come back. To make up for her absence, she stays by my side most hours of the day. I encourage her to swim or play with Hikari, but she says she wants to be with me.

Gwen runs the white tips of her nails up my neck and massages my scalp. It no longer startles me. She adjusts the collar of my lab coat and runs her other hand down my face. The way she touches me reminds me of being played with, like a toy. I sit still and hear the rattlesnakes behind me.

Things have been awkward between me and Hotaka. He wasn't expecting this either. Neither of us knows how to respond to this. Hotaka is a professional but also my friend. Gwen is devastated. She can be the love of my life, but may not be able to be the mother of my child. She doesn't say anything, though. Her cheek is on my shoulder and I want a cigarette so badly.

"You don't want me to go," she states.

I swallow the rock in my throat.

"I don't want you to get hurt."

"Nothing can hurt me anymore," she says and pulls away from me.

"Please, be careful."

I'm nervous Gwen is going to be careless.

"I'll come back to you."

She touches my face but doesn't look in my direction. The glowing eyes focus intently on preparing to kill the Mantodea.

"Are you angry with me?" I ask.

This gets her attention. Her gaze is burning my eyes out of their socket.

"No. I can't be. You do everything for me."

"It's okay if you are."

"I'm disappointed. My heart makes it hard to think properly. I'm sorry."

"Don't apologize," I say and kiss her.

She goes back to leaning on me. The device has enhanced her mind. It has created a god. How cruel for it to take away her ability to make life. The rest of her organs benefit from the steel infusion. Nobody bothered to think about the Ex Machina's desires.

Gwen refuses to eat dinner with me. She inserts the metal jacks into the battery and continues to ponder ways to defeat the Mantodea. The time comes where she is expected to leave. Nori, Isamu, and Katsuo carry out the magnificent weapon. I see them inspecting it by the front door. Shira holds Gwen's oxygen tank and respirator. Yui, Hotaka, and Hikari are standing off to the side, taking in what's happening. Tonight may be the night Gwen destroys the ship. But what if she doesn't come back? Hikari and I exchange worried glances. We both have long faces.

I'm standing by myself. This is my team, my lab, my project, yet I have no sense of control. Everything is happening to me instead of resulting from me paving a way. Gwen comes up to my side. Her arms are around my neck.

"I love you, Bellamy."

"I love you."

I want to say more, but the words are lost to me. She walks off and lets her hand fall off my shoulder. I stand frozen in time. Nori hooks up her oxygen tank and inserts the respirator. Katsuo and Isamu hand her the trident. I turn my head to face Hotaka. He nods at me and Yui looks down. So does Hikari. When I look up, Gwen is staring at me. She puts two fingers to her respirator and holds out her hand in my direction, signaling she is blowing me a kiss. I catch it and she waves goodbye to me like a normal girl.

CHAPTER TWENTY-FOUR
BEETLES

Waiting is agonizing. I sit on the couch and fidget like a child. It brings no peace of mind and I go into my room. I pull back my sheets and fan the wildflower scent across the bed. Light of my life, the girl of my dreams, the soft scent of deadly white flowers brings her back to me. I wrap myself up in the memory of her.

"Bell?"

Hotaka has let himself in my room. He sits in the chair next to my bed and rubs his left shoulder.

"Hey," I whisper.

My voice is quiet and hoarse.

"You shouldn't worry so much," he says in a friendly way.

"How can I not?"

"I know. She is quite remarkable, though." There is a deep silence between us. It builds and boils over. Black water foaming gray and indigo.

"No one seems to understand that she is more than a machine," I declare to the pillowcase.

Hotaka takes off his glasses and sighs.

"I do. Gwen is my friend. She isn't just something made in a lab. I care about her," he says.

I sit up and white knuckle my sheets.

"Then why do we insist on her saving us, even if it means sacrificing herself?" I ask through gritted teeth.

"I never asked for her to do that."

Hotaka gives me a grave look.

"It is implied," I say and lay back down.

"Nobody is telling you what to do. You sign the checks. This is your lab.

We are your employees, and Gwen has chosen you. It's not up to anyone else."

"The others make me feel like a reckless playboy," I admit.

Hotaka stands and brushes himself off. I don't know if it is the dust in the air or the bullshit.

"I know who you really are. So does Gwen," he says and exits my room.

I lay back down and ponder the life I've lived, the life I have, who I am. What I was.

The days before the Mantodea weren't peaceful, but in comparison, they were calm. Almost unnoticeable in their normality. There was school, homework, baseball, and all the things in between. We didn't seem busy until my life came to a halt. Then I realized how much I was missing out on. I never skipped a class or pranked someone. Although I've seen it a thousand times in movies, I've never danced with a girl. I don't know what it's like to graduate from college. I've never driven a car.

Waiting feels like being dead, but goes much slower. Death in suspended motion. Hotaka says Gwen is his friend, but is he injured by her absence the way I am? No. It's like a paper cut, an annoyance. For me, it's a deep gash across my chest. I feel it completely. Pain can be a satisfying emotion if there is enough of it. Looking at my watch, I see it's been an hour. Gwen should be back soon. Should.

I get up and head back towards the front door. The others are already gathered around. Shira is tapping her foot with folded arms. Katsuo is frustrated trying to calm down Hikari. Nori and Isamu nod at me but turn the other way. Yui gives me a small smile. I stand next to Hotaka and he puts his hand on my shoulder. She should be less than eleven minutes away.

There is a slight rumble. We all look out the window. Nothing. The pen Yui dropped is rattling on the ground. It's barely audible as I kneel to pick it up, but I notice it. Yui has a worried expression as I hand it to her. I walk closer to the door and my team stands behind me. Their eyes bore into the back of my head.

Outside, there is nothing out of the ordinary. Up in the sky is a battle between angels and demons. A story of gods and monsters. I stare at the black pines and cedars. There is the hill where cosmos grow and I get a twinge in my chest thinking of Gwen and I laying in the tall grass like yin and yang. To summon her back, I put my hand on the glass as I did when she was in stasis. Science is magic we don't understand and somehow it works. Gwen is cutting through the sky at breakneck speed. I feel proud of her—until I see that thing. It's not like the other Mantodea.

This thing is massive. It looks like four female Mantodea intertwined. The exoskeleton is shiny and black. There are no dents or nicks in its armor. This thing looks untouched. It chases Gwen, and she flies back and forth trying to shake it. The wings penetrate the air and the sky rumbles. Gwen is fast, but this thing is faster. It strikes her and she hits the ground. She gets up immediately and takes off before it can squash her into the earth.

The battle between a goddess and a monster continues. Gwen doesn't seem to be attacking. She is only evading the Mantodea's advances. The creature nears her again. My stomach seizes up. It comes down on her but strikes the oxygen tank. Gwen takes out the respirator and flies straight up. The monster follows. I'm not sure what it is. The Mantodea have been around for twenty years, but I've never seen one that looks like this. Gwen lands in front of the door and begins hitting it with her fist.

"Bellamy," she calls for me and I watch the alien land behind her and screech. Hitting the button on the door, it opens. I grab her and pull her inside right as the creature lunges at us. The door closes just in time. It's all black body is flawless despite being hideous. It roars and backs up. The monsters are smart, but have never been able to access the electronic keypad to enter the lab. I assumed when Gwen was sneaking out, she learned how to get back in by guessing all the possible number combinations. Thankfully, the aliens haven't caught on.

"Gwen, are you alright?" I ask.

She is clinging onto my lab coat and staring outside. My team and her all have their eyes on that thing, but my eyes are on her.

"I...couldn't do it," she says and starts to cry.

The older male scientists look pissed off, but everyone else is sympathetic.

"What happened?" asks Isamu.

Nori and Katsuo wait eagerly to learn about their weapon.

"I was making progress eliminating the exoskeleton from the ship. The trident worked efficiently. I was sure I could destroy the spacecraft," she starts. Her gold eyes are back on the beast. "Until they sent that thing after me," she whispers. The alien screeches one last time before flying back into space.

"What was it?" asks Yui.

She has her notepad out, hand ready to write. Always ready to learn.

"I'm not sure. During Procreation, all the Mantodea go inside the ship. At least, that's what I thought. Because they have been aware of me, they are more and more prepared to ward me off. They made it to protect them during their vulnerable season," says Gwen.

I tighten my hold on her and try to hide my worried face in her hair.

"The aliens made another one of them?" asks Hotaka.

"Yes," she says.

All the scientists turn to each other in confusion and horror. Hikari breaks away from his dad and runs up to Gwen. He puts his little arms around her waist and stares up at us.

"I'm glad you're okay, Gwen," says Hikari.

I let her go so she can hug him.

"I'm sorry I didn't win," says Gwen.

She takes Hikari's face in her hands. Katsuo is agitated by this and I smile to myself. The Ex Machina has a better connection with the kid than any of us. My smile fades, realizing we may never get to experience having our own child.

"It's okay. I still love you," says Hikari.

This makes Gwen's eyes flicker.

"I love you," she says it back as Katsuo takes Hikari's hand.

Shira is at his side and the three of them walk away together. The other scientists scatter. Gwen and I go back to my room. Now that she's back, I feel the weight of my aching muscles, so I lay down. I don't have to ask her, and she curls up to me. She is disappointed. I run my hand through her hair and keep her close to my chest with my other arm.

"I'm so happy you're back," I say.

"But I lost."

"Don't say that." I hold her in blissful silence but notice an off-putting sensation on my hand touching her back. Peeking over her shoulder, I see red. There's blood on my fingertips. "Gwen, you're bleeding," I say in surprise.

She sits up and I check her spine to see claw marks. The Mantodea landed a hit. Gwen is startled by the sight of her own blood.

"It knocked the weapon out of my hand in space. I didn't stand a chance," she says.

"Promise me you'll never go into space again. I don't care if you go outside, but please don't go back to the ship."

I cling onto her.

"But then I can't save you, Bellamy."

"I don't care."

She stays in my grasp and this time I know I won't wake up alone.

***

I'm spitting up blood in the sink. Gwen bit my tongue. Not very hard. It wasn't aggressive like the time she bit my lip. I don't think we should try again, but it's what she wants. Her womb is inhospitable, and so is the earth. Everything about this is impracticable and illogical.

Cold water on my face helps me get it together. I go back and forth from happiness to merciless dread. When I'm ignorant and acting like we are a normal couple, I'm fine. It's when I'm reminded of her purpose, what she's become, and what I've done, I feel the walls closing in on me. My headaches make me sensitive to the fluorescents. I dim the lights in my room. Gold eyes greet me if I'm lucky.

In the dark, I'm cradled by fatal arms. She holds me the way a child holds a toy. I am held captive but seek no escape. Gwen is my hideaway. Not truly a place, more of a feeling. I can't find the word for it. A mixture of love, fear, and devotion. During the day, I have a million racing thoughts. I do my rounds, go over everyone's notes, and plot a way to free us without sacrificing her. I can't do it.

"I'm sorry," she whispers.

In the mirror, I watch as her arms slither around my waist. The wires fan out behind me. The illusion makes me appear as the Ex Machina. I look over my shoulder to see Gwen's face pressed against my back. "I didn't mean to."

"It's okay."

I rinse my mouth with water. It's a sheer red. The bleeding has almost stopped. The side of my tongue stings from the tiny incision her steel canine has made.

"Please don't be mad at me."

"I'm not mad at you. I've been having these awful migraines. They make me tense," I say.

"Anything I can do?" she asks.

"No, I just have a lot on my mind. Don't worry about it," I say to comfort her.

Gwen doesn't seem content with my answer, but she lets it go.

I suspect my team is turning rabid. Animals with jagged teeth, ready to pounce. Nori has softened his demeanor towards me, but Isamu and Katsuo are most annoyed by my presence. Hikari likes me, though. That's all that really matters. He holds a piece of Gwen's heart and that makes him not only unique but valuable. Like me.

Yui has also been quite kind to me. She sits with me if she sees I'm alone. Not longer than ten minutes, but she makes a point to show interest in me. It's like the miscarriage made her see me as more than just Adam Krim's son, her boss, the guy who is screwing the Ex Machina. In a way, I think Yui sees me as an actual person. Maybe as a friend.

Around Shira, the air turns thick and imperious. She is cordial, but fake. We make small talk and I have a tight jaw the whole time. I can tell she's using our brief conversations to survey my mood. She watches me with a cold, but intense stare. "Are you happy now?" they seem to say. The vexing part is I'm elated but also deeply depressed. I don't think I can give my girlfriend what she wants. She can't give me what I want without killing herself. I'm running out of time. The others will turn on me, eventually.

Hotaka is a true friend. A glorious being. He cares about people with intimacy. Not in the distant way most medical professionals do. His eyes smile when his mouth doesn't. When the team comes to rip me apart, he'll probably try to put me back together. Gwen tugs on me and guides me back to my bed. I lay down, but she doesn't.

"I'm going to go swimming," she says.

"Okay." I'm exhausted.

Rest without the nagging sensation of being next to an apex predator would be appreciated.

"Sleep well."

She kisses me and the wires rattle as she slips down the hall. Blackness takes over too quickly and consumes me.

Everything is monochromatic blue tones. I'm walking through a field of tall grass. There are cosmos and lily of the valley lining the path I'm on. A waning crescent disappears from the sky and it turns out the lights. The waxing crescent illuminates the forest and I can see where I'm going. I keep walking deeper and deeper into the dark.

"Bellamy," I hear my name and open my eyes.

Gwen is calling for me. I turn around. She's standing in front of the lab. I'm outside, standing right by the woods. Black pines and cedars loom over me.

When I was seventeen, I started sleepwalking several times a month for a year. It drove my dying mother insane. The men who worked for my dad thought I was more and more unusual by the minute. At least three nights a week, I wandered around the lab like a zombie. I must have been quite a spectacle.

I attributed it to the stress of isolation. My family was falling apart. Although incredibly wealthy, I felt like I had nothing. No sense of purpose, place, or personhood. How does one know who they are if they are never given the chance to experience life? I tried to be grateful for the comfortable lifestyle we retained after the Mantodea invaded, but resent the empty void that has grown inside me. It's a part of me. Like a nerve or tendon.

By the time I was twenty-two, I stopped sleepwalking. I only did it once while with Sophia. She said she found me in the room where Gwen was. Apparently, I was standing in front of the tank with my eyes closed. Sophia said she guided me back to my room, where I went back to bed without any problems. I never thought anything of it.

"Bellamy!"

She calls my name again. I hear rustling in the bushes behind me. A shrew comes running out in a hurry. It rushes past my left foot. I sigh in relief. Then I hear a much louder noise from something bigger. It shakes the ground and pebbles vibrate in the dirt. A roaring screech is echoing from the dark forest.

A bat flies out and over me. I take my first step towards Gwen. She is running at me with impressive speed. Somehow, she isn't fast enough. The Nymph is right on me. It's not as massive as the females and adult males, but this won't stop it from killing me. I dodge its attack that tears up the ground. This agitates it and the creature rears up and screams. I keep running towards Gwen, who is so fast but can't close the gap before I feel a sharp claw in the middle of my back.

The Ex Machina reaches me as I collapse. As the Nymph aims to crush my skull, Gwen sinks her stingers into its head and abdomen. I cover my eyes, but the gravel in a blender noise brings on a dreadful headache. It rattles my brain and vibrates in my heart. I can't tell how bad my wound is because I'm not here anymore.

CHAPTER TWENTY-FIVE
DEVOTION

There is a beep. Then another. I think it's my heartbeat on the monitor. My hand is gripping the crisp sheet. I'm not in my bed. This is the infirmary. I smell the sterile cleaner and hear equipment buzz and hum.

"Please, wake up," says Gwen. I'm not ready to open my eyes, but I hold my palm open and she takes it. "Don't die." I hear her start to cry.

"I'm right here," I say.

My voice is raspy. We sit together and listen to the symphony of the machines. My head hurts. I have a raw, burning sensation between my shoulder blades where the Nymph struck me. In my half awake state, I thought it penetrated my heart. Gwen is touching my hair and face. I wish my eyelids weren't so heavy.

"Bellamy?"

Hotaka's voice is in my ear. I turn in his direction and open an eye. It's too bright. Hotaka dims the fluorescent bulbs.

"Hey," I cough.

"You really gave us a scare," he says and adjusts his glasses.

His smile is wide.

"Am I going to be okay?" I ask.

Gwen has her hand in my shirt. I put my palm over hers.

"Yes. But you're going to have to take it easy the next few weeks. I had to cauterize the wound. It's susceptible to opening again and getting infected. No harsh movements or strenuous activity, okay?"

"Got it, doc," I half joke and regret it.

My lungs are made out of metal.

"I'm serious, Funny Guy," he teases and gets up.

Gwen waits for him to exit the room to crawl into the infirmary bed with me.

It's not as big as the beds in our rooms. She is careful laying down next to me. Now that I can open my eyes, I see hers are hazel with tears spilling out.

"It's okay, Beautiful. I'll be fine," I say and put my hand in her hair.

Making a fist is difficult. My muscles reject the idea.

"Watching the Nymph hurt you...it made me feel powerless. I was afraid," she says into my shirt.

"You tried to help me."

"But I didn't make it in time."

"Yes, you did. I'm alive because you saved me."

"I want to save you. All of you," she says, and it heals me in a way I didn't think possible.

"I'm glad you do."

I slip in and out of consciousness. It's like the tide going out and coming back in. I touch the same sand but move further towards the horizon. It's been years since I've seen the beach. I smell salt and rosemary. My dad never went to the beach with us. That didn't stop my mom from taking me and my friends. At the time, I didn't think it was bizarre how estranged I was from my father. He was changing the world. I was just a child.

I wake up and grab the blanket with white knuckles. She's not here. The lights are low and I'm alone. I pull off the electrodes and remove my IV. My migraine is gone, but the pain in between my shoulders is a fiery sting. I get out of bed and stand on my feet. No shakiness to my surprise. I make my way to the bathroom. In the full-length mirror, I examine my back.

There is a hefty amount of gauze wrapped around my chest and left shoulder. Looking at the middle, I see a large bandage. It's covering the surely horrendous wound. I put my shirt back down. I've seen enough. My heart is loose in my chest and bounces when I walk. I'm faint and should probably eat.

It's the middle of the night, 3:13am. I make my way to the kitchen and make myself a cup of tea and have one of the nutrition bars meant to supplement a meal. I don't feel like eating actual food. It's a necessity, not a luxury. What I really want is to go back to sleep in my bed. I sip on my jasmine green tea with my eyes half closed until it's cold and unsatisfying.

In my room there is no one, but I smell something fragrant, white, and dewy. I search around my bed. At the foot of it is a green stem with bell-shaped flowers. I lay down and hold them to my chest. I fall asleep and when I dream I dream about gold butterflies being crushed by a mechanical praying mantis.

"Bellamy," she says my name and puts one hand in my hair and the other on my heart where I'm guarding the little white flowers.

Over my shoulder, I spy glowing eyes in the darkness of my room.

"Hey Beautiful," I whisper.

She traces my collarbone and pauses on the stem of the lily of the valley.

"You shouldn't be walking around. You're hurt really bad."

"I wanted to be in my bed." Gwen slips in beside me. Lethal arms hold me and I couldn't be happier.

"Sweet dreams," she says into my ear as she kisses the side of my neck.

Visions of poisonous insects with fatal stingers come to mind. Her lips hit me like morphine and knock me out as if she punched me.

***

I got the flu when I was twenty-four. Eva took care of me. My back ached. I was throwing up everything—including water, but somehow we laughed it off. It was the end of the world and I was bedridden. It was kind of funny. Irony was something we both noticed. Maybe because we sought it out. Everything is funny if you think about it.

Nothing compares to the connection of being taken care of. Thousands of years ago, people would break a bone and die. It's not until someone takes care of the ill and tends to the wounded that a foundation can be built. To gain trust, some must be given. Civilization couldn't exist without this fundamental exchange.

Hotaka changed my bandage. I saw my injury in the mirror. It's a large blister in the middle of my back with a ripple effect of smaller burns. I'm lucky it hasn't reopened or gotten infected. The color red sickens me and I dismiss inspecting it further.

Gwen has been insistent on me staying in bed and only allows me to walk around with her assistance. I let her tell me what to do. She wants me to be safe and alive. I haven't thought about it until recently, but I wonder what the Ex Machina would do if I died.

The Mantodea don't always eat people. Many of them shred flesh apart for entertainment. During the beginning of the invasion, I saw the news broadcast about the aliens attacking gazelles in Africa, taking down a moose in Canada, and folded arms with claws rip apart a Siberian tiger. The one that aimed for my heart could have been hungry or bored. I'll never know which.

In a way, this is like having the flu. The ache in my spine leaves me defeated. I have fever dreams. My stomach isn't sick, but the constant anxiety makes it tight. A balled up fist in my core. Gwen brings me mint and chamomile tea to make me feel better. She's left my side to go swimming. I suspect she needs a break from seeing how miserable I am. There's a knock on my door and I sit up.

"How are you feeling?" asks Yui.

I'm surprised to see the young scientist visit me. She is peeking at me from behind the door but hasn't stepped into my room yet. I wave her in.

"I'm doing much better. Gwen has been taking good care of me."

I finger comb my bedhead and shake the sleepiness from my crown. Yui sits in the chair by my desk. She picks up a peony. It's fresh and unwilted. I wince at the pink flower in her hand.

"What will we do now, Dr. Krim?" she asks.

Yui is strong enough to withstand the answer.

"I'm not sure. I can't sacrifice her for our freedom."

"No one expects you to."

"The other scientists act like she's not a person," I hiss.

It's angry and impulsive. An instinct I didn't know I had.

"I don't see Gwen as a tool," says Yui with a grave gaze.

She takes notice of the other items my girlfriend has collected. Yui holds a glittery quartz in her fingers. She sees me eyeing her and sets it down gingerly.

"The Mantodea have proven to be more intelligent and ingenious than we thought."

I change the subject.

"That thing they created is horrifying," starts the young scientist. She cradles an acorn in her palm, another gift from my girlfriend. "But it's spectacular," she finishes her sentence and sets down the small treasure.

"How are they able to formulate these plans? Why are they always one step ahead?" I ask the ceiling as I lay back down.

"We don't know much about them. They are from deep space. Who knows the creatures out there they have encountered? Perhaps they are on the mild end of the spectrum. I wonder if all aliens are violent," says Yui.

She is thoughtful in nature. We sit in a silence that isn't unbearable or awkward. I break it with what's been on my mind for months.

"Am I the bad guy because I fell in love with the Ex Machina?" I ask, because I am ready to hear the truth.

Yui turns up the corners of her mouth. She leans back in the chair and brings the peony sitting on the desk with her. Twirling it around, she puts together her answer. I hold my breath.

"No. How could anyone predict such an incredible phenomenon? Who is to say that it is wrong? No one like Gwen has ever existed. She is robotically enhanced but still human. A heart is a heart. Love has never been out of the realm of possibility," she says into the pink blossom.

"Sometimes I wish I wasn't the one," I admit, but regret it immediately.

Yui stands up and hands me the peony.

"You would hate to see her bonded to another, though," says the young scientist.

She leaves and I hear her tiny feet take fast steps down the hall. The pink flower is fresh. Gwen has been going outside. I said that she could, but it vexes me. Being controlling has never been a trait I wanted to have. It reminds me of my dad.

I stand on wobbly legs and put the peony back in the teacup with water. Underneath all the little gifts, I see a piece of paper with writing on it. I push the glittery quartz, acorn, pinecone, and purple blossoms the size of quarters out of the way.

I've seen planets and stars/The depths of the sea/No matter where I am/You are always with me

Gwen wrote me a note in cursive. Love letters in the movies couldn't compare. I worry at times her feelings are ingenuine. That she could turn them off like a faucet and I'd be left dying of thirst. My guilt consumes me. Gwen hasn't been going outside to get away from our relationship. She searches for things like peonies and white flowers to cheer me up.

***

She rides me like a Nor'Easter wind. The tornado in a glass is a cyclone. I have small bruises on my chest from her steel finger tips. They leave black and blue fingerprints. Giving her what she wants hurts me. There is no turning back from what I've done.

My wound is almost completely healed. The huge scab has fallen off, revealing sensitive pink skin. It's no longer tight and itchy. For a while, it was driving me crazy. I couldn't sleep without it bothering me all night. No one has mentioned my sleepwalking episode, not even Gwen.

I did an ultrasound on her this morning. She's pregnant again. I'm happy, but my heart thuds in my chest, thinking about the metal wires in her womb. The image of a squished cherry has me ready to vomit. We are a typical couple, keeping secrets, and avoiding unpleasant topics.

If we pretend nothing is wrong and everything is normal, can we make it so? In what universe can one believe so wholly that they can make it reality? Gwen is smarter than all of us, but her decisions perplex me. She might be putting too much emotional strain on herself. I should stop her. But I don't. Maybe I don't try to because I'm not sure if I can. Nothing can stop a natural disaster.

Our child will truly be spoiled. I thought I was someone else before Gwen. I realize now I'm a push-over. With no true compass, I end up in every corner. I'm a "whatever" type of person. For someone of great introspection, I didn't know myself well enough to be aware of this bad habit. Not only am I a push-over, but I'm an enabler as well.

I let my dad lose his mind and work himself to death because that's what he wanted. My mom and I had a good relationship, but I let her pretend her husband wasn't an emotionally neglectful man. We summed it up to "all families have problems." No one had problems quite like the Krims, though. Now I've knocked up my girlfriend who is prone to miscarriage, and I let her be excited. Good thing I don't have experience with drug addicts. I would probably be the guy who bought their friend a bad batch or lent them too much money in hopes of "helping them."

Looking in the mirror, I'm not sure who I see. A scientist, a fraud, a regular guy, a shitty boyfriend? I shave my face and knick the lower part of my cheek.

A perfect red drop builds and falls. It lands on the white counter with the faintest splash. On my neck, I notice a scratch mark about four inches long. It stops at the top of my shoulder. The white arc of Gwen's nails could shred me apart and expose the muscle underneath.

Perhaps it's better my life turned out this way. If I were a normal kid who played baseball, who knows the trouble I would get into? At least here it's controlled and contained. An extraordinary kind of chaos. I could have been anybody: a teacher, a coach, a junkie, maybe a musician. Instead, I'm the sole master of the Ex Machina who also happens to be pregnant with my child. This is what it means to be Adam Krim's son. It means sacrificing any normalcy for the fantastic.

I leave my room in search of her. She is playing with Hikari. The little boy laughs as Gwen dances with him. He kisses her cheek and runs off down the hall towards his father. Katsuo glares at me but waves. She turns around and shows me her teeth. The eyes flicker between hazel and gold. Her wires make fierce swishing noises from her joy. She embraces me with steel arms and gives me a hard kiss on the lips.

"Hey Beautiful," I say.

She is hugging onto me the way a child squeezes a toy. Pulling back, I see her eye my neck. The scratch peeks out from the collar of my lab coat. I yank it up higher, but Gwen pushes it down and examines her work.

"Does it hurt? I didn't mean to. I'm sorry."

"I'm fine, don't worry."

"I'll be more careful," she says and takes my hand.

We walk around the building with no destination in mind. Yui passes us and gives Gwen a friendly smile. It delights Gwen, but I can tell she is analyzing it thoroughly. I don't want to think about what might happen, but I want to talk about our baby.

"Do you want a little boy like Hikari?" I ask and put my arms around her so I can touch her stomach.

Gwen nods excitedly and the wires whip. They startle me and she calms herself.

"Yes. But I wouldn't mind a little girl either," she says.

I stop to look at my girlfriend. She might have the answer.

"What makes you want a baby?" I ask.

All my life I've avoided the topic of fatherhood. It never seemed important or necessary. Now I'm ill prepared. Gwen's eyes flicker as she holds her body like she is feeling it for the first time. Her hand moves up and down, side to side, as she races through her thoughts like a runner in a maze.

"There are...no words for it. Only that I feel it," she says as she brings her palm to her heart. "Right here."

I put my hand on hers.

CHAPTER TWENTY-SIX
INSOMNIA

I told Gwen I had a migraine and wanted to be by myself for a while. Not a total lie. For once, I can think clearly without the foggy pain building behind my eyes. I want to be by myself, but I don't want to be alone. Alone implies its chronic and ongoing. "I want to be by myself" sounds much better. It has an air of adolescence. Fleeting and moody. As I lay in bed and try to solve my girlfriend's problems, I hear a knock on the door.

"How are you feeling?" asks Shira.

I wasn't expecting her to drop in. She hasn't spoken to me much for so long I forgot the sound of her voice. It seems flatter than usual.

"I'm okay. A bit of a headache," I say to keep up my charade.

Shira sits at my desk and picks up a white flower. I want to scold her.

"So this is it," she says and holds the blossom in her open palm like a butterfly.

I'm waiting for her to close her fist on it.

"What?"

"No matter what we do, the Mantodea throw us a curveball we can't catch. I'm saying," she pushes the flower in her hand with her index finger, "we're giving up."

"I didn't say that."

"You don't have to. We have tried our best. I don't think there is anything Gwen can do to stop them," she says and puts the flower back.

Shira doesn't know the truth, that I could tell Gwen to fry the ship, killing her in the process. I gulp and hope the lump in my throat isn't audible. Lies tend to be louder than the truth.

"What are you getting at, Shira?"

"I'm sorry. I guess what I'm trying to say is that you and Gwen can focus on your family now."

"Why are you concerned with our relationship all of a sudden?"

"I'm trying to wish you happiness."

"Oh. Thank you," I say in discomfort.

The migraine I lied about is returning with a vengeance.

"I'll let you rest," she says and exits my room, leaving a jagged edge.

I am relieved the others don't know about Gwen's ability to destroy the ship. The lies are building up, though. All towers come crashing down. It takes a few hours, but Shira's words seep in. She wants us to be happy.

Does this mean the others could accept? I don't want to give up, but at this point, there is little proof we can come up with a plan to outsmart the Mantodea. My team may not be as rabid as originally expected. I thought they would seek to ruin me if I couldn't deliver on my promises. They may understand now that they've seen how hard Gwen tried for us. She may not be their savior, but she's my angel. I smile through my splintering headache.

Unable to relax, I get up and search for her. How I long to see her smile and hold her in my arms. Realizing we can be together and give up on this suicidal plan gives me a surge of energy. I've kept her at a distance because I've been afraid of losing her. I'm weaving through the halls and run into Nori.

"Bellamy, how are you?" he asks.

Nori may not trust me the way he did in the beginning, but he is neutral. He isn't open about his disapproval like Katsuo and Isamu are.

"I'm fine, thank you."

"Congratulations," he mumbles and looks at his shoes.

"I'm a lucky man."

I'm not sure what to say.

"The probability of such a union is rare. Quite lucky indeed."

"Yeah," I agree.

Nori steps back and really looks at me.

"What?" I ask.

"I'm glad you were the one she bonded to. I don't mean to insult your father, but I don't think the Ex Machina would have progressed as much as she has if she imprinted on him."

"I'm sorry she couldn't defeat the Mantodea. It must be a big disappointment to everyone."

"She is spectacular."

"What?"

"Gwen didn't annihilate the aliens, but she has been a joy to study."

"You think so?" I ask in shock.

Nori has been most professional. I never thought about his personal feelings towards the project or Gwen.

"Yes. Watching her learn what it is to be human while using her robotic brain has been fascinating. She has proven the human heart holds more power than we think."

"The heart wants what it wants," I offer.

"Love is stronger than logic."

"Huh?"

"The heart will almost always win in a battle against the mind," he says and continues down the hall.

What an eccentric man. His words stick to me. They cling onto my coat and weigh me down. I go in and out of rooms looking for her. The lights buzz as I turn them on and off. She's in the room where she was born staring at the tank. I walk up next to her. She turns to embrace me but keeps her eyes on the glass. Our reflection is altered and we morph together into an undistinguishable being.

"Are you feeling better?" she asks.

I pull handfuls of blonde hair over her shoulder.

"Much better," I laugh.

"What's so funny?"

"Nothing."

"Are you going to make another one of me?" she asks.

Gwen seems sad. Her wires are droopy and drift in listless motions.

"No, why would you think that?"

"All the other rooms…" she starts.

"This is my father's lab. He anticipated," I pause and move the hair out of her eyes and touch her soft face, "a much different project."

"How so?"

"He was a genius, but not good at reading human emotions or understanding their complexities."

"He didn't expect me to want children," she states.

"No. He thought you would be scientifically driven."

"Is it bad I came out this way?" she asks and breaks my grasp to touch the tank.

"Of course not. You're wonderful just the way you are," I say and reach for her.

***

A little boy playing pretend. That's what I feel like. An imposter. I don't have the slightest idea of how to manage my girlfriend, run this lab, and I've run out of ideas as to how to fight the aliens plaguing our planet. I do my rounds and keep everything functional. If it looks like I know what I'm doing, but most people take it at face value.

I make a list of supplies to order and I add things for an infant. It seems out of place on the starchy white paper. I consider erasing it. But I can't erase my actions. I'm embarrassed to be asking for these things. I know the man who brings our deliveries will go through the checklist. He may think it's one of the female scientists. My paranoia is getting the better of me.

All this money and power has me walking on eggshells. I don't want to be like my dad. What if I end up as oblivious as he was? He wasn't a bad person, but he wasn't a great father. His projects, his intentions, his dreams, they consumed him. I don't think that's grounds for punishment. Still, I resent my dad. It makes no difference, though. He's dead, I'm not.

"Hey," says Hotaka as he emerges from behind stacks of paperwork.

"Hey, didn't see you there," I joke.

Hotaka looks at the clipboard in my hand.

"Are you ready?" he asks.

"Ready for what?"

"Now that we can put aside our need to use Gwen as a weapon of mass destruction, you two can start your life. Are you ready for that?"

Hotaka smiles at me and plays with his glasses.

"I think so."

"You have been waiting for her for longer than you think."

"Huh?"

"I apologize, it's just that, in a sense, I knew you would fall for her."

"How?" I ask in confusion.

Hotaka smooths the collar of his shirt and chuckles.

"Call it a friend's intuition."

"Do you agree with my father? That I was inappropriate?"

"Not at all. I don't think you fell for her until she chased after the elk."

"What does the elk have to do with anything?"

"You ran after her into the forest one hundred yards away from the lab with no hesitation. In that moment you decided she was more important than your life," he says.

I didn't put two and two together. Since the beginning, I've been childishly attached to her, summing it up to her being my father's project, my life's work. But she is my world. I've chosen her over the one out there time and time again.

"I did, didn't I?"

"You have been in love before, but Gwen hasn't. Imagine feeling it the way she feels it."

Hotaka grips my shoulder in a brotherly way. I remember what she said. That she wished I could be damaged by it the way she is.

"I'm so stupid," I laugh.

Hotaka joins me and we smile at the floor.

"Your father was a brilliant scientist, but you, my friend, are a great person."

"Maybe that's why my mom chose my name. Bellamy is French for 'beautiful friend.' I hated it as a kid because I thought it was too feminine. My mom was wiser than she let on," I say and get a twinge in my chest thinking about her. She deserved so much more. I should have convinced her to leave my father.

"Go be with Gwen. I'll finish the order," says Hotaka, and he takes the clipboard and pen from me.

"Thank you, Hotaka. You're the best."

My lab coat sways and hits the doorframe on the way out. If she is in my heart like an atom bomb, then what am I doing to her? I think back to Sophia and Eva. How I loved them, what I believed, and how it felt. I fell so hard for Eva I constantly thought my heart was on the verge of exploding. That doesn't compare to this. Love is miserable and wondrous. How the Ex Machina experiences it, I can only imagine. I thought she was distant, but she is a vulnerable person beneath the exoskeleton.

The walls waver from the flickering blue lights. Gwen isn't in my room. She's not in hers. A teddy bear sits in the middle of her bed, holding a pink rose. I go in and out of the rooms with the artificial wombs. Yui and Nori are at the computers entering data into the system. They smile at me, but I'm anxious. I walk past Katsuo, Shira, and Hikari. They fall silent as I walk by.

She's been enjoying swimming. I turn around and head towards the water reservoir. Isamu looks sleepy as we approach each other. He is snacking on an apple and I wince as he takes an enormous bite. The crispness adds to my tension.

"Bellamy, can I say something?" asks Isamu.

I nod, but my mouth is tight and I can't talk.

"I'm sorry for my rude behavior. To be honest, I've been afraid. But I realize there is nothing to be afraid of. Gwen isn't a weapon. She is a person."

Isamu shoves the apple back in his mouth. Probably trying to keep in his tongue. I pat his shoulders like we're old friends.

"It's okay," I say, and we part ways.

The empty clang of my footsteps seems louder. They ring out in the empty hall. I'm halfway there when I notice something on the floor. I kneel to inspect the spot on the ground. It's blood. I stand up and follow the trail of red splotches. There are droplets the size of a dime, followed by smears of blood. Partial footsteps lead me to the room with the reservoir. As I near its edge, there is blood with grey matter in it. I try to keep it in but cannot do so and vomit. Not bothering to roll up my sleeves, I stick my arm in the water. I wipe my face with my other hand. Steel fingers grip my wrist and I pull her into my chest.

"Gwen," I say her name, but it's no use. She's sobbing and practically ripping the collar off my coat. "I'm so sorry."

The front of my shirt and sleeves are soaked. Her wires are swishing erratically with despair.

"Why is it making me cry like this?" she asks as she tugs at the front of my lab coat.

I have my arms around her shoulders and my right hand in her white gold hair. In my attempt to find the answer, I find nothing but tears myself.

"Because it's sad."

***

Gwen can't sleep and neither can I. She climbs over me like star jasmine and hangs on me. I hold up white flowers heavy enough to leave craters in the earth. She smells like spring rain and I can't figure out why she comes back.

I'm not sure Gwen even likes what I'm doing to her anymore. She says she loves me but I have my suspicions that I'm just a means to an end; I think it's hurting her as she begs me. We could have a baby another way, but she becomes volatile if I bring up the subject. She says I could never understand, and she's right. I've never understood any of my girlfriends.

I haven't been sleepwalking, but I feel myself going somewhere in my dreams, so I stay awake. In my nightmares, I go to rooms with empty tanks and broken respirators. I go to baseball games played in slow motion. Some nights I go to the room where Gwen was born and envy my father doting on her. I end up with blood on my lab coat.

Does Gwen protect me out of obligation? Or is that what love is? If my heart aches, then hers must be obliterated. She doesn't say much, but I can see it in her eyes and she doesn't smile like she did before. I can get her to light up, yet it's not the same. Everything has changed.

"Do you want to go outside tomorrow?" I ask.

"Yes," she says and her teeth graze my neck as she talks. "You should get some rest."

I don't flinch.

"I love you," I say and barely feel the sentence escape my mouth before I fall asleep.

As I should have known, I wake up alone. I use the opportunity to shower by myself and examine the tiny bruises and scratches she marks me with.

Spring is here. The ground is littered with pink cherry blossoms. Daisies, daffodils, and dandelions have taken over the tall grass. It's breathtaking. Hopefully, it will cheer her up. In the mirror, I run my finger along the small cluster of bruises on the top of my shoulder. The wound in the middle of my back has healed, but Hotaka said I should still be careful.

I remember my favorite spring break with my mom. We went on a road trip to a concert. I was eleven and had fully developed my love of indie electronic pop music. My mom liked it, too. She was the one who introduced me to most of the stuff I like.

Of course, my father didn't join us. It didn't bother me at the time. We were having too much fun. The beach we went to was lined with azaleas. It seemed exotic for the east coast of the United States. The sky turning orange as the sun set sticks out in my mind. My mom kept her hair in a ponytail and it whipped her face.

I head out and begin my search for Gwen. It's early but I feel like I slept in. Everyone seems to know what's going on except me. I don't carry a notepad or pen. It's been weeks since I've bothered to read anyone's notes to do anything other than the bare minimum. We have food, supplies, and everything is stable besides me, so no need to burn myself out.

"Do you have a moment?" asks Katsuo.

He snuck up behind me. I should get him a bell like a cat.

"Sure. What is it, Katsuo?"

I try to be cordial. To keep from fidgeting, I put my hands in my pockets.

"I don't think you and Gwen should keep trying."

"What?"

"It's just that it seems..." Katsuo shrugs with nonchalance, "a bit ridiculous."

"Excuse me?"

My core temperature rises and I feel my face becoming hot.

"C'mon, Bellamy. Do you really think it's safe to keep fucking around with that thing?"

"What did you say?" I find my fist gripping onto his shirt. "Don't call her that," I snarl and shove him against the wall.

His back hits the metal, and it reverberates.

"She's not human like me or you."

He has no shame saying these words to me. I tighten my hold on his collar.

"Don't even."

"I'm sorry, I mean your little girlfriend," he says in a mocking manner.

I lose it and deck him in the nose. Blood gushes out and falls to the floor like red rain. It sprays my chin and stains my lab coat.

"Fuck you," I say and drop him.

Katsuo smiles with blood in his teeth.

"I'm taking my son and leaving first thing tomorrow. The military will transport us to our new location."

"Safe travels." I walk off without looking back.

My anger fades and I remember Gwen. She will be heartbroken to know Hikari is leaving. I'm not sure, but I think it's all my fault.

CHAPTER TWENTY-SEVEN
IMPULSE

"No!" screams the little boy with an intense shrillness.

"Hikari! Come here!" shouts his father.

Katsuo is not pleased. Hikari is gripping the hem of Gwen's dress. She is trying to usher him towards his father, but he is refusing.

"You need to be with your dad," she says to him.

Hikari is still struggling. Huge tears pool down his face. Gwen is wearing a powder blue dress. It makes her look sadder. The most heartbreaking shade of blue.

"I want to stay with you," whispers Hikari.

Gwen kneels down so she can embrace the little boy. Katsuo disapproves and taps his foot in annoyance. The military guards are waiting behind him.

"I know. I'll be thinking of you always," she says and kisses his cheek.

Katsuo winces at the sight of her lips touching his son's skin.

"I love you," says Hikari, and he throws his short arms around her neck. The Ex Machina ruffles his hair like a real girl.

"I love you," she says.

"I'll never forget you."

"You will be in my heart," she says and stands.

Katsuo walks up and yanks Hikari away from her. She keeps her head down. He doesn't check her out so I reconsider decking him in the face again.

"Goodbye," says the little boy.

"Goodbye," she says and waves him off.

It's not until they leave in their armored vehicle and it's no longer visible in the distance does she fall to her knees. She covers her face and sobs. I kneel so I can put my hands on her shoulders. The wires whip with despair.

"Gwen–" I start to say her name, but she cuts me off.

"Leave me alone," she hisses.

Her voice is low in her throat. I back up. Gwen has snapped at me, made me nervous, but she has never lashed out at me like this.

"Okay," I choke and make my way down the hall. Nori and Yui saw the whole thing but act like they were just walking by. I want a cigarette. The craving is warm and empty in my chest covered in tiny bruises.

In my room I dim the lights and lay down. I feel a migraine in the works. Tossing and turning, no side is the right side, I can't relax. A cigarette sounds better and better. Gwen would be angry, though, and she is already mad at me.

All I wanted to do was defend her from Katsuo's nasty comments. I end up tearing out her heart. Hikari had a genuine bond with her. One I can't replicate. She belongs to me, but she gave a piece of herself to the little boy. My girlfriend is fickle. She fascinates me. I hear my door being opened and I sit up.

"Shira? What are you doing here? I thought you left with Katsuo."

"I was going to," she says and steps into my room without permission.

"What do you want?" I ask.

She slips next to me in a slinky way resembling a cat. Her hand is on the sheets.

"I can't figure you out."

"There's nothing to figure out," I say and roll my eyes.

"The rich playboy son of a madman falls for the Ex Machina his father created and is now attempting to impregnate her. What a mess you are."

"Piss off," I snarl. She reaches out and touches my face. The opposite of what I thought she would do. I pull back. "What are you doing?"

"She is incredible, but there's something about you," she says and puts her lips on mine. I push her off me.

"Stop it, Shira."

"You stay completely still when she kisses you."

Shira is in my lap and forcing me to kiss her. I stand up and she falls off me.

"Get out," I say, but she is grabbing at my shirt. She stands on the tips of her toes and sticks her tongue in my mouth. "Knock it off, Shira!" I shout.

She is speechless. We stare at each other. Looking down at the same time, we see blood staining her blouse. She falls face first on the ground. Gwen has snuck into my room and inserted her metal jack stinger into Shira's chest. "What have you done?" I ask. Gwen retracts the bloody wire. It wags with satisfaction.

"Did you like her kissing you?" she asks with a glowing gold glare.

"Of course not," I sigh.

Shira is bleeding out on my bedroom floor. Sweat collects at my hairline and the collar of my shirt. I take off my tie.

"Have you been cheating on me?"

Gwen closes the gap and knocks me to the bed. She is hovering over me like the angel of death.

"No, I'd never do that," I say. She lowers herself so she can look into my eyes. "Why did you kill her?" I ask.

"I...did not expect to. When I saw her kiss you, I lost myself."

"We need to do something before someone finds her," I whisper.

Gwen gets off me. Standing up, I assess my situation. My girlfriend murdered my employee. I let out a loud exhale and start thinking about what to do.

"I'm sorry," says Gwen. She is sheepish now that she realizes what she's done. "I'll do anything for you. Please, don't be mad at me."

"Gwen, I need you to get one of the carts. Empty it and wheel it here."

"What are you going to do, Bellamy?"

"We're going to put her in the cart, clean up this blood, and wait until everyone is asleep."

"What then?" she asks. I think it is amusing to her. Watching me cover up her mess proves my devotion.

"We're going to dump her into the incinerator where we dispose of our garbage," I say.

She leaves me with Shira's corpse. A ghost is touching my face, I know it. The coolness of the room makes me shiver.

***

I make Gwen get the cart because if anyone walks in, I want them to think I'm the one who killed Shira. For some reason, I'm making excuses for her. She didn't mean to. It was an accident. It's my fault—none are true except maybe the last one. Using all my towels, I sop up the blood seeping out from beneath Shira's small body. Her eyes are glossy, staring up at the ceiling. I close them for her.

Gwen killed someone. I knew she could, but never thought she'd resort to it. After all, she is under my control. She does what I say. But when the Ex Machina saw Shira kissing me, she made a most impulsive decision. My girlfriend could have murdered me, but she chose to strike Shira. I don't know whether or not she will be hostile after this.

"Bellamy..." she whispers my name as she steps in with the cart. I look up at my girlfriend. She has an angelic face. Moving my gaze back to the dead body, I know that is fictitious. "I'm sorry. I don't know what came over me." Gwen is crying and I'm becoming agitated.

"Help me move her," I say, and Gwen does as she's told.

Her face is streaked with tears, but I ignore them. I have to take care of this mess. Tearing the sheets from my bed, I have Gwen set Shira down and I roll her up before placing her in the cart. I wipe up the remaining blood on the ground. Somehow it doesn't sicken me like usual. The color red disgusts me, but I can't let it distract me from the task at hand.

I toss the bloody towels into a garbage bag and throw them on top of Shira. It makes me feel guilty, so I move the bag over. Then I take off my crimson stained lab coat and shirt. These will have to be disposed of as well. My khakis have blood splattered across the knees. I get rid of them, too. Going into the bathroom, I see my cheek has been sprayed with Shira's blood. I wash my face and dispose of the fluffy white towel with red fingerprints along with the others.

"What are you going to do to me?" asks Gwen.

I'm pulling my arms through a clean shirt.

"What do you mean?"

"I did something horrible. Aren't you going to punish me?"

The Ex Machina stares at Shira's body, crumpled like a rag doll.

"Do you want to be punished?" I ask, perplexed by Gwen's strange question.

"I feel like I deserve it," she says and to my surprise she reaches in and moves Shira's bangs out of her face.

"Do you regret what you did?"

"Yes," she whispers as she continues to play with Shira's hair. "I didn't like seeing her touch you, but I shouldn't have reacted the way I did. I'm...afraid of myself."

"Afraid of yourself?"

"I thought I was in complete control. But I'm not," she whispers in her airy way and lets go of Shira's black tresses.

I put my arms around her.

"We can't tell anybody," I say into her ear, which is half hidden by blonde hair.

"You want to pretend nothing happened?"

"Gwen, promise me you won't tell anybody."

"If that's what you want. I promise."

Gwen doesn't face me. She keeps her eyes on Shira's lifeless form, that is surrounded by bloody cotton towels.

"It's what I want," I say and pull the top over the cart.

It startles Gwen, and she steps back. For once, I'm the one making her nervous.

"What do we do now, Bellamy?"

"I'm going to wait a few hours and then wheel the cart to the incinerator."

"What do we say when the others ask about her?"

"We'll say she left with Katsuo," I snap, more angrily than expected.

She should have left with him. Why she decided to stay and try to kiss me is beyond my level of expertise.

"They'll know she's not with him, eventually. Isamu and him are friends.

I'm sure they'll talk at some point," Gwen says with certainty.

"Shira was fickle. We'll say she must have changed her mind and went to work for someone else."

"Are you sure we should be doing this?"

"Doing what?" I ask.

"Lying," she says.

I'm at a loss for words. I throw my arms around her to stop her from talking.

"Just let me take care of it."

Gwen agrees but not without reluctance. I tell her to take a bath. There's blood on her dress, so I add it to the evidence I'm going to burn. I leave my room to walk around and survey the place. It's quiet, no footsteps other than mine. In the kitchen, I make two cups of tea. No one passes by or enters. As though nothing is wrong, I take the hot beverages back to my room with no incident.

Gwen is making small splashing noises in the tub. The wires are whipping, probably sensing if it's me or someone else. I open the door and hand her the tea. I sit on the ledge of the tub and sip mine. We don't make eye contact or speak until both our drinks are gone.

"No one is walking around. I'm going to take the cart," I announce.

Gwen's wires droop like I've scolded her.

"Okay," she says into the clear water.

I touch her face and get her to look at me.

"Everything is going to be okay," I say.

It's frightening how willing I am to do anything for her.

***

Like a rat, I keep to the walls and stay in the shadows. The cart's wheels make squeaky noises. The perspiration is building on my face. There are no cameras in the hallway with the incinerator, so no need to worry about that. It's my own shameful guilt recording everything I'm doing.

The more steps I take, the further away it seems. The illusion finally stops because I'm here. Peeking over my shoulder, I see no one walking by. I listen for the sound of steps. Nothing. Only my racing heart and heavy breathing. I sigh as I open the lid. Shira's face is slack and innocent. She looks younger than Gwen.

I gulp to keep my heart in. In one swift motion, I heave her into the incinerator with the towels, the bloody clothes, and press the button. Covering my mouth stifles my vomit. I really just did that. It wouldn't have been possible if I didn't love Gwen as much as I do. It's toxic and my veins burst from the poison.

With heavy feet, I push the cart back into the storage room. I make sure there isn't any blood left on it. There's some on my hand and it leaves a fingerprint. Taking the inside of my shirt, I wipe off my fingertips and the evidence on the metal handle of the cart. Paranoid, I scour the cart for any sign of anything amiss. I hold my sickly stomach and choke on air. I leave the room and am met with Hotaka.

"Hey Bell, what are you up to?"

"Oh, just taking inventory," I say as calmly as I can.

"I know it might be too soon to ask but," Hotaka pauses and the pulse in my temple is threatening to give me away, "are you and Gwen going to try again?"

"Yes, she still wants to try."

"Do you?" he asks.

I'm not in the right mind for this conversation. First, I'm disposing of a body and now I'm being reminded of what my girlfriend really wants.

"I wish she'd let us use another option, so she doesn't hurt herself," I admit.

Hotaka nods and smiles apologetically.

"She wants to feel it," he says and touches his heart.

"Yeah," I don't know what else to say and the word hangs there like a stubborn cloud.

"Take care of each other," he says and pats my shoulder.

I smile because he is a good friend, but I think I might be a bad person. Hotaka goes back towards the crops and I head back to my room. Gwen is waiting for me like an abandoned puppy. She is on me as soon as I walk in.

"So?" she asks.

"Everything is fine. No one saw anything."

"Are you sure?"

"I'm sure."

"I'm scared."

"What are you scared of, Beautiful?"

"Myself," she says and kisses me.

I'm stunned when she brushes past me and leaves me all alone after cleaning up her mess. Taking a shower eases me a bit, but I can't wash away what I did. I can't change what I've done. Maybe my dad was right. I'm not good enough.

It takes practice to unclench my jaw. The headache starts to fade. I lay down and try to get some rest. It's been a grueling day. Sleep is impossible, though. The ghost keeps playing with my hair and touching my face. I open my eyes to no one. Gwen isn't here. The room is cold. I turn the heat up and pull the blanket over my ears. It's no use. The ghost continues to haunt me and send shivers down my spine.

It goes on like this all night. The cold spots in my room move over my face, arms, and blow on my neck. Covering my face and eyes stops it, but only for a short while. This is purgatory. A place between sleep and no sleep. It's walking nightmares and freezing fingertips. The image of Shira's blood on my shirt and hands causes me to get out of bed and empty my stomach. I dry heave there is so little substance.

I take a bath. It's soothing, but only at first. The memory of Gwen miscarrying in here fills my mind, and I have visions of bathing in my baby's blood. It overflows, and the cup falls over. Splashing warm water on my face brings me back. The moment is now, but now is far from where I am and where I should be.

When I get back into bed, I smell white flowers. My blankets smell like her, but she isn't here. I try to sleep once more but have dreams about monsters with wire tentacles reaching for me from under my bed. Childish as it is, the thought of something under my bed has me hiding against the wall. It's funny, really. How I can sleep next to something poisonous but nightmares about monsters hiding in my room has me covering my face with the pillow.

CHAPTER TWENTY-EIGHT
EXTRAORDINARY

It takes nine days for Isamu to confront me. I've been on my best behavior. Everything is calm and organized, or so it seems. Gwen is pregnant again. She is hopeful, but it hurts. I pretend to be happy, I am, but I'm drowning.

"Where did Shira go?" asks Isamu.

He looks cross and serious. It reminds me of my father.

"I thought she left with Katsuo," I play dumb.

"No. Katsuo told me she changed her mind."

"Oh. She didn't say anything to me. I assume she went to work for someone else."

"All her stuff is still in her room. Her bags were packed, but she didn't take anything with her," he says with suspicion and steps closer to me. "Isn't that odd?" he adds. He emphasizes the last part.

"That is odd…" I trail off. We stare at each other for a moment before I continue, "Shira and I didn't talk much after…" I can't finish my sentence.

"You started having an intimate relationship with Gwen," he says.

"Yes."

I have phlegm in my throat, making me sound older.

"Since we can't go forward in our plans to create a weapon strong enough to kill the Mantodea, I am resigning from my position. The military will pick me up tomorrow."

"Of course," I say and I analyze Isamu, who is trying to read me like a magazine.

"I hope Shira is okay," he says over his shoulder as he walks off.

"Me too."

Isamu stops, and my blood turns cold.

"It would be a shame if something bad happened to her," he says and stomps off.

I think he is calling me out, but I can't be sure. Once I'm sure he's gone, I head for Shira's room. The door opens. The smell of her perfume and books float around me like a ghost. Her bed is made. She is always immaculate. I pick up a bracelet with an oval diamond from her nightstand that holds nothing else. Correction, she was. The word hits me in the ribs. Shira was always very neat.

Her suitcase sits by the door waiting to go somewhere. A dog begging to be walked. It's bulky and black. Kind of ugly, but Shira was a practical person. That word again: was. Her gym bag sits in the middle of the bed like a big fat cat. I swear it growls at me as I reach for the zipper. My hand shakes and I pull back. The laptop and her books surround the bag, guarding it, glaring at me.

I run out of the room. What am I looking for? I know where she is. Maybe I played dumb so good I believe myself. No, that's not true. I know what I did. What we did. The walls close in on me. The hallway is too skinny. I can't catch my breath. Rounding the corner, I see Gwen. She is standing at the front door, looking out the window. It's almost summer. The sun is high in the sky and it hits her right, illuminating my girlfriend's pretty face. What touches me, though, is Gwen's smile at the beautiful day as she rests her palm on her stomach.

This moment is too perfect. I don't deserve it. My father was cold, neglectful, and a brilliant scientist. What does that make me? I can't rid myself of the vision of crushed cranberries or water pouring into a respirator. As I walk up beside her, my cough gives me away. She turns to me and opens her arms. I let her play with me like I'm no more than a stuffed animal.

"What are you thinking about?" I ask.

"You," she says and touches my nose.

I flinch, but she brushes it off.

"Yeah?"

"How I want us to be outside all the time, Bellamy."

She pulls away from me and puts her hand to the window.

"I know."

"Are you okay?" she asks and embraces me again.

I keep my gaze on the forest. To ignore the intrusive thoughts of a watermelon splattering on concrete and berries being squished by too eager of hands, I look into the vast greenness of the outside. Aquatic blue tones, earthy hues, and the swirl of clouds center me.

"I'm fine, Beautiful," I say, but Shira's dead eyes are staring into my soul. The temperature drops and I shiver.

"You're cold," she says and pops up my collar and buttons my coat.

"Thanks."

It starts to rain, but it's barely a mist. A rainbow appears. It looks like it ends beyond the lake.

"Can we go outside? Just for a minute?"

"Yes," I say and usher her out the door. We hold open our hands and touch the sky. It's warm with no breeze. The rain is so light on my skin. I look over to see Gwen with her eyes closed and her nose pointed at the sky. "Do you like the rain, Gwen?"

"I love it," she says with a smile. A raindrop lands under my eye. It's soft summer rain, but the image of Shira's blood being splattered across my face returns. Gwen still has her eyes closed. I kiss her, harder than usual, and she wraps herself around me. A wire slithers around my waist. "But I don't love anything as much as I love you," she says.

***

She is docile when she gets what she wants. A playful kitten or loyal dog, I can't disguise the Ex Machina as a house pet. Acting like nothing is wrong is easy. It perturbs me. I don't know what it means to be a good person, so I attempt to be a good boyfriend, someone who would be a good dad. Gwen is eating a carrot. She doesn't spit it out, so I assume she likes it.

"How are you feeling?" I ask.

Gwen keeps her eyes down but has a grin on her face.

"Content," she says.

Her titanium teeth sink into the carrot with a distinct crunch. I cover my left ear with my hand. Everything has been too loud. The volume is up and the bass echoes in my brain.

"That's great."

I go back to my work. The thing the Mantodea created won't leave me be. I think about it all the time. What it was, how they made it, and when they will die. Will they die at all? Does earth belong to them forever? I ponder the possibility of other kinds of aliens.

"Is something on your mind, Bellamy?"

"I'm reading the same stuff again. Seeing if I missed anything important," I say and give her a weak smile.

It doesn't help that I also keep wondering what kind of person I am. I hear Katsuo behind me, "Do you know what it means to be a father?"

I was cocky. It was stupid for me to brush him off the way I did. He knew something valuable. As a scientist, I'm disappointed I didn't question him about fatherhood. As a man, I'm pleased with myself for punching him in the face. My dad would call me an idiot. I would call him a selfish megalomaniac.

"Anything I can do to help?" she asks and slides into my lap.

Her steel fingers lift my chin, and she gazes at me with intense glowing eyes.

"No, it's nothing. I want you to relax."

"Okay," she says.

Gwen hardly fights me anymore. The duality between the needy puppy and deadly scorpion is astounding. I kiss her on the cheek and she gets up.

"I'm going to do my rounds. Wait for me here."

I can tell she wants to go with me, but we are together every minute these days and I need a break. Gwen nods but in a defeated manner. I ignore it and she kisses me, anyway. Walking down the hall, I sense eyes bore into my head. I let my shoulders fall when I'm out of her sight. She can sense me, though. Does she hear or feel the thud, thud, thud of my heart?

The rounds are necessary. I take my time. Steady paced steps and meandering buy me time for myself. I don't want to be alone again. Yet I'm starved of my autonomy. She is ivy, climbing up my torso, and hanging on my arms. I hold completely still as she constricts around me.

"Hey Bellamy," says Yui.

She is peeking out from one of the research rooms.

"What's up, Yui?"

"Are you busy?"

"No, not at all."

"Can we talk for a minute?" she asks and coaxes me into the room.

I sit in the chair across from her. The tiny green lamp on the table is a pleasant change from the drastic fluorescent lights.

"What is it?" I ask.

Yui fiddles with her pen. She smiles out of embarrassment.

"Can I speak freely, as though you are my friend and not my boss?"

"Sure," I shrug.

"Before I came to work for you, my older sister and her boyfriend were trying to have a baby," she starts. I sink in the chair. The young scientist goes on. "She had a miscarriage. They were devastated, but she got pregnant again rather quickly. My parents were so excited. We were anxiously waiting as a family. Then one day in her second trimester she lost the baby. Her boyfriend broke down. She was a mess. My mom tried to help them both by cooking their meals and distracting them. It didn't matter though because in the end, my big sister killed herself."

"Yui...I'm so sorry. I had no idea," I say.

"She was only twenty-five. The postpartum depression destroyed her psyche."

"You think Gwen is going to hurt herself, too?"

"I'm not judging or offering advice. I just wanted to tell you what happened to my family," she says.

Yui won't look at me. I keep my eyes on the green lamp. The mossy glow is soothing. Something green in the metal wonderland.

"I don't know what to do other than give her what she wants. I'm really bad at saying no," I admit.

Yui smiles a genuine smile this time.

"It's sweet how in love you both are," she says. I must have a look on my face because she apologizes. "I'm sorry, that was out of line. I shouldn't have said that."

"No, it's fine. Don't worry about it. I guess I'm surprised. No one has said Gwen and I were sweet before," I laugh.

"I know the others don't understand. I don't fully comprehend it myself but I'm..." Yui puts her chin in her hands and searches for the word. "Grateful."

"Grateful? For what?" I ask.

"The Ex Machina is more than we ever thought she could be. We assumed she would make us more than what we are. In actuality, we made her who she is, a genuine human woman. Her love is not only authentic, it's...impressive."

"I'm glad someone else is in awe of her," I say as I rise from the uncomfortable chair.

"Thank you for your time. I'm sorry if I was too personal," she says.

Yui seems shy, so I let her be.

"No problem. I'll talk to you later," I say.

I end up in the room where Gwen was born. My hand is on the glass. There is nothing in there, but the memory fuels the habit. Her palm touching my palm. Gwen reaching for me in the darkness. She said my voice reminds her of the stars.

If Gwen loses our baby, this will be her fourth miscarriage. I've never met a woman who openly talked about it. It's painful to witness. Surely it has to be physically and emotionally unbearable to experience. My girlfriend listens to me but doesn't agree. She wants what she wants. If she was any other woman, I wouldn't be doing this.

***

I watch Gwen swim on camera. She blows me kisses. The wires know where I am at all times of the day. I find myself in her room. My hands pass over every book, dried flower, and her blankets. I lay in bed and when I wake there's a thin layer of perspiration on my face.

I look over last week's footage to see where she goes when she's not with me. She's been outside twice. I knew she would, but it's irritating to watch. Gwen doesn't wink at the camera. No, she ignores it now. I wonder if it's because she wants to drive me crazy.

I sit in his chair. The one by the tank she's not in anymore. My tornado in a glass is free. But what am I? I find myself so tired some days I sleep sixteen hours. Gwen worries about me those days. I find myself wired other nights. Those are the longest. I read, work out, make tea, pace around, and so on. The hours tick by at the rate of a sloth. Gwen leaves me alone when I'm like that. I think it makes her uneasy.

My father, a revolutionary leader in science, was not a sane man. Most people knew this. The world thought it endearing and that it added to his eccentric personality. His inventions made people's lives easier, better, and unbelievable. He unified the scientific with the realm of the mystic. And I think he was in love with Gwen.

I find myself in the storage room. They delivered everything I asked for, including a bassinet. I haven't wanted to show Gwen yet. I find myself in the infirmary. There are several pictures of her ultrasound. A strawberry being smashed pops up without warning, and I set the photos down.

I stand at the front door. Dusk is here. The stars are on the pink and indigo horizon. Waiting for them gives me a sense of aliveness. No matter how miserable things can be, there are certain beautiful things that never cease to be riveting: sunsets, the moon, forests, and stars. I long to live in my old house with a porch and a backyard. I find myself in the past.

I anticipate the future. Is it possible to find myself in myself? Someone else living my life as though I stepped out into the astral world and returned to another entity parading around as me.

Sleeping to the sound of rain and rattlesnakes no longer frightens me. It has become my lullaby. I find myself in her arms. This is where I surrender to the gold glow in the darkness. The monster under my bed is a distant dream. I walk to a cliff with a fistful of blonde hair. Where I was going? I do not know.

"You were having a nightmare," she whispers and kisses my earlobe.

"I can't remember it," I say.

Lying has become a reflex. A white lie isn't an actual lie, is it?

"What is it like to have dreams?"

"It's like a strange story unfolding in your mind. They don't make sense most of the time. Many people don't remember them."

"Have you ever dreamt of me?" she asks.

I remember the dream I had where my dad threw me down in front of Gwen's tank and said I wasn't good enough for her. The nightmares of Gwen's respirator leaking flash through my mind like a flock of birds.

"I used to dream about you waking up," I say.

"You did?" she asks with enthusiasm.

It makes me chuckle.

"Yes. I couldn't wait to meet you."

"Did you know we would fall in love?" she asks.

Her breath tickles my chest, but hits me hard enough to knock the wind out of me.

"No. But I'm happy we did."

"You are?"

Gwen sits up and leans over me.

"I am."

She lays back down. The wires rustle under the covers. One of them tore through Shira like puncturing a tube of paint. I think about red acrylics on the sands of a beach.

198

CHAPTER TWENTY-NINE
SURROGATE

Her tongue in my mouth has me at a loss for words. Not that there is anything left for me to say. I'm not fully paying attention to what she's doing to me because cold spots caress my face and arms. A ghost in the room. Shira's body haunts my mind and her icy fingers graze my skin.

"Is something wrong?"

Gwen stops kissing me and takes in my disheveled appearance.

"I've had a lot on my mind," I say and touch her stomach. She knows what I mean.

"Are you okay?" Gwen lays down next to me and rests her palm on my heart.

"Yeah."

She props herself on her elbow and stares me down. I don't feel threatened, but I'm well aware of her wires as they swish back and forth. My girlfriend is watching the pulse in my neck. She is noticing the thud of my weak heart and trying to figure me out.

"What do you want from me?" she asks in an airy whisper.

Her tone is neutral but lilting with childish wonder. It stuns me with no metal infused sting. I turn to her and the heat of glowing gold eyes starts melting my face.

"What if we tried things my way?"

I put my palm on her stomach and pray the tiny metallic threads don't shred them apart.

"You want to have our baby grow in an artificial womb? Like me," she says with a stern flatness.

"I just..." the words get caught in my throat. There's phlegm again and I cough.

"What?"

"I just don't want to hurt you anymore," I say.

Regret hits me like the scent of death. Gwen's eyes cease to glow and she recoils from me.

"Don't say that. You could never be damaged by this the way I am," she hisses.

The wires rattle as she speaks venomously.

"I'm sorry. I—"

"You should get some rest," she says and walks out.

I'm left alone with the ghost again. Shira is screaming at me. Small but fierce footsteps clank all over my room. I sit up and cover my ears. She is still whispering to me. Shira keeps asking me why I let Gwen kill her. I have no excuse other than I love her.

I get out of bed. Stormy white flowers are on my shirt, so I change. My hair is unkempt and sticking out in different directions. I comb it and try to put myself together. In the mirror, I see the bathtub behind me fill up with blood. I see it in the sink and taste it in my mouth.

Gwen has left many tiny scars on me. There's the spot on my lip where her canine first marked me and a scratch at the bottom of my neck. I take off my shirt, curious to see what else has happened to me.

On my back are eight scratches, four on each shoulder blade. She keeps digging into the same spots, leaving a multicolored layer of scars. Gwen draws blood when she orgasms. My hand feels the skin changing from her nails' impression. A wound is a wound, is a wound. I put my shirt back on and head out into the hall to get some air.

Walking allows me to expel some anxious energy. I'm tired but can't shake the adrenaline coursing through me. I pace around, going nowhere in particular, and avoid Gwen's room. I'm tempted to knock but refrain. She's furious with me. I should let her cool down. Continuing down the hall, I run into Nori. He seems nervous but has sleepy eyes.

"Dr. Krim," he starts, but doesn't finish.

Nori looks down sheepishly. He's wearing his slippers and a beige sweater.

"Hey Nori."

"What are you doing at this hour?"

"Same as you. I can't sleep," I say with a hint of a grin.

"I was waiting to talk to you, but since neither of us can sleep, this seems like the right time. I will be going back home next week," he says.

Nori has a kind voice. His family must miss him.

"Thank you for the work you did here. I know we didn't complete our goal, but maybe someone will figure out a way to defeat the Mantodea."

"I hope so. I wish I could have been of more help," says Nori as he keeps his eyes on his slippers.

"You did plenty. You all did," I say, and he looks at me.

"Bellamy, can I ask you something?"

"Go ahead."

"What is it like being with someone like Gwen?" he asks.

His voice is shy despite being a decade older than me.

"It's...incredible. I can't explain it."

"Are you afraid of her?"

Nori's eyes are shiny and looking into mine.

"Yes," my voice shakes as I utter the one syllable word.

"Will you be alright?" he asks, like a dad would.

I know nothing about Nori's personal life.

"I'll be fine." I try to say it with confidence and comfort him. He seems unconvinced but won't say so. I decide to ask about his family. "Do you have kids, Nori?"

"I do," he says.

His face lights up when he answers me.

"How many?"

"Two. One boy and one girl. My son is eighteen and my daughter is twenty now."

"What are they like?"

"My son is rowdy, like most boys. He plays guitar and drives my wife up the wall." Nori chuckles. He seems proud of his son, who is the polar opposite of him. "My daughter is very sweet. She takes care of the family while I'm gone."

"You must be excited to see them."

"Yes. I look forward to our reunion. Thank you, Dr. Krim. I have never met anyone as interesting or as courageous as you," he says, and my eyes widen.

"Thanks," I say and turn away.

Nori might not trust me, but at least he admires me. I couldn't win them all, but perhaps Nori didn't turn against me when Katsuo disapproved of mine and Gwen's relationship. He seems like a good person. I hope he gets home to his family safely.

✳✳✳

"Wake up," an airy voice whispers in my ear. Everything is dim shades of blue, black, and grey. "Open your eyes," she says. Hands are on my face, neck, they move to my shoulders. "You need to wake up," says the voice.

I'm jolted by a cold breeze. We're outside. The moon is a waning crescent. I open my eyes in time to see a shooting star. Gwen is gently shaking me and trying to get me to look at her. I can't focus.

"Gwen?"

I say her name and take in her serious face with bleary eyes.

"We should go back inside. I sense them. They're coming this way."

There is a slight rumble in the atmosphere. I don't need wires to know they are nearing us. The air changes when they draw closer. It becomes acrid and too thin. Tall grass droops and the scent of wildflowers is replaced with an alien odor.

"You're right," I say.

She lets me walk on my own back towards the lab. Her wires whip with nervous anticipation. Gripping me with an iron fist, she holds on like I'll be taken away by the wind. Once we're inside, she chastises me.

"What were you doing out there?" she asks.

My back is up against the wall. Outside the window, I see them. A swarm of low flying Mantodea. The scar in the middle of my back throbs in pain, looking at their folded arms.

"I'm sorry. I must have been sleepwalking again."

"You could have died. What if I didn't notice you weren't in your room?"

Gwen raises her voice at me. It's shriller than expected and I cover my ears. I'm taller than her, but I cower as she cuts me down.

"I...I don't know," I stutter.

"Why won't you talk to me? I love you," she says, and lowers her voice.

"I'm not sure what to say."

Gwen grabs my hand and pulls me down the hall. She practically pushes me into my room. Nimble fingers start taking off my shirt and she's slipping out of her dress. This doesn't really seem like the time. I try to say something, but she shoves me into the bathroom and starts the shower. She gets in and gestures for me to join her. I'm put off, but go along with it.

"I know you're upset because I killed Shira," she says.

I gulp, and it sticks in my throat like a piece of lard.

"I've been feeling guilty about what we did."

"What I did. You didn't do anything."

"I burned her, Gwen. I got rid of her like she was no more than a bag of garbage," I say and my icy grey eyes must have something dark in them because Gwen backs up.

Her features are severe, but her face is irritatingly young. Full lips pout and make her look sad but pretty the way girls in magazines do.

"I'm the guilty one. I don't want you to suffer."

The water hits my shoulders and soaks my hair. Gwen notices the scar on my neck. She kisses her fingers and then places them where she hurt me in the past. Giving me a kiss on the cheek, she also steals a glance at the damage done to my back. Gwen studies my mouth, the tiny mark where she first made me hers. "I'm sorry. I need to be careful," she says.

"Why did you pull me into the shower?" I ask to break the tension.

"I didn't want anyone to hear us discuss what happened to Shira."

The Ex Machina is clever and still has her best interest in mind. It's just

Yui and Hotaka here with us, but she is correct. We can't let anybody know.

"Thank you for saving me. I should work on lowering my stress. That's usually when I sleepwalk."

"I shouldn't have left you alone," she says and wraps her arms around me. "I'll always protect you, Bellamy."

***

Gwen is eight weeks pregnant. Summer is here and the baby roses are in full bloom. I wake up to white flowers on my nightstand. She likes to do sweet things like that. Her moods are stable but I worry they may become erratic. My girlfriend can be unpredictable like a storm in the summer. She can go cold and it's November in July. There's a knock at my door.

"Hey Bell," says Hotaka with a glossy smile. He hands me a glass of water and a bowl of what appears to be a broccoli and mushroom stir fry.

"Thanks."

"How have you been? I don't see you much these days," he says and sips on his tea.

"I'm okay," I say and pause. I don't take a bite of my food and Hotaka stares at me. "I've been really worried about Gwen."

Hotaka nods his head politely. I know he knows what I am saying. We speak with our eyes and he sits back in the chair. He taps his fingers for a moment. I look at my food, no red in it but it's all I see in my head.

"This is the furthest she's been along," he says.

"Yes. Gwen won't listen to me. She becomes furious anytime I mention an alternative."

"It's because you're not listening."

"What?" I ask.

"You hear her but you're not listening."

"I don't think I understand." I must be stupider than I thought. Hotaka laughs and gets up to sit with me.

"You are only thinking of the end goal. She is talking about the whole experience," he says. I feel like an idiot.

"Thanks Hotaka. You're a good friend. To both of us."

He has been there for me and her this whole time. When I couldn't remember to eat he subtly helped me out. Gwen and him formed a bond. She likes his music and poetry books. Hotaka is her friend. He cares about her, too.

"I hope you two get what you want."

"Really? You don't look down on me for what I'm doing?" I ask. Hotaka takes off his glasses and rubs his eyes.

"No. Why would I?"

"Because deep down I feel as though I'm doing something wrong," I confess. Shira's face flashes before me. I flinch and Hotaka looks at the center of my room confused. For whatever reason I fear he'll know her body was there. That I cleaned up a pool of blood and threw her away.

"Don't let Katsuo and the other scientists dictate how you feel. They could never understand because they don't have what you have. No one ever will."

"I should be grateful. What I have is special, unique. I worry I'm ruining it."

"Try and cheer up. One day at a time," he says and walks out. I know I should eat but I'm not hungry. I force it down anyway. Then I drink the water. I need to take care of myself. If I sleepwalk again, who knows what might happen.

I decide to walk around. Gwen isn't swimming. She's not in her room. I check the cameras to see she went outside about thirty minutes ago. Sighing at her absence from the building I head for the storage area. In the far left corner is the bassinet. I touch it. It's mine but feels like it belongs to someone else.

I go into the room where Gwen was born. The glass has my handprint on it. I should wash it off. My father would scold me for such a thing. Imagining a baby in the tank again makes me wince. Not that I want it to be that way. I understand now what Gwen has been trying to say. I can't feel it the way she feels it. In a way I am hurt I can't be damaged by it the way she is.

Sitting in his chair I'm a fraud, an imposter. There is no way he would've known what to do if he were in my situation. Yet I can't help but think he would be more confident and it pisses me off. I want to rip my hair out as I ruminate. My elbows dig into my thighs as I rest my head in my hands. The heaviness in my heart pulls me forward.

"Please, don't be sad," says Gwen. I look up to see her holding out a sunflower to me. She pushes it into my palm.

"I'm not sad. I was just thinking," I say.

"Do I make you happy?" she asks.

"Of course." Her hair is so long. I reach up and pull my fingers through it. She grabs my hand. I'm not ready for it and it shocks me.

"You don't seem happy." Gwen is frowning at me.

"I've never been a dad. I'm really nervous." My life is spoken in half truths.

"Why are you nervous?"

"I'm worried I'll be like my dad. We didn't have a good relationship. I get nervous thinking we won't be close."

Gwen studies my face for a moment before focusing her gold eyes on the tank. She walks up to it the way a child walks up to a tank in an aquarium. Killer whales and great white sharks have nothing on her.

"Would he and I have been close the way we are if he didn't die?" she asks. Her question has me falling out of the chair. She is quick to scoop me up. I can't recover though.

"Yes."

CHAPTER THIRTY
SAMSARA

Hotaka and Yui have been attentive towards me. Yui seems focused on my state of mind. She keeps asking me how I am and having me sit with her so we can go over my father's notes that don't have anything to do with Gwen. The young scientist can simultaneously admire my father and accept who I am.

I notice Hotaka taking an interest in Gwen. He seems concerned about her. The other day, I overheard her tell him how excited she was. Hotaka smiled, but it stung. I know because he grimaced when she looked away. He checks on her daily in the infirmary. So far, the metallic threads haven't pierced them. Not yet. We're at ten and a half weeks and I'm falling through the earth.

Gwen's question about my father has me rattled. I can't get over it. Why did she bring it up? It's like she wants to break me. For what, though? I'm already hers. She thinks I control her, but it's the other way around. I'm holding a blanket I bought for our baby. It's mint green. I didn't want to get blue or pink. The other one I got is lemon yellow. Neutral colors seemed most appropriate, but then again, what do I know about these kinds of things?

The Ex Machina is all wise with an infallible mind. Incredible intelligence but so very reckless. Here I am encouraging it. I think about the day Gwen told me all the things she liked: swimming, flying, and me. Not knowing any better, I said I liked her, too.

I'm angry with my father. How could he—I stop myself? How could he do what? Fall in love with Gwen? I bite my tongue to hold it back from myself. He was a frigid person without meaning to be. Neglectful but not abusive. I can't imagine what he would do in my position. The tiny bruises on my chest ache in places. I touch them individually. They belong to me.

Missing her draws me to her room. She's not here. My next stop is the water reservoir. I stand at the ledge. The water is green black. I see gold and blue in the darkness. She breaks the surface but stays where I can't reach her.

"Come here," I say with a laugh.

"No, you come here."

"What?"

"I want to show you something," she says.

Gwen's hair swirls around her. A dangerous mermaid. The wires aren't visible, but they must be swaying underneath the dark water. I hear Nori's voice. Are you afraid of her? Yes. But I trust her.

"You want to what?" I ask, dumbfounded. Gwen motions for me to kneel, like she is going to tell me a secret. "What?" I ask again.

She is so quick I don't know what's happening and by the time I do, I can't scream. Gwen's dragged me into the green-black water. I flail in her arms but she calms me with a kiss that also breathes air into my lungs. I relax, realizing Gwen will not hurt me.

Gwen focuses her gold eyes behind me and points. I turn to see what she wanted to show me. Hundreds of aquatic plants have grown on the bottom of the reservoir. From the view of the camera, it looks like there is nothing but rock walls, but further down are an array of purple, red, and lime green plants. They have almond-shaped leaves. Gwen kisses me and breathes into me again. I feel guilty for thinking she had bad intentions.

We admire the beauty of the bottom of the reservoir for a moment. The aquatic plants reach up with long arms. The stems are waxy and shiny. Gwen heads for the surface, but I keep my eyes on the red and purple plants. I'm anxious to be out of the water. She and I sit on the ledge. I think she finds it amusing watching me choke on what's left in my lungs.

"Did you like it?" she asks.

"I did. Thank you."

"I wanted to show you something beautiful."

She smiles and I bring her closer to my side. I like how she grips my coat. It's all too romantic. Too good to be true. The color red catches my eye and I look down. To my horror, I see sheer crimson bleeding through Gwen's peach colored dress.

"Gwen," I whisper her name and touch her leg with my index finger.

Her smile disappears as she looks down.

"No, no, no..." she cries.

I throw my arms around her. Even though I knew this was going to happen, I can't take it. Gwen's wires swish in agony. She parts her legs and the hem of the dress is soaked with blood. Why couldn't we just try it my way this time?

"I'm sorry."

There is nothing else I can say. Nothing more to say. I'm a fool to have kept playing this game.

"It's been obvious I wasn't going to be able to stay pregnant. But I really wanted to try," she sobs into my neck.

I hold her platinum hair in my fist and clench my teeth.

"We could try the alternative," I say it without thinking it all the way through.

Gwen stops crying and I know I fucked up.

"It's not the same, Bellamy."

"I know, but can't we—"

"No," she says it gently, and reaches for my hair. Brushing it out of my face, she touches my cheek and runs her thumb across my lips. "I love you so much, Bellamy. I know now what I need to do now."

She gets up and walks away from me, leaving a trail of blood. I think about a trail of rose petals, but that's not what they are.

"Gwen, wait! What are you doing?"

"What I should have done a long time ago," she says and heads for the front door.

"No. Gwen, whatever you are planning, please wait. We can talk about this!" I'm chasing her down the hall. Blood gets on my shoes and leaves a red streak in the hallway. I ignore it and keep running after my girlfriend, who is about to do something outrageous. "Gwen, come here, right now!" I yell. She stops in her tracks and turns around. I grab her and refuse to let go.

"Bellamy—"

"No, you're not going out there."

She says my name again, but I grip onto her tighter.

"Listen to me," she says and pushes me away. I give her some slack but keep her in my arms. "I love you too much to let you live in a world with monsters."

"But—"

"Don't forget me," she says and gives me a kiss, nearly knocking me out.

It must have been her plan. It works, and she wriggles out of my grasp. Gwen flies out the front door and I can't stop her. Yui and Hotaka call for me. I see they have also stepped into Gwen's blood. They approach me and hold my shoulders while I lose myself.

The sky turns stormy. Lightning strikes and the wind moves through the tops of the pines. The three of us witness history. A gust of wind rips the flowers from their stems and they blow listlessly with nowhere to go. Electricity lights up the indigo sky. It's daytime, but it looks like the middle of the night.

Hotaka rubs my back and tries to comfort me. I can't hear him, but I appreciate his kindness. Yui is holding my hand that I'm apparently squeezing. We haven't been friends until recently, but I'm grateful for her support. The clouds swirl in the sky. Lightning strikes and burns the grass where it hits.

Gwen is up there sacrificing herself. She and I couldn't have a family. Now I can't even have her. She loves me enough to make the right decision when I couldn't. I've been selfish. But how could I give up the thing I love the most?

We keep our eyes on the sky, changing from indigo to gray to bright blue. The storm stops abruptly. Yui and I look at each other with perplexed faces. Hotaka steps closer to the window. He lets go of my shoulder and we all approach the glass. There is a strange sound outside. Its pitch is similar to a firework right as it's about to go off.

Alien bodies pour from the sky. They crash into the earth and kick up the dirt. Green blood oozes from their cracked exoskeletons. Shiny black pieces explode upon impact. Their folded arms and heads shatter. Red eyes glaze over with defeat. It's hard to be proud and destroyed at the same time, but I am.

***

The Mantodea were gone but so was she. After the Queen was killed, the Mantodea dropped like flies. It appears they were all connected to her and possibly the ship. Alien bodies littered the ground. Asphalt cracked, and the dirt caved in around them. They decomposed rapidly, turning to dust, and were carried by the wind. We will never know where the Mantodea came from or how they operated. Most of the world is content just being alive. No need to further educate ourselves on the eradicated species.

It took me four months to retrieve the device. After the explosion, I turned on the device's tracker. She landed in the middle of the Gulf of Mexico, nearly eight thousand feet under the sea. No team would go at first. I threw more and more money at them. At that point, nothing mattered other than being with her again.

Once I had the device in my hands, I cried tears of joy. I cried tears of anguish and regret. The floral metal piece fit against my fingers like she was holding me back. The men I hired thought I had lost my mind. Perhaps I did. I paid them with cash.

Then came a difficult obstacle. Securing a donor. The Mantodea were defeated, gone, and humanity slowly began rebuilding itself. Most countries commended my creation and thanked me for saving our planet, but were hesitant in giving me another chance.

Finally, someone agreed to give me a donor. A baby girl from Scotland. She was less than thirty weeks old when I received her. I implanted the device myself and the hardest part came. Waiting for her. The years dragged on. Hotaka and Yui returned home, but not me. The lab became my home. She is my home.

Earth was returned to the humans. I prayed for her to return to me. Not that I believe in karmic justice, but I have a sick smugness. It tells me I deserve to have her back. If I didn't finish my father's work, we would have never rid the planet of aliens. She has to come back. For me. I'm the one she killed herself to save the world for.

I'm sure what I'm doing is illegal and immoral. It doesn't matter. The government, the people, they all turn a blind eye to what I'm doing. They never asked why I wanted to make another and I didn't tell them. People want to keep their heroes on a pedestal. If they knew their heroes personally, they'd be sorely disappointed.

I've been waiting for so many years. A lifetime, really. Almost eighteen years. She doesn't need to be indestructible or have fortified skin tough enough to withstand space. I just need her to be her. I've been debating waiting the full twenty years as my father instructed. But why? Why wait when I don't need her to be our savior? I simply need her to be who she was.

The Scottish girl has the longest, curliest red hair I've ever seen. It swirls in the tank, a flame in a glass. Her skin is quite fair with different shades of freckles on her face, the tops of her arms, and thighs. She is petite, 5'2 and weighs one-hundred pounds. The hand has touched the glass. I say her name and hope she's in there.

There is no time like right now. I hit the button. Blue liquid drains from the tank. It sloshes and splashes against the sides of the glass. I remove the respirator with numb fingers. Her eyes are closed and she coughs up the amniotic fluid. I hold her shoulder and whisper to her. She reaches for me, grabbing the collar of my coat.

I brush her hair from her face. It's sticking to her freckled cheeks. She has thin bow-shaped lips. Her face is pretty like a Renaissance painting. Coughing up the liquid, she gasps one last time before opening her eyes. I thought they would be green but they are hazel. They light up gold and stare at me in amazement.

"Bellamy?"

She says my name.

"Yes," I choke.

It's her.

"You look different."

She has a higher voice, but it's definitely Gwen making a joke. I smile like I haven't smiled in eighteen years.

"So do you," I say.

She touches my hair that is turning gray. Her fingers trace the lines in the corners of my eyes.

"You're still beautiful," she says and kisses me.

I've waited forever to see her again. While everyone else returned to their ordinary lives, I sought another chance to be with a goddess. She is our savior. Gwen sacrificed herself against my wishes. She is the one with a good heart.

"I missed you."

We lock eyes. The imprint has already happened, but I sense its revival. I look at the floral device. The blue stands out against the red. I thought I hated that color, but on her it's the most divine shade. Gwen's hair before was silky smooth and straight. Now it's a wild, tousled mess. Curls pile on top of one another.

"I'm so happy to see you again," she says and we embrace.

We are chest to chest. I kiss her bow-shaped lips and she wraps around me. Gwen is back. I know because she holds me the way a child holds a toy.

THE END